THE EMPTY GREATCOAT

THE EMPTY GREATCOAT

Rebecca F. John

Aderyn

First published in Great Britain in 2022 by Aderyn Press
Gweledfa, Felindre, Swansea, Wales, SA5 7NA

www.aderynpress.com

A CIP catalogue record for this book is available
from the British Library

ISBN 978-1-9163986-0-3
eISBN 978-1-9163986-1-0

Cover design: Kari Brownlie
Text design: Elaine Sharples
Printed in Great Britain by 4edge Limited

To Sergeant Francis Albert House, for all he did.
And to the millions whose names I do not know.

One

'Listen!'

A low, muted moon striates Captain Burrows' face as he leans in to whisper to the men. Beneath, the water flutters and gasps. *Listen. Hush.* Corporal Francis House concentrates on the orb of spittle which glints from the corner of his Captain's ruckled lips and waits for it to drop.

'Listen,' he hisses again. 'When we're within six yards of land, we're to step into the shallows and wade ashore.'

The men strain to hear him over the tattling waves. They hunch, fidget, sniff. Burrows adjusts his position, props his elbow on a muscled knee and continues, splaying his fingers with each word until his knuckles are tight and pale.

'Be cautious. Men have drowned under their kits in these waters, but whatever happens you must – not – make – a – sound. Do you understand? Here are your orders. If you are drowning, drown – quietly.' The fingers stretch further in the black air, as if reaching for something they cannot find. 'If you are shot, bleed – quietly. You will not touch that beach if you utter a single sound, I can promise you that. Bill will hear you. Silence is your only hope.'

At this, the men sit back, withdrawing as far as the crowded barge will allow them from Burrows' blunt words. Francis bites down on the inside of his cheek and braces himself against the movement: he will not shrink with them.

All around is darkness and stifled silence. Francis swallows the urge to cough. In his throat, the scratch of that morning's square of kommissbrot and sea salt.

'Do you understand?' Burrows asks.

• The men have been warned against speaking, and so they wait, shuffling on the spot, while Burrows shifts his attention from one pair of gleaming eyes to the next and extracts their nod of confirmation. *Yes, Sir*, their juddering chins reply. *Yes, Sir*, say their gathering tears. But the claggy stench rising from their underarms claims otherwise. They can feel war on the stagnant air now. Ashore, the glimpsed flare of guns and spit of rifles mount to a pip-pipping firework display, and their mouths fish open as they realise, man by man, that they are at last under fire.

Francis tastes someone else's stale breath thrusting over his tongue and clamps his mouth shut. He is nauseated. He hadn't known, until now, that dread could melt your innards.

A few gasps go up as a Turkish bullet, two, dent the tramp's funnel and, with a dissonant clang, arc away. Francis peacocks his broad chest, keen to demonstrate control of his nerves: he is Corporal House now, for Christ's sake; he has been entrusted to lead these men in Captain Burrows' stead; he must slough away that idiot who'd spotted an orange box floating off the Maltese coast last summer and, thinking it a submarine, brought hell down on its splintered slats; he must inhabit his bravest self again.

A second cluster of bullets pings into the funnel just above their heads and, this time, Francis cannot help but duck. Despite the heat, gooseflesh rises along his neck. This really is it. They are under attack. And how different it is to the imagining. There is no room for bravery or heroism here. They must simply teeter together, forty-two men trapped on a round-topped barge, attempting to hold on to their kit and their rations and their balance. They cannot lift their guns. They cannot strike the enemy in close combat. They are jammed between the six-inch howitzers and their fear and, try as he might, Francis cannot even sight the beach. They are drifting slowly towards Anzac Cove. Helpless. And Francis had wanted this. Begged for it even.

Six months earlier, chin to the ceiling in the coffee and pipe tobacco fug of Lieutenant Cruikshank's office at St Elmo, he'd demanded to be taken off that great, weather-beaten star fort. He wanted off Malta. He wanted action. Whatever far-flung post Berto Murley and Busty Leonard were destined for, Francis House was determined to follow. He was puffed up with bravado and ignorance.

'You don't know what you're asking,' Cruikshank said evenly. 'And I won't hear you ask it again. Now go, hmm.'

Hmm. Always that hmm with Cruikshank. Francis wanted to shake him: for the way it signified that he was mulling you over; for the pretension. Had Francis been told then that someday he would take comfort from that repeated hmm, that someday he would miss it, the disbelief would have led him to laughter.

And yet, as the men await Captain Burrows' next command, Francis finds himself listening for it. He understands now that Cruikshank was correct: he hadn't known what he'd been asking. He could not have foreseen any of this. He and the forty men he cajoled off Malta with his grins and promises are about to stumble into unknown silt, in deepest black, without the slightest idea of the conditions they'll be under, and their sole objective is silence. They are not to disturb Bill. But none of them knows who Bill is. Francis cannot begin to guess, and it makes him feel a clown, and that is no way to proceed into battle. He cannot write to his father of confusion and cowardice. He is under his own orders to make Frederick House proud.

He is under his own orders, more importantly, to find Berto.

Fear drops through Francis' chest, heavy as an iron bullet. He needs to move – to drag off his kit and dive into the waves and swim until his every muscle hurts. After all, he belongs to the sea. He always has. He marvels, even now, that only Lily ever understood that.

The last time they went to the beach together, just the two

of them, it was fallen-leaf brown and disappointingly flat under a wet grey slick of afternoon sky, but Francis didn't mind a jot. He was not yet ten. He was a sea child, a salt sprite.

'I don't think you're a House at all,' Lily called, laughing, as he swooped around her. 'I think you're a sea urchin.'

Oft, Lily told him stories of how some quick-finned creature had stolen in through the window one moony night while the true Francis House lay asleep in his cot and replaced her little brother with a swaddled merchild. She had no better explanation, she said, for the way he seemed to transform when the coast winds battered him, until he was composed of feathers or scales or spindrift. When he tore off his shoes and raced across the sand, he was a herring gull, complete with hungry beak and ready wings. When he dove into the waves, he was a glimmering bream.

He aches suddenly for the sister he has not seen these past four years. He aches to show her the actuality of all that adventure they had dreamt of; to stand alongside her again and peer outwards instead of in; to kick and overarm himself all the way back to Plymouth and say, 'Wasn't I foolish, thinking myself capable of so much.'

But Burrows' warning has wormed too effectually into his thoughts to allow him to move. He mustn't wake Bill. Whatever else happens, he must not wake Bill. He opens his mouth wider and drags at the dark, aware that already the volume of his hauling breath is countering Captain Burrows' orders, but he cannot persuade the muggy Turkish air into his lungs.

Silence, he reminds himself. *Hush. Listen. Hush.* The water purls and plashes.

Soon, the steam pinnace towing them towards the enemy slows to a bobbing halt, and the men begin lowering themselves charily into the water: first Edwards, with his always-startled eyes; then Henley, the only one amongst them who stands taller and broader than Francis; next, Farrelly and Whitman, so similar in stance and slight build that they might well be twins;

then Hodgson, with his bandy legs and turned-out elbows; followed by Carson, the oldest amongst them, sporting a badger's streak in his slicked-back hair; and finally Goskirk, who Francis discerns by his woolly farmer's scent.

The water is not cold. It would feel pleasant, were it not for the fact that it is pouring over the cuffs of their boots, swirling into their bags. It ruffles around their waists and chests, and immediately Francis is aware of the pull of his sodden kit. Burrows was spot on: should a man panic, it would prove all too easy to go under. Francis attributes each inhalation a three beat and concentrates on counting through the unexpected syncopation of his breathing. In, two, three. Out! In, two, three. Out, out! The exhalation he hasn't yet garnered control of. His lips are trembling. But he is surrounded by water, at least, and it is familiar and soothing and he knows, somewhere beneath his terror, that he is strong when he is held by the tides. That he is the sea urchin his sister named him. That he is pearl oyster and starfish and wolf eel and pinniped and grey reef shark.

Though the guns have stopped now, he senses movement on the beach. He trudges slower, hoping to gain more time to assess whatever aberrant situation he is approaching, and, none wanting to be first ashore, the others slow with him. Now and then, there comes a faint knocking against his shin bones, and Francis grits his teeth and hopes to God there are no skeletons swilling around in the shallows. At their head, Captain Burrows presses on through the softening silt. Occasionally, he snaps around to call them forward with a glare, but the bulge-eyed instruction does little to hurry the men. They are gathering all the information they can. Knowledge, Francis has taught them during their training hikes and their target practice, is as important a weapon as any.

To his surprise, he soon discerns that the beach is only five yards or so deep. Though it arcs some way down the coast, its depth is diminutive indeed. A man might take only ten or twelve strides in one direction before finding himself trapped up against the sheer scrubby hill which rises from the sand into Turk territory. Surely, Francis thinks, Johnnie Turk is defending that hill. He's heard rumour that the British haven't yet made it off the beaches at Gallipoli. As such, he had expected them to be vast affairs, freckled with soldiers, not these curled white fingernails, gripping at the lapping sea as they sink under the weight of overcrowding.

Reluctantly, they drip onto dry sand, a clump of deliquescing men. All around are piles of ration boxes, arranged in neat cubes so that Francis feels he has been dropped at the entrance to a labyrinth. And into the maze, Aussies move their ammunition, and barges unload their stores, and bodies are wrapped up and carried into the afterlife. The moon greys the hair of a passing boy who bites an unlit cigarette possessively between his teeth. By fine, cloud-roaming light, Francis contemplates the shroud of a thin figure, laid out in slanting shadow; the white tented roofs of the rowed and mismatched huts; the curved lip of a rowing boat sitting, tilted and abandoned, on the shoreline; the rounded helmets of the men already installed at Gallipoli; the spokes of five enormous gunwheels, leant against each other and in need of repair; and, further away, the slatted stretch of a narrow jetty into the sea. Everyone is busy. Everything is practised motion. Yet, there is never a noise. Perhaps these soldiers have simply learned to stop opening their mouths to the gruesome tang of decaying flesh and disinfectant. Francis tries clamping his lips closed and relying on his nose, but the effect is not much lessened; his tongue is already ripe with it.

So, this is Anzac, he thinks. It tastes of death.

Down the line, one of the men bends double and vomits over his own boots. Burrows arrives before him forthwith to grasp his shoulders, straighten him up, and nod his head in encouragement.

'Stand tall,' he mutters. 'You'll get used to it.'

I enlisted in the Royal Garrison Artillery on the 12th Dec 1907, being then of the tender age of 15 years and 3 months. By mistake the latter was officially recorded as 15 years, 1 month. My rank was 'boy', a fret which caused me much annoyance since, being a soldier, I considered I was very much a man.

Two

Francis drops on to one knee and, rummaging around in his sodden kit bag, locates and removes his rolled Witney blanket. Likely, the grey wool was gentle over its first owner's skin, but it has since grown flat and stiff and faded. He bumps a forefinger over its frayed edge. Someone, he supposes, has been boiled out of it. He imagines a courageous lad, a few years his junior perhaps, with a very ordinary name like William – no, Joe – clenching his teeth and wrapping the blanket around a severed foot or a bleeding head in silent determination.

This Joe would have been able to fashion a bandage from just about anything, he decides, having always wanted to be a doctor, and practised earnestly on the knotted legs of his father's herd of sad-eyed cattle. Or perhaps Joe had wanted to be a veterinary surgeon. Or perhaps wrapping cows' legs in linen was simply a means of liberating all the kindnesses he possessed but felt he ought to hide.

Francis need not decide now. Thus far, his experience of soldiering has taught him that there will plenty of time for imagining ahead.

In deference to his invented ghost, he spreads the blanket over the gritty sand carefully, to ensure it does not snag on the jaggy shrubs or stones which mark the boundary of the invading forces' progress – a pitifully narrow curve which lies but nine of Francis' leggy strides distant from the glimmering shoreline.

It was the measuring of it which had caused him to lose track of Captain Burrows and the others in the writhing darkness. On the off chance, he had stopped and listened for

Burrows' familiar whistle – it was always a snippet of Mozart – but, in truth, he knew the Captain would not be careless enough to break the order for quiet. Francis was a stranger on Anzac Cove, and, since he could not yet think how to make himself useful, he reasoned it was best to grab some sleep and wake rested, ready for action, on the morrow. He felt his way towards a crudely erected hut and propped himself against its facade, thinking to enjoy the last gusts of salt air the retreating tide had to offer.

Some thirty minutes later, he had been disturbed by the combined and hasty movement of those men already dirtied into Gallipoli: towards the huts; towards the cliff face. They were taking cover.

Though he ached from the soles of his feet to the ends of his hair, Francis forced himself mutely upright and followed suit, shouldering his way along the moon-tipped foreshore until he discovered a deep cleft already scooped out of the scrubby cliffside.

Before it now on his hands and knees, he crawls forwards into shadow, stores his kit bag at the back of the narrow cave, then wriggles inside, rolling into his damp blanket as he goes. Within, it is darker yet, and Francis' eyes dilate desperately, as though in widening they might find something solid to fix on. From his makeshift pillow, he can sight no other living body but the sea, shone under the stout, marled moon. He closes his eyes and hopes that Henley and the others have managed to find similar shelter, for he is certain trouble is approaching. Why else should the beach have emptied so uniformly? Why else would they have been ordered to Gallipoli in the first? Scores of men – Berto and Busty included – have been posted here before him.

It seems that mere moments have passed since that slow falling, ginger-spiced June eve, when he and Henley sat in the shadow of the ship's funnel to observe the five-hundred Maoris aboard the *S.S. Massilia* go about their war dance, their teeth gnashing and their tongues thrusting and their eyes popping as they let out their snorts and yells and stamped their feet against the quivering deck. Though it was as exhilarating as watching a streak of tigers snarl together for a hunt, Francis expected Henley – who had proved himself such a bloody con-'sistent fool on Malta – to grow sated and wander away, but he remained as stock still as Francis, fascinated by the foreigners' rippling chants.

'Well,' he said finally, slapping Francis' thigh with an enormous paw. 'Haven't we got something to live up to.' And the words convinced Francis that, yes, in the absence of Berto or Busty, this was the fellow he'd have beside him when they waded ashore at the Dardanelles.

But now Henley is lost, Francis thinks as he finally submits to sleep. Great, square, burly Henley, with his booming voice and his soft eyes and his reddened knuckles. Gone. As easily as that. Francis had kept him close in the water: closer than young Whitman or poor Drowning Edwards. But he'd discarded him on the sand, like a vest dragged off and thrown to the sky in readiness for a midnight swim. Like the women he had shoved aside at the slightest inducement. Like the sister he had so readily abandoned. Like the friend he had failed and has come here to find.

Anzac, Cruikshank had confirmed when Francis had rushed into his office and demanded he check, had been Berto's posting. There was no reason to believe he hadn't made it on ship.

It is only right, though, that Francis approach his first morning in action amongst strangers. It is precisely what he deserves, given how selfishly he has behaved.

In his restless sleep, he touches the place where the damnable lifebelt he was sworn to wear all the way across from Malta smarted his skin: the sore extends above his navel like a hyphen reaching for the second part of himself; the missing component which will make sense of the man Francis Albert House must become.

He starts at the clap of a flattened palm against a proud chest. The hollow thwap of skin against skin is chased by a second, then a third. Pap-pap-pap, goes the beat. Pap-pap-pap. They sound in quick succession. It is not like the Maoris to rush into their dance. It is not like them, Francis realises slowly, because it is not them. The Maoris were bound for Cape Helles, not Anzac.

Francis' eyelids peel open at the sudden flare of a shell shattering the sky. He jolts upright to the illuminated sight of heels disappearing behind ration boxes; of, further away, the glinting breakers being dulled by the whirring infiltration; then, close to, of the toes of his boots, which stretch beyond the protection of his shallow cave, glowing as if freshly polished for parade; and, when he finally works up the courage to acknowledge them, only a foot apart from his boot soles and looming in towards him, their faces obscured by the inquisitive angle at which they protrude from their necks – two men, waiting, with shovels held aloft.

In the next shell flash, he glimpses the black holes of their eyes.

Francis lifts his arms to display his palms. 'Hello, fellows,' he says. 'What can I do for you?'

But neither man answers him. The shorter of the two simply lifts an erect finger to his invisible lips and exhales.

'Shush.'

Three

Bill reveals himself with the slanting sweep of first light. From his elevated position, he takes a deep breath, aims his one eye down over the beach, and peppers every inch of the exposed shore with shells.

None moves on Anzac Cove but those grains of sand flung up into a thousand spitting eruptions by Bill's relentless battering.

Knees tucked up to his chin, Francis stares out from his cave and attempts to tally them. He cannot keep track, and he soon grows frustrated and gives it up, but he knows that if he is to keep his limbs from twitching into movement, he needs to occupy his brain, so he begins instead to plan his letters to Lily, to Ethel, to Ivy, to his mother, to his father.

It ought to be raining, he begins.

How Frederick would scoff at such a sentence. 'It is or it isn't, lad,' he would chide, in his more lucid moments. 'Speculation is enough to get a man killed.'

It ought to be raining, but...

And there Francis stalls. He cannot get past the opening line. He cannot reconcile the idyllic view with the violent onslaught of shells, for though he is not sheltering from the grey assault of cold sleet on the Plymouth front, it is raining on sun-softened Anzac Cove. It is raining pig iron.

'Well, there's your Bill,' says Farmer, who is hunched now against Francis' right side, smelling sweetly of damp. His rusted shovel is tucked behind him. To Francis' left sits Farmer's companion, who has rested his head against the inside wall of the cave and now snores steadily into the dawn.

'He's a measure more forward than I'd imagined,' Francis replies.

The corners of Farmer's mouth flirt with a smile.

Already, Francis likes Farmer. Hours previous, when he had woken to find two men looming over him with weapons raised, Francis had supposed himself about to be murdered. But while he'd shuffled desperately around inside his blanket, attempting to extricate his limbs in preparation for lunging forwards and throwing punches for all his worth, Farmer had calmly thrust his shovel into the sand, extended both arms, and said, 'Won't you shake a fella's hand?'

Looking up, Francis saw that he was grinning and, obliging, felt his hand enveloped by two firm, stony palms.

'Look about you, princess,' the Australian said.

The near view showed Francis that the Anzacs had dug a trench right up to his blanket and, apparently loathe to disturb him, continued on the other side of his crossed ankles. Evidently, they needed to lay a wire. These two had arrived to complete the portion he was sleeping on.

'I'm so sorry,' Francis said, rushing to disentangle himself from his blanket and remove the obstacle. 'I didn't realise. Why didn't somebody wake me?'

The Australian hocked back a glob of catarrh and, putting a finger to one nostril, ejected it from the other with a sudden snort. 'Didn't see the need,' he replied. 'Who am I to keep a man from his rest?'

Throughout this exchange, the second man remained silent. Francis studied him momentarily.

'I don't know what language he speaks,' the Australian said, thrusting a thumb over his shoulder at his companion, 'but it ain't English, we've established that much.'

Having now righted himself and dusted the sand from the seat of his shorts, Francis offered his hand again. 'Francis House,' he said.

'Bill Farmer,' the Australian replied, pumping his arm heartily.

'Not *the* Bill?'

Bill Farmer smiled. '*The* Bill?'

Francis shrugged stupidly. 'Our Captain said we weren't to wake Bill.'

'Ah! I should say so!' Bill Farmer answered. 'Regardless, you'll meet him in the morning.'

And already, Francis thinks, he wishes he could rescind the acquaintance.

'How long will it continue?' he asks. Jammed as he is between Bill Farmer and his unnamed friend, he is growing stiff and prickly. He longs to walk down to the sea and plunge in. It might loosen his muscles. It might make him feel cleaner. Since the moment he clambered off the *Massilia*, he has yearned for nothing so much as a good thorough soak in a tin tub. Morning is clawing at the waves now, wild as a hunting cat, made splendid by that same pale gold glint of movement, and Francis wants to revel in the swelling heat of it. Partly, he had joined up for this. He never did deal well with small spaces, and the army had promised him the freedom of mountains or fields, deserts or oceans. As a boy, he'd hungered for all that was open. On those weekends before the House family settled in Plymouth, when they were still gypsying along the coast, his parents would take Francis and his sisters to the beaches and immediately his feet hit new sand, so he would tear off his shoes and run and run until his chest flamed. There was no better sensation than charging away from his family and feeling that gap open up between himself and the deckchairs and the picnic blanket, than savouring the rush of air around his straining body, than hearing the desperate drumming of Lily and Ethel and Ivy's paces as they tried to catch up to him.

Inevitably, hysterics followed when Ethel or Ivy stumbled and gave up. But Lily never was one to be beaten. Whatever the terrain, however great the distance, Lily would run until she reached him.

He'd played the same game with Berto at Woodlands. It was,

he supposed, a test of loyalty. At midnight or just before dawn, he would sneak out of number three room and into the streets, to run between the flares of the streetlamps. Then he would pause in the shadows, listen for the footsteps of the ferocious lad thundering along in his wake, and leap out at him as he passed. Rarely they managed to silence their laughter afterwards, those two innocent boys. They would shove and scuffle the whole way back to their bunks and, when they rolled into their blankets, their stomachs would ache with the simple effort of calming down.

Francis always had felt he needed a brother to cover him in the silent war he and his father were engaged in. In brash little Berto, he knew he'd found one. Though he never could have imagined how much he would ask of him before they even passed out of Woodlands.

'All day?' Francis asks, because he has not been listening properly to Bill Farmer and he thinks he must have misheard.

'On and off,' Farmer confirms. 'There's no work on Anzac Cove after daybreak, that's for certain. Bill's a grumpy old fella.'

Francis estimates that he has slept for only a few hours. Likely, Burrows won't be too angry if he returns now, with the light. He scans the fan of beach visible from inside his cave, but he can pick out no sign of Captain Burrows and the others through the morning's misty exsufflation. All is achingly unfamiliar. Though it is, at least, more equable than the view he encountered when he arrived those few drenched hours previous. Where men had shifted between the rows of ration boxes, lifting and carrying and depositing, now Francis can see only two pals, cupped in the sand, legs spread before them, their heads lowered as they share out pinches of tobacco.

One is half a foot shorter than the other. Berto and I, he thinks, with a smirk.

'And don't imagine you can outfox him,' Bill Farmer continues. 'The bastard'll take your head clean off if he catches you in his sights.'

Francis does not admit to his intention to trudge through the spilling sand, searching any one of the cobbled-together company he dragged off Malta. He is boot-heavy and glad of a reason not to follow it through. He does not want, either, to sit in wait for the rowdy scattering of Bill's next round – that would do nothing to improve a man's nerves. What he wants is to retrieve the letter in his breast pocket, unfold the rumpled paper, and let his eyes trail the words down the page again to the scrawled *Mrs Lily Carter* at its bottom.

But his letter is not for sharing, and he will not open it while there are ready eyes so close by. He resorts to counting, and plods through a three-minute silent spell before realising what is missing.

'There's no birdcall,' he says. On Malta – whether masked by the hissing expulsion of the steam ships, or the unrelenting hubbub of the harbour men, or, at night, the gentle song of the dghaisa men as they sprawled pot-bellied in their vessels, pulled their straw hats down over their faces, and hummed their way into a refrain which rose to haunt the stars – the choked yodelling of the gulls was a constant.

'Nope,' Bill Farmer replies. 'Seems everything can find a way off Anzac Cove but the men.'

Francis wonders if Berto or Busty have managed it.

Last time he'd seen Berto Murley and Busty Leonard together, weeks back now, they were sitting on the harbour wall at Valletta, picking from a leftover plate of cold pastizzi and mussels, and flapping their hands at the swooping gulls. Over the water, dusk skulked, mauve and magenta and minatory. Francis and Berto were teasing Busty about the photograph of his girl he had tacked above his pillow: 'To watch over us,' he always said. Jenny-Jane herself was too sweet, too owl-eyed and plum-cheeked, to subject to mockery. But it was imperative they hide the fact that they all took comfort from her motherly plumpness, her honest smile – twenty-year-old Jenny-Jane became their guardian angel long before any of them knew

16

they needed one – and so instead they ribbed Busty. Francis admired Busty's ability to brush it off. Beyond the quietening quay, and the loafing dghaisa men, and beneath strands of cloud the colour of watermelon flesh which blew across the sky like ribbons, a great, hulking trooper sat, marring the ruffling waves with her dark, cumbrous body and awaiting his dearest pals.

The lucky devils. He'd made jibes at them so that there was laughter to hide his jealousy behind, when what he should have done was stop teasing and insist that they stay there all night and watch the new day begin together. What he should have done was throw his arms around them and hold tight as they said goodbye.

But they were only lads, drunk on weak Maltese lagers and goading each other into a race they knew Busty, with his too-tight belt and puffed cheeks, would lose. They had not yet been to war. When they stood to retire, they left a forgotten plate of pastizzi crumbs and mussel shells on the harbour wall, to await those persistent gulls.

'How long have you been here, Farmer?' Francis asks. Rather than look into Bill Farmer's weather-mapped face, Francis concentrates his attention on the other man's wrist and the wisps of shining blond hair which curl out from under his sleeve. His boots, Francis has noted, are scuffed and encrusted with lumps of some sort of clay: the lace of one has snapped; the sole of the other is working open. The knees of his trousers are faded. He smells, most pungently, of cigarette smoke and sweat. Francis has already studied Bill Farmer and decided that the man is coming loose. What he needs to know is how long it has taken for Gallipoli to unpick him.

Farmer shrugs. 'Three, or maybe four... Four weeks.'

Francis turns back to the pair who sit perhaps thirty yards distant, sharing their tobacco. He expects to see two shimmies of smoke rising away from them now, as though from a couple of chimney stacks in the early light, but their heads remain bent over their task, their shoulders slumped.

'Those two…' he begins.

Farmer shakes his head. 'We'll get them buried after dark.'

'They're…'

'Christ knows what it is that takes them,' Bill Farmer replies, hardly noticing Francis' shock. 'There's disease here, though, House – that's for sure. You'll see as many go without bullet holes in them as with.'

But again, Francis is hardly listening, because he had not realised, and it is worse than seeing a shape wound tight inside a shroud, this… This… The mistake churns his stomach. He'd thought they were pinching tobacco. He'd thought they would share a cigarette then stand, pull up their trousers, and wander away, shoving at each other and joking just as he and Berto had done the morning they arrived at Malta, almost four years since now. He'd thought he would hear their voices, carried on the quiet. It is such a simple thing to expect that to be denied it unbalances Francis, and he pitches a few degrees forwards over his knees, a retch rising in his throat.

Bill Farmer's arm halts the movement. 'Not yet,' he warns.

Francis swallows hard, tasting the bitterness of bile being forced back towards his roiling gut, and when he looks to Bill Farmer again, he finds the corners of the older man's eyes crinkled in sympathy. His irises are slender loops of sapphire rimming his dilated pupils. They tell Francis of sights he does not want to see.

'Our orders will arrive with the moon,' he says, removing his arm by slow degrees. 'Sit back, House, and look out for the moon. Until then, we wait.'

'For what?' Francis asks.

And Bill Farmer, who has hitherto been so garrulous, replies with only a glance of silence.

At 4am on 12th Sept '11 we marched to Butts Head behind the 1st Welch Band and boarded the 'Alligator', which took us to Hayland across the harbour. Here we were locked in a 1st class carriage – 10 men and no conveniences – and there we stopped for 12 hours, arriving at Southampton at 6pm. I had again written to my sister to say at what time I would be passing through Britton Ferry, but our special was travelling fast as we approached the station so I got a man to hang on to my heels while I leaned far out of the window and waved my handkerchief. The station is on a bend in the line and is flanked by a bridge. Consequently, I only caught a glimpse of my sister and then had to duck to save my head. The poor girl was waving at every uniform until she saw me and then she collapsed. Little did I think of the events that were to take place before I saw her again. It was my birthday (12th Sept '11) when I waved farewell. Suffice it to say I was very happy, for I was a full-blown soldier and was off to see the world. In those days I only asked for action and excitement, and if wars were to be fought, well, I would be one of the first to volunteer.

Four

Fresh orders arrive with the moon, just as Farmer predicted. Captain Burrows, a Sergeant Patterson, and Corporal House are to gather twenty-five men and take a gun behind the Australians. With Bill satiated by the long day's shelling, and the moon revealing itself like a sky lantern above the dissolving clouds, Francis has had no difficulty in locating the rest of his company on his second night on Anzac. Indeed, and against Farmer's best advice, he has taken the opportunity to comb the cove like a fortune hunter, asking after Berto. *This high*, he has said, holding a flattened hand out in line with his chest. *This slim*, pointing one erect finger at the heavens. *Blue-eyed. Sharp-jawed. Thick-knuckled. Quick-tongued.* But, as desperate as he soon becomes, there is little worth in offering more detail. No man here will recognise Berto by his loyalty or his sarcasm. No man will meet the intensity of Francis' gripped hand as they shake and say, 'I know him. Saw him yesterday. The dependability was just seeping out of him.' So many of the things Francis knows about Berto cannot be seen.

At the passing of a third hour, Francis finds himself face-to-face with a lumbering bear of a fellow he has already approached twice, and is forced to give it up. Berto is not on the beach. Unless Francis is able to leave this sorry place at his back, he will have no luck in finding his friend. He returns to his counting, and tallies the minutes he must wait before he discovers where, exactly, they are to follow the Australians.

By true nightfall, the assembled party and two hundred assisting Australians stand braced to begin their labours. They have gathered in a semi-circle, like a rugby team awaiting their match talk, and Francis, positioned before them alongside the Sergeant and the Captain, feels the clammy heat of their bodies as a hand, pushing hard against his chest. They are looking to him and their stare has reduced him to boyhood.

'The position,' Captain Burrows announces, 'is within one hundred and fifty yards of Johnnie Turk. It is not – too – safe.'

And that is all the information they are given before they are hitched up like mules and instructed to sweat and grunt their way forwards. It is soon let slip that they are to drag the cumbrous gun three hundred yards along exposed beach, around a Dead Man's Corner, and thence uphill until they are able to drop the trail in a gun pit on the cliff edge. Off the beach, then, Francis thinks, nodding encouragement to himself. Off the beach and towards hope. But naturally it is not so easy. The men have barely budged ten yards before they are cursing loudly enough to call every last Turk from his sleep, and Francis cannot blame them. The sand shifts impossibly under their boots. Better the clumpy items were removed so that they could easier grip the ground beneath their feet, but the British Army would not have its men barefooting across Anzac Cove, whatever the benefit – the lessons Francis learnt on Malta assure him of that much.

What ease the steam-engine marches Cruikshank and Dad Rymills forced them through seem in comparison to this. Francis always enjoyed the twenty-milers. They were hot and smoky and difficult. They made his evening sea plunges all the more pleasurable.

Every night from their first in Sliema, Francis had taken to the sea. Often, Berto came with him, but he swam further and faster without his friend, hauling arm over arm in an even front crawl until his lungs were fit to rupture. It was by watery moonlight that he learnt the country, the waves barging at his chin when he stopped to tread water and gather his bearings. He wanted to know the jut and ebb of the coast in the darkness. It would benefit him, he considered, if it came to a fight. He couldn't understand why that thought hadn't occurred to the other men, why he wasn't swimming about in a discovery fleet of pale limbs, but he was glad of it. Offshore, with everything silenced but the deep whirling charge of the Mediterranean Sea and the dull thump of his heart, Francis was nearer home than he ever could be in barracks or out on a march or even practising with his guns.

But the Turkish waters which gleam now to the peripheral left of his vision, he does not know. He has not had the opportunity to explore them. He has not had a chance even to eat since he stepped off the *Massilia* and, at the thought, he finally recognises the gnawing which has started in his stomach. Scritch-scratch, it seems to go. Scritch-scratch. He must be starving.

'We could sing our way to the top,' Francis suggests, as they stand in the shadow of the cliff, fists on hips, and peer questioningly upwards.

'And what of our orders for quiet?' an obscured face asks.

Francis speaks in the man's general direction. 'We can speak at a whisper,' he replies. 'Why can't we sing at one?'

'It's an idea,' says Farmer. 'The rhythm would help.'

'What about 'Who Were You With Last Night?''

There comes a general hum of concurrence as they shuffle back into position. From the front, Francis raises a fist straight up over his shoulder and gives a count on his fingers. He swallows a laugh as they move off to the jolly four-beat of their whispers.

When, hours after the moon's first peeping inception, they finally crest the hill – foreheads dripping, chests heaving, lips curling at each other's damp hot niff – they find that Captain Burrows' warning was warranted: the position is not safe. Compared with the Turks, they have barely risen above the beach, and yet, one hundred yards behind and below them, waves crash against the cliff wall, dragging away sizeable fragments of rock at their retreat. To the right, the Turks wait to defend their heightened situation. On the postage stamp of land the Anzacs have claimed, small shacks have been erected, rising just above ground-level to shelter the trenches which have been dug into the cloddy earth. The gun pit, too, sports a low wooden covering. Walker's Ridge is nothing but a crease in the cliff face, and beyond it is the sea, the sea, the sea. At no point can the Anzacs or the British remove themselves by more than a single mile from the strange and endless sea. And on the jutting bluff an entire Army Corps clings.

Burrows allows them thirty minutes of slumping recovery before he delivers their next orders.

'We're to ensure she's operational – by – tomorrow – eve,' he says, nodding at the offending weapon. 'So we have to go back for the shells. Now, I'd wager we're not going to get them all shifted before sun up, so, here's the real bitch of the thing, we're going to have to run the gauntlet on that exposed section.' Burrows indicates the smooth bowl of sand between Walker's Ridge and Plugge's Plateau. 'Who's willing to take first shift?'

Francis is proud to note Henley's arm spring up and lifts his own in response. They'll go together. He needs the company. And he'd sooner go now than later, when the day rises to shine them again into Bill's waiting graticule.

He touches the folded paper in his breast pocket. His reward, upon completion of the task, will be to reread Lily's letter. For now, though, he will only contemplate the word-pictures he has committed to memory: the tailored shamrock-green coat; the red-apple lipstick; the pages of the magazine she and her friends have printed lifting and fluttering.

Soon, Francis, Henley, and two other of the wiser chaps find themselves scurrying at a peculiar forward hunch across deep sand, the darkness corrupting their footsteps, the cliffs echoing their panting breaths, and the hundred pound shells cupped in their arms like cradled babies. The shells stink, like a penny or a farthing held in the palm too long and clammily brought to the nose. The weight of the things, when running, is near unbearable, and Francis grits his teeth against the slow, even tearing of his rhomboid muscles. He will suffer for this. They all will. It doesn't seem a sensible use of manpower when they might have hitched up some donkeys. But Burrows is in charge, and Burrows has his orders, and Francis is determined to be respectful of them. There are games he must play if he wants to step ahead.

Perhaps that was what Cruikshank had wanted them to think on when he had moved down their line at Sliema barracks, pointed his knuckled cane at them, and said, 'What games do you play?'

'All of them, Sir,' Francis had replied, thinking he had bested the old man, but what if Cruikshank, in his wisdom, had only been waiting for some keen boy to announce, 'Games of war, Sir.'

Francis curses himself for not having found that answer earlier. It might have impressed Cruikshank. It might have meant for swifter promotion. It might have allowed him to follow Berto to the Dardanelles sooner.

And those are his greatest wishes now: to progress the ranks, and to explore every sand-grain of Gallipoli in search of his friend. And, perhaps, himself.

He had imagined he wanted to earn his stripes for his father's sake. Or his sisters'. Or even, on occasion, for whichever woman – Agnese, Lorenza, Marija – whose bedsheets he was sneaking between. But he thinks now that, truly, he wants it for himself. Plymouth had offered him only grey skies, cold sleet, and secrets. Malta: frustration, fatigue, and the riddles of dissatisfied women. Gallipoli, then, might prove the site of his greatest opportunity. Here, he will show everyone that his father was wrong to accuse him of being fly-by-night. Here, he will show them all that Francis Albert House is driven by ambition and altruism.

But first, he must find Berto. He needs to say sorry.

'One more?' Henley gasps, gripping Francis' bicep. 'Have you got one more in you, Sir?'

Faint moonlight shows him the purpling of Henley's flat cheeks. The chap is near spent. And so, too, is Francis, for he has not slept for more than one sweep of the clock in many a night.

He nods. 'One more, and then we've done our share. Agreed?'

'Sir,' Henley says.

'Alright, then.' He exhales, short and sharp. 'Let's at it.' And they take off across the beach for their final sprint, their ankles throbbing, their backs burning, and only God knows how many rounds of ammunition waiting to strike them down. There is a pressure in Francis' ears and chest which he recognises, somehow, as the deepest sort of dread. But beneath that, hidden in the pitch hot pit of himself, are the swellings of another secret feeling: purpose, perhaps.

How long it will sustain him, he cannot suppose.

At the dusking of the next evening, they are declared fit for action. The line in front of Francis' is defended by the 7th Light House – a fine set of fellows, Francis has already discovered, containing the same Bill Farmer who'd woken him on the beach. Then, to the left come the 10th and 12th Battalions A.I.F., which, Francis discerns, stands for Australian Imperial Force and sounds impossibly grand. To the right, they are touched by a small clutch of their old friends the Maoris, washed up at Anzac after all.

The sorry party Captain Burrows hauled ashore, Francis included, are deemed to no longer constitute a company, as such, and are promptly attached in name and order to the Australians for the foreseeable. The impersonal nature of this arrangement leaves Francis dejected, but he suspects he will have no trouble making the best of it in the long term. His pluck and spirit might have been shocked into hiding by his landing on the cove, but they are returning to him now, moment by moment. So long as there is action to chase, Francis House will charge forward into it. It will prevent him, at least, from looking back.

Their gun position is merely another round hole cut into the side of a bank. The army are making mice of themselves in Turkey, scuttering about after nightfall, gnawing little holes here and there to cower in. And since they have gained nothing, surely a new approach would be welcome. He'll think on it, he decides, as he finishes connecting a wire with the observation post Captain Burrows and Sergeant Patterson have found behind the 12th Battalion. He'll take all the best of his learning and his training and he'll think out a solution.

Cruikshank's last words to him had surely been designed to boost his confidence. 'I need thinking men to show the way out there,' he'd said. And Francis might just be the very thinking man required in Turkey. He is desperate to show the way, for he cannot tolerate this stasis. It will send him mad. He ponders the quadrilateral organisation of the men around the poorly protected gun, and the location of the gun on the cliff edge, and the seeming futility of it all.

Yes, he can make a difference here.

He reports along his wire. Two words. Two words he wholly believes in, having consumed no food and managed no sleep in two – or perhaps it is three – days. He speaks them proud.

'Ready, Sir.'

And then comes the shelling.

Five

They are eight inchers, Francis learns when the first pen-
etrates his Witney blanket to graze his thigh, and, unlike
those Bill issues during his morning shift, they make their
visits day and night and any time between. The graze leaves
a blood stain on his blanket which resembles scattered grease
spots. Francis wishes it were more impressive or not visible
at all.

I am wounded, Father, he might have written of a deeper gash.
I've taken a shot to the leg, but I'm trudging on all the same. Such a
boast might have satisfied the man who, after every school
rugby match, had stood his young son on the kitchen table and
turned him about inspecting him for 'war wounds', then,
finding none to his satisfaction, declared Francis 'soft'.

But Francis cannot bring himself to commit to the lie. He
spits on the blanket and rubs at the stain, his head already
lowering under the whir of the shells.

In the days that follow, the men are provided a sheet of corrugated iron and ten feet of four-inch timber, between three,
and told to set about protecting themselves.

For a full week, Francis tunnels and hammers and tinkers
with his dug-out, flanked by Henley and Farmer. So soon he
has become one of those rodents, burrowing into his hole. But
burrow he does, splitting the lined skin of his palms and
knuckles, sucking blood and dust from his fingers, hammering
an index nail black. He can, as yet, identify no better option.
Pounding plank to plank, he envisages the words of Lily's
letter, chiselled into the wood, and feels better for knowing that
they will be part of his canopy when he sleeps.

Each night, when he is spent, he settles in his dug-out, unfolds her letter, and reads.

She writes exquisitely – her thoughts and truths flooding forth in a cursive Francis is so familiar with, he fancies he can hear it – and he sees every incident she describes as though he is sitting in the dark before one of the new Gaumont or Pathé films and having his eyes lit for him.

He welcomes the distraction. He sinks into it…

I was waiting at the top end of Temple Street…

Francis rushes to close her words back into the envelope when he hears approaching footsteps. Henley's thick legs appear over the lip of the dug-out and he drops clumsily in, causing a thud which Francis feels through his thighs and buttocks. Francis does not bother to shove his letter into his breast pocket, where he most often hides it: Henley has seen him secret it there before and does not trouble him to reveal its contents. Instead, he uses the corner of it to scratch at the crease of his nose, as if it is unimportant, a mere tool. He manages to leave a straight red scrape along his cheek.

Henley lowers himself to the ground. Francis, seeking a new occupation for his hands, runs a fingertip along the line of his jaw until he finds some imperfection to pick at, and waits for Henley to settle. But Henley cannot seem to. He shifts twitchily about, his hand returning at rapid intervals to his bulging pocket.

'And what have we here?' Francis asks, leaning closer.

Henley's finger flies to his lips. 'Shush!' he hisses. Despite his size, Henley is child-like in expression and mannerism. Francis wonders if he has yet left his teens behind.

'All right,' Francis laughs, raising his hands in mock surrender. 'Caught you in the act, have I?'

This time, it is Henley who leans in closer. Francis grips the letter tighter.

'Don't tell the others,' Henley begins, his voice a skittering autumn leaf. 'But I've pilfered us a little treat.' Pushing his hand into his right pocket, Henley retrieves a battered round tin and grins at Francis as he holds it up triumphantly between thumb and forefinger. The tin is army green, with an ovate white sticker-label. Saliva pools in the well of Francis' held tongue.

Henley glances over his shoulders to left and right, as though expecting some creature to swoop in and pluck it from his grasp.

'Plum duff,' he whispers. His pupils gleam deep black with excitement. 'We'll have to wait until the others are sleeping though.'

Francis nods agreement. 'Don't want Burrows catching on.'

He watches, disappointed, as Henley slides the tin back into his pocket. Francis has not eaten since dawn; his stomach is the gaping mouth of a monkfish.

Then, for a trice, they sit back and listen to the shells.

'It's enough to break your nerve, isn't it? The persistence of it.'

Francis nods. The sound of the shelling is as much a weapon as the shelling itself. It is as though a woodpecker has been set to work at each man's temple and ordered not to stop until it has penetrated the skull and reached the sweet reward of the swilling consciousness within.

'Do you want to hear a story instead?' Francis offers.

'What kind of story?'

He lifts Lily's letter and gives it a wave.

'Is it interesting?'

Francis shrugs. 'It might be. It's from my sister. She…' He pauses to consider which words to choose. It is the first he has spoken of his sister to anyone on Anzac. 'She's started something of a protest, I suppose. Joined up with some friends. They've published a magazine…'

'Have you read it?' Henley asks, sitting up a little straighter. He is intrigued.

'No,' Francis replies. 'She lives in Swansea now. Moved there with her husband to open a butcher's shop. But she's written to me about it.'

'And what's it for, this magazine?'

'To help those at home decide whether what's going on out here is right or wrong. To better inform those boys who want to join up what it is they'll be facing. That's the gist of it, I imagine. By all accounts, it's proved quite incendiary.'

'Go on, then,' Henley says. Leaning into the wall again, he crosses his arms over his deep chest, tilts back his head, and closes his eyes to listen. 'I could do with a story.'

Francis unfolds the paper carefully, then glances at Henley, to ask whether he should start by introducing him to Lily's friends, or the contents of the magazine, or... He notices the steadying of Henley's breathing, and the streak of dirt which javelins his left cheek, and the tired slump of his shoulders, and quietly Francis does as he has promised and tells Henley a story.

It's the best he has to offer. He has been inventing stories his whole life.

We would be formed up about three times a week and go on a march of anything up to 20 miles and this distance combined with the heat and the fact that we had to follow the smoking steam engine was by no means a joke. I soon got used to it and became as fit as a fiddle, but needless to say, I was always glad to plunge into the sea, and soon became a strong swimmer. At night I would meet my friend Berto and we would go off on the road near the sea and open our hearts to each other. Berto is the only man who knows my inner being and he has always been worthy.

Six

The poppy-plush cusp of some other day – he cannot say which, for already and so soon, he has lost his grip on time – sees Francis crawling towards the cliff edge on his belly. His men are sleeping still; last night, they had swilled their worries away with pint after pint of stolen rum. Those Maoris who have been washed back to Anzac Cove from Cape Hellas are about their silent prayers. The world is suspiciously quiet. There is only the swooping of the birds which remain far offshore, and the pressing weight of motionless air, and the steady cuffing of the waves against the butterscotch rocks below, and the thumping of Francis's thoughts, matched to his heart, as he slithers forward like an infant learning to use its limbs and tries to swallow the taste of that flaming rum.

On the cliff edge, he knows, perched like gulls in the breakfast light, are the words he will write to his family.

He has no paper to scrawl them on, but, he considers, once he has caught hold of them, he can pin them down and keep them until he knows the order they must be placed in. Later, sobered, he will know what to say. He will know how to admit that, as suspected, he's been a fool; that he's only just begun and he fears being unable to sight the finish line; that, truly, he understands nothing of the world. Because it has been a week – just seven days – and already there is a dead man less than four feet beneath the earth beside his dug-out.

There is a dead man sprawled in the broken rowing boat abandoned down by the shore.

Everywhere Francis looks, there are dead men, and he cannot drink them away, however much rum he, Farmer, and Henley steal. He is forced, instead, to sober up and face them – as he has always suspected must be his fate.

He begins with the dead man standing in front of the gun. His name is Tom Merton.

Tom is Francis' bombardier. Tom's job, whilst they are fixed in this unfortunate position, is to retrieve rations from the beach. Less than an hour before he had gone down through the shaded gulley between the cliffs to fetch water, and now here he is, as white as only death can render a man, and haunting the very stony aperture through which Francis is to observe the Turks. He has retained a firm grip on the billy cans, but Francis can tell by the long creak of their swinging that they are empty.

'Tom!' Francis snaps. 'You're in the line of the gun, man!'

Tom only gawps at something far beyond Francis' head, his mouth open, his eyes unblinking, his shoulders slack. The billy cans clang as they swing.

'Merton!' Francis calls.

Tom responds by turning his stare on Francis, and Francis wishes instantly that he had not called: Tom is as empty as those penduluming billy cans.

'Merton! Move!'

Burrows' thick neck thrusts his head into view above the wall of a nearby dug-out. 'Would you listen to your Corporal, Merton?' he barks.

It is apparent, however, that Tom Merton cannot. He is lost. He is spattered with blood, but he is not bleeding. He is dead, but he continues to breathe. Somewhere between stepping into the water queue and climbing back to their position, he has entered the realm of the unnatural and Francis cannot stand to look at him.

Just as he could not stand to regard poor Edwards when they

perched like twisted harpies along the Valetta coast and ached for sight of a submarine or a German boat.

Then, mornings slicked by, timed by the sea's steady breath, and they saw nothing. Days dwindled. Nights swelled and waned. Through some endless watches, Francis did nothing more than doze and think of cold Plymouth rain. Through coruscating dawns and afternoons that dried even their perspiration, through sunsets that tore open the heavens and slow, clement evenings, the men lamented the inglorious beginning of their war. They stared out to sea and spotted little more than the occasional gull. Somewhere, there were barbarians to shoot at, but since they could unearth none, the guns stayed silent. And only Edwards amongst them was wise enough to settle quietly and accept the situation.

'Sir,' he would say promptly whenever Francis made a request of him. 'Yes, Sir.' His voice was timid as a drowsy child's and it irritated Corporal House. The man just hadn't been the same since his near-drowning those few months before during a tough training exercise. He crept about as though always part-way into a slow apology, his head low, his shoulders slumped. His eyes were permanently popped, still evidently awaiting the disaster he had somehow evaded. When Francis looked at him, what he saw was a body perpetually suspended in water, the movement of arms and legs softened, the mouth shocked open. It was a haunting thing to behold, but Drowning Edwards, as they began to call him, drowned all day long.

And instead of wondering, as he ought to have, whether it made things more difficult for Edwards, to be sat atop the cliffs, staring out at the surreptitious sea hour after hour, studying and questioning it, Francis had spurned the man. Even after he'd ventured to the Dardanelles as one of his volunteers, Francis had kept his distance. He keeps it still.

He shall have to do better by Tom Merton. The boy cannot be more than sixteen-years-old. Perhaps – hindered in love by his delicate chin and softly curled hair – he has joined up to impress a girl back home. No doubt he imagines himself returning, triumphant and muscled, to sweep her off her size threes. His shoulders are not yet wide enough to support a greatcoat. He reminds Francis of … someone else.

Captain Burrows clambers from his dug-out and, grasping him by the tunic, half-walks half-pushes Tom away from the direct threat of harm.

'What happened, Merton?' he asks.

All around, men have stopped to await Tom Merton's answer. They lean on their rifles and pinch their tobacco, they pause part-way through lacing their boots, they halt in the process of loading shells, they slow-chew their bully and biscuits and swallow away their tea, and they wait. Only Bill Farmer moves amongst them, affecting his usual gutsy detachment. Reaching Francis, he whispers into the younger man's ear.

'You'd better find a new fella for your fatigue party,' he says, nodding in Tom's direction. 'His nerves will never be right after that.'

'After what?' Francis murmurs.

Bill Farmer only shrugs and nods again at Tom, who has folded to the ground now and sits, legs splayed, between his discarded billy cans. The uncomfortable extension of his legs coupled with the slow labour of his movements puts Francis in mind of a toddling child, slackening into sleep.

'What happened, Merton?' Burrows asks again, and in the silence, Francis lifts his boot onto a shell box and pretends to polish it. He does not look at Tom Merton, or Captain Burrows, or Bill Farmer. A response will not be drawn from Tom, he thinks, when so many eyes and ears are waiting on it.

It was always so for Francis, when he sat at the end of the dinner table opposite his father – the two House men positioned to make a two-headed beast of the contrivance – to be poked at by Frederick for responses to questions about science or history, philosophy or mathematics. Though ideas sailed like galleons across invented oceans in Francis' mind, it was only rarely he knew the answers Frederick wanted.

'You have to commit yourself to the retention of this variety of information, Francis,' Frederick would say. 'Without a thought in your mind, what kind of man will you become?'

By asking question after question after question, Captain Burrows is eventually able to establish that, down on the beach, Tom had joined a single queue for water and struck up a conversation with the chap in front of him: they were discussing where home was, he reports, and shuffling forward inch by inch, when Johnnie started shelling the Jacks.

'But you're not hit,' Burrows assures Tom, shaking him by his upper arms. 'Listen, lad, you – are – not – hit.'

'No,' Tom agrees.

'Then you must get up.'

Tom locks eyes with Captain Burrows and, after a thud of silence, releases the sob he's been holding so tightly on to. Every soul in camp, even Farmer, bows their head then, wanting to block out its shuddering heave. For a minute or more, over a hundred men contemplate their own shadows, laid out as they are before them on the patchy earth, and wait for Tom Merton to stop crying. When eventually he speaks, two-thirds of them have unwittingly traced out their own graves.

'Tom,' Burrows urges. 'Speak, lad.'

And so he does. Past the trembling of his lips, and the dryness of his tongue, Tom manages to tell the end of his story. The words fall into an infrequent well of calm.

'They shattered him to atoms,' he says.

Seven

Every aching morning, they lay their dead out in an orderly line near the gun, then walk back and forth in the manner of children picking a new member for their football team. They stare into each pale face; they consider each broken body; they decide that this one is not theirs, and they move on. Sometimes, Francis identifies chums who have been called: he knows Carson by his silver-streaked hair and, for decency's sake, does not pull down the shroud to consider his face. Sometimes, he stares into the eyes of departed Turks and wonders at how many he has killed. Always, he holds his breath until he reaches the end of the line and can be certain that Berto does not lie at his feet. Only then can he keep believing in the story he is telling himself.

Whether friend or foe, the bodies are treated each the same: anyone handy stands around and uncovers through the snatched minutes of an inadequate burial service, then the unfortunates are rolled into a soldier's blanket and committed to the earth.

Mostly, their graves are marked by crosses mustered together with a couple of split planks and a tat of rope, though some have civilised memorials, brought in from who knows where. Francis notices the acquisition of neither. He pays his respects and he returns to his duty, as he ought. There are more enemies to fight here than just the Turks. And some, he has learnt, are invisible. Submarines shift steadily towards land, unseen and unheard. Diarrhoea and dysentery attack without warning. Rats scuttle about the dug-outs, indiscernible in the wallowing darkness until their teeth tear a diseased chunk of flesh free from a bared toe, an ankle, a hand, and deposit infection in its stead.

The men tend their guns and eat their paltry rations and troop down to the sea to wrap their infested garments around a stone and drop them into the water, and Tom Merton says in a low stammer, 'They shattered him to atoms'.

At bleary daybreak and hungry nightfall, Tom Merton says, 'They shattered him to atoms'.

At empty dawn and shell-shot dusk, Francis asks, 'Do you know a chap called Berto Murley?'

But when a voice says, 'Maybe down by the…' or a finger points towards a sleeping possibility, Francis does not need to investigate. Were Berto that close, Francis would have felt him. Were Berto within earshot, Francis would have heard his wheezing laugh as he fell about at the punchlines of his own jokes.

He recalls him reclining in the narrow rhombus of shade behind sixty-five company's block after one of their twenty-milers, his ankles crossed and his socked feet resting damp on Busty's knees. Sweat dribbled down his temples still as he flicked open a Maltese newspaper and started to read.

'Do you suffer from a bad case of optimism?' he said, clipping his round northern vowels so that they more closely resembled Dad Rymills'.

'Do you enjoy peeling blisters from your toes and sucking splinters from your fingers? Do you long to inhale the noxious gases of fifteen sleeping men as you dream? Then join the British Army and you too could be issued your very own mis-sized uniform and complimentary punishment schedule.'

He crumpled the paper into a messy globe and threw it at Francis.

'How can you still be smiling after that slog?' he demanded. And Francis had no response to offer him, but that he was happy on Malta, for a time. It was he – not Lorenza, nor his father, nor Berto – who had ruined it all in the end.

With the curling heat of August, comes the realisation that twenty of Francis' twenty-five men are dead. Four weeks of cowering from Bill's bombardments and rising with the moon to stretch their legs and backs, four weeks of tinkering with their dug-outs and cleaning the six-inchers and firing shells into the invisible distance, four weeks of growing ill and losing track of time and waking up not knowing whether they've slept or not, of smoking and waiting and scratching, and all they have to show for it is twenty rudimentary crosses, sitting crookedly against the sky. Twenty tormented shadows. Twenty fewer voices to converse into distraction with.

'What do you suppose,' Bill Farmer says, settling alongside Francis so that they sit shoulder to shoulder, looking out into the copse of crosses, 'the Captain writes about in that book of his?'

Along their tunnelled dug-out, Captain Burrows sits hunched over his scribbled words.

Francis shrugs. He should like to write in a notebook about all the different sights he has seen; all the scents he has inhaled; all those fleeting moments which he has, over the last four weeks, begun to fear forgetting. The flat, misty damp of Pembroke Dock. The sight of that ragged coast where he'd been woken untold times by the seaweed spoor of the incoming tide. His father's hand, proud on his shoulder the day he received his uniform. Standing on the hurricane deck of the *Sudan* on the voyage to Malta, listening to the waves slapping at the ship's hull and chatting with Berto until their bones grew cold. The ship anchoring off the Needles and him and Berto hanging over the railings, watching morning blanch the rocks which rose like fins out of the sea. Their first sight of Fort Tigne: the almost-circular harbour, with a small heart-shaped island at its centre; the rolling waves which shone white at their idle crests; the drooping explosion of palm leaves. The busy harbourside. The water, dotted with small rowing boats in which natives lounged, awaiting but seemingly not encouraging their fares. The straw-hatted workers who milled around at the water's edge, heaving carts or dragging loaded donkeys to and fro. The ladies standing in bunches, choosing fruit from carts heaped with fat water-melons and cascading grapes. Marija's rose and beech tree skin.

But here in Turkey, his hands are always dirty. He cannot imagine holding clean white paper between the fingers Bill Farmer thrusts a lit cigarette into now.

It's a Maltese brand. Francis recognises it from Agnese's lips.

'Perhaps he writes love poetry,' Henley suggests from the opposite dug-out wall. So close is he that if Francis were to straighten his leg, he could kick Henley in the kneecap. He chooses not to. It is not the hour for playfulness.

'Or his confessions,' Farmer counters.

'Perhaps it's a report,' Francis mutters, 'for the Fortress Commander.'

'Or for Churchill himself.'

On Malta, Francis had made it his business to read the papers, to study the companies' order and movements, and he knows that Winston Churchill believed that if he sent enough of his Navy battleships through the Dardanelles and on to Constantinople, they could hammer Turkey clean out of the war and establish supply routes along the narrows to Russia to boot. But the Turks' defence has proved stronger than antici-pated. The Gallipoli Campaign has been at a bloody stalemate since the first landings, in April. Already, Francis has lost twenty of his twenty-five men. Tom Merton has lost his mind. They've gained no more than the grains of sand which work into their boots and pockets and weigh them down.

War in no way resembles that which Francis dreamt of when he tucked himself into his childhood blankets and touched the wall his older sister used to sleep behind and found the paint cold under his fingertips. There is no echo, in the Dardanelles, of what he and Berto envisaged on their first night in Malta.

'Come on,' he'd whispered.

Berto shook his head and turned over onto his back but did not wake. Holding his arm out straight, Francis tipped the jug again. A string of water escaped the spout and rushed along each of Berto's eyebrows before disappearing behind his slightly protuberant ears. This time, he did wake.

'What the hell are you doing, Nellie?' Berto had called him Nellie since their training days at Woodlands, when he had noticed an unfortunate likeness between Francis and one of the serving girls. His friend's accent added a length to the word that Francis' south-westerly burr could not find.

Francis held his laugh between his teeth. 'How did you know it was me?' he asked. Berto hadn't yet opened his eyes.

'Who else?' Berto grumbled.

'Come on. We're going out.'

And before Berto could properly get his bearings, he was being dragged out of barracks, through the muddle of little stone houses, and back towards the sea they had marched away from hours earlier.

There, Francis discovered a wide, empty road which swerved along the coast and, at his insistence, they began following it. The moon sat so heavy in the sky that it looked liable to drop into oblivion at a blink, and whilst Berto stumbled along next to him, Francis explored the misshapen dark by its pearl-shell glow. He moved like a hunting dog, nudging Berto now and then as he doubled back and forth in front of him. Now, he scuffed his boots against the rocks that lined the place where the road succumbed to nature and climbed again into cliff face. Now, he rushed towards the spot where the road collapsed into rocks and spilled into the water.

Half a mile further along, they stopped and looked out together. Francis inhaled until his breath caught in his throat and he coughed. That familiar smell pitched towards him over the waves: the sting of salt and deep cold.

'The sea always smells the same,' he said. 'Have you noticed that, Berto?'

'Can't say I've thought about it.'

On the opposite side of the harbour, Valetta skulked: a long, smudged mystery.

'We should go across.'

'On one of the boats? I didn't bring any money.'

'No. We should swim.'

'I'm not swimming about in there. The natives'll have our clothes.'

'Off the point, then,' Francis said, whipping around to face Berto. 'Off the point and out to sea. Come on, Berto, let's see if you've managed to persuade any hair onto that chest of yours.' And, slapping his friend's back, Francis took off.

Berto let out a shout of foul play but he was soon at Francis' heels and, pushing up clouds of dust, they dashed left, leaving Valetta at their backs and veering around Tigne's blunt point: Berto's wiry strength ensured he kept pace easily enough with Francis' longer lope. Their panting breaths broke on the air like mortars. Unknown scaled creatures scattered into roadside shrubs or scurried up the cliff walls as they tore past. And then, with only the black sea before them, they hopped from rock to rock until they felt the water at their toes.

'You don't think we'll be bitten, do you?' Berto said, wriggling out of his shirt and swinging it around his head as a cowboy would a lasso before releasing it. It floated down onto the rocks like some ghostly, foreign bird.

'By what?'

'I don't know. Whatever's in there.'

'Well, what's in there?'

'I don't know… Octopuses?' Berto said, his eyes round as pennies.

'Octopuses,' Francis repeated, and they began to laugh, their voices cutting through the thin night air.

Pulling off his trousers, Francis felt spits of water splashing up from beyond the rocks against his legs. The cold spray was welcome after the day's heat; his muscles burned furiously. He dragged off his socks and then, with nothing else to remove, dropped his underwear and tottered over the last remaining boulder stones. The sea called to him as wistfully as ever, and now he waded straight in, taking huge graceless strides and causing the shone surface to roll and tilt and shatter. Soon, his feet could no longer find ground and he began to tread water. He took a few shivering, misdirected strokes, to acclimatise to the temperature, before twisting around to look for Berto.

Berto was standing onshore still, naked and white as virtue under the moonlight.

'Get in, man,' Francis called, flicking water in his direction. 'You look like a plucked chicken.'

'And you, my friend, look like a side of pork,' Berto returned. Then, scrunching his nose, he oinked for all he was worth, leapt, tucked, and plunged in.

Reaching Francis' side, he said, 'Been trying to impress a girl down there in wild Wales, have you?'

Francis sniffed. 'No –'

Putting his palm to the top of Francis' head, Berto thrust him underwater and held him there a while. Francis did not struggle. He knew that Berto would soon let go. It was only that he did not want to look at the way the lines of Francis' back shifted as he moved, or the swelling of the tendons in his neck, newly thick and ropy beneath his skin. Berto had told him as much when they'd marched up from the harbour that morning, and Francis had joked that, from the rear, his friend gave the uncanny impression that he had shoved two pitchforks into his tunic to fill the space his flesh did not.

'Better a scarecrow than a fattened bull,' he'd winked.

On the count of three, Francis resurfaced, slow and slippery as a seal.

'How long do you think we'll be here, Murley?' he asked, turning in Berto's direction. He wanted to know what Berto really thought, not what he was willing to say in front of Busty and the others. He'd come out here searching truth. Excepting the trouble at the Llanelly and Cardiff strikes, Francis hadn't yet been called upon to prove himself. And during the strikes he'd had numbers to back him up, and superiors too. What if he had, in Malta, to act alone? Now that he was here, he wasn't sure he could do it. Not absolutely. And he didn't know how to settle that doubt with the craving he had to see a real fight.

But Berto would know what to say. He always did. Berto might look bony and pale as a sickly youth, but his soul belonged to the boldest of terriers. He'd enlisted when his mother still ought to have been scrubbing his face clean – orphaned, Francis had always imagined, though Berto had never been forthcoming on the subject. He'd served three months with the Marines before he'd even reached age. He might pretend to grumble now and then, for the attention it gained him, but Berto Murley was and always would be bursting with pep. For that, Francis loved him. For that, and for the fact that, since the day they'd met, Berto had chosen to stand beside Francis, all bristle and snarl, and remain there regardless, in case he should be needed. Even after the accident, he had not flinched.

Francis searched the answer to his question on Berto's face, but he couldn't make it out. In the darkness, his friend's eyes were beads of oil.

'Who knows,' Berto answered finally. 'Long enough for you to get your way, I wouldn't mind betting.'

Francis stared up at the cliffs and, with the lapping of the sea, began to feel calm again. It had been a hiccup, that was all – a moment's uncertainty brought on by the search for sleep in a new country. But here was the sea, right here, and he could dive into it any time he wanted. In Malta, he decided, he would become a fish.

'Long enough to see a fight, perhaps,' he said.

But he'd thought they would charge into it together, Francis and Berto, House and Murley, friends since the day of enlistment and bound by their secrets and their trust.

'Did you ever envisage this?' Francis asks now, biting away sudden tears.

'The heat, Sir, or the bugs?' Henley replies, applying his teeth to his knuckle and tearing at something which has embedded itself there.

'The waiting.'

There comes no answer from Henley or Farmer, but into the empty wedge of earth between the dug-outs they hear a voice rise.

'They shattered him to atoms,' Tom Merton says.

It is not my scheme to give the impression that I looked for trouble – one did not need to look in Malta.

Eight

The dead men are replaced, soul by soul, by Australians, but these Francis must train on the heavy gun whilst in action, and he soon finds himself worn to a rake with a sporadic and unstoppable sickness. No woman would look twice at him now, skinny and black-eyed as he is becoming. Where once his thick curled hair sprung away from his face, now it hangs limp and dull over his forehead. His easy smile has shrunk under chapped and bleeding lips. A Dr Marks – following a most cursory examination – supplies him with opium, to ease the pain that is forever picking at his ribs. Francis takes it without question that first time and for an hour or two afterwards cannot remember where the pain originated. It is so much more effective than the rum that almost immediately he requests more, and is rewarded with dose after dose.

Within five days, he knows only that his brain is too large for his head; and that the diarrhoea has stopped; and that even when he wakes he is as weighty as a sleeping man; and that perched still on the cliff edge, and now on the cannon of the six-inch, and the corrugated roofs of the dug-outs, and the mismatched crosses of the vast cemetery they have built in front of the gun, folded and angled like flighted origami creatures, are the fluttering words he must write to his family.

'Coward!' they caw. 'Guilty!'

But he cannot spell them out until he has spoken them to Berto. It is the only way to say sorry for what he has done.

Sometimes, when he is lucky enough to be awarded a larger measure of the opium, the words of Lily's letters dance before him.

She has written to tell him that Hopkins Street has thrown a party. He thinks his way through those bitten sentences to Lily's fear and disgust now and considers that perhaps he finally appreciates it as he pops a stone into each of his socks and, standing barefoot on the shingle, drops them into the sea to wash them. They disappear with two muted plops, spitting salt-beads back at his feet. The day is little more than a silver trace at the furthest reaches of his sight. Mists coil around his ankles like fussing cats. He inhales the murky sea salt smell, in hopes that it will offset the rotten stench which lingers over Walker's Ridge. He has twelve hours of nothing but Bill's relentless song to get through before he can return to the howitzers and begin playing his countermelody.

Carefully, sculpting the soles of his feet over the wash of jagged stones and shells at the tideline, he turns and teeters towards the softer sand, and then over it, and thence in the upward direction of his breakfast. Or rather his supper. On Gallipoli, they breakfast at the cessation of their efforts, then settle into sleep with their stomachs bloated by weak tea and their dreams warmed by crisped bacon and stacked toast and plump blue duck eggs.

Francis notices light close into dark and dark peel into light, but he finds he has no need, here, to count the regularity with which it happens. At dawn, Bill peppers the shore. At night, men move about the greyed beach like miners or dock workers: synchronous; ghostly. This is his new nocturnal existence. It does not contain days of the week. There are only the hours, and what they signify.

When they are manning the howitzers and awaiting their next round of tea and straw-packed bread, the hours mark degrees of hunger. When, in the dead of day, they creep down to the shore to wash, and the Turk guns awaken and jolt life after life into the invisible depths, the hours tally the number of graves they will dig once they have hauled the wet, dangling men out of the shallows and carried them back to their dug-outs – as they had poor Goskirk, who, as bound to the hills as his flocks, never had managed well on the coast. When they catch sight of a supply ship in the distance, they wager their empty stomachs on how many minutes will pass before it is spotted, shot at, and sunk: then, the hours are a game.

Walker's Ridge is a quadrangle of rising steam and smoke when Francis returns from the shore. The damped air puts him in mind of a laundry, but no clean white sheets billow here. Nothing is clean here. All about, billy cans have been set over fires to blacken and boil, and men sit around the fires, cross-legged and slumped, chatting and sharing cigarettes and scratching.

Bill Farmer has a small pan positioned over one of the fires, and in it he is frying three thin sausages. Their muscular scent greases the air. Francis has opted for a pint of porter over the rum this morning and, though he doubts he is destined for any share of the meat, he is already imagining chasing it down with a bitter swig of warm beer. He touches a palm to the few ounces of dried fruit he has wrapped into a squared cloth in his shorts pocket. It will do.

'Forgotten something?' Farmer asks, nodding at Francis' naked feet and the boots which swing from between his clamped fingers.

'Nothing but your sense of humour,' Francis replies. 'I'm afraid I let the tide take that.'

Farmer picks up an abandoned cup and flings it at Francis. Francis catches it deftly in one spread hand, hooks a forefinger through the handle, twirls it around, and winks. Today, he recalls something of the man who paraded around Malta, charming women and teasing his friends.

'Sit down, won't you,' Farmer urges. 'We're waiting on another of your letters.'

For want of a kinder sound to drown out Bill's continuous crank and shell, Francis has taken to reading Lily's letters aloud to the men. By turns they huddle around – Henley, Tom Merton,

Bill Farmer, Drowning Edwards, Farrelly, Hodgson – as if in anticipation of the bedtime stories of their childhoods, and listen pensively to the faraway cadences of a woman's voice.

Francis shrugs into his tunic and probes around in the pocket for the envelope, then settles just outside the lick of the fire's heat and unfolds the paper. He lets his eyes play over it for a beat or two, deciding where to start, before he speaks.

'The celebrations were in honour of the first of the local boys to volunteer for Kitchener's Army,' Francis explains, settling alongside Henley's salt-cleaned scent as he describes the party Lily had detailed: the tables dragged from sheds and back rooms and lined, end to end, down the middle of the street; the stiff white cloths laid with cheeses and cold meats, scotch eggs and cucumber sandwiches, biscuits and jellies and fruits; the music crackling from a gramophone positioned on a swept front doorstep.

Occasionally, he borrows her words and twists and reshuffles them so that they sound, to the men, like a tale written in a novel. Sometimes, he plays for laughs. But today a melancholic streak persuades him to recite her words just as they were put to paper.

The music was grinding on and on, and at the bottom of the street, a group of boys were transforming their football match into a game of soldiers. One small chap filched a broom and, positioning it under his arm, aimed it at his former team-mate. Pew-pew, pew-pew! *He fired four bullets in rapid duplets.* Pew-pew, pew-pew, pew-pew! *Six more, and three of his comrades slow-motioned to the ground, arms rotating like airplane propellers, chests bucking, legs crumpling. A few more boys – little Gwilym from next door amongst them – lifted invisible weaponry and took aim. It was a barrage, Francis. Bullets scuttered and streaked, and the boys smacked their lips in imitation of the dampened drub of metal finding flesh.* Pew-pew-pew! Thwack, thwack! *they were all going, dying again and again, until they were a battling ghost army.*

And I said to Elaine, 'They're little boys; their mothers will die of this.'

But the women didn't care to think on it, Francis. Not a jot. They were too full of pride and bragging, sending those poor lads who had joined up up and down the road like show horses on lunge lines, primed for admiration. They hardly looked older than the little ones about their play fighting.

How much of them will come home, I wonder, and how much of them will be lost to the earth.

Don't let that be you, Francis, she had written at the foot of the page. *Do what you must, but promise me. Don't let that be you.*

Francis does not speak that sentence aloud. It is private, his very own, as nothing else is on Gallipoli.

He thinks back through Lily's earlier letters, for some details to replace the truth with, but he is saved the effort when, a heartbeat later, a sniper objects to the Jacks' breakfast preparations and, with a quick pap-pap-pap, holes three of their billy cans. The last spills its contents over the flames and, with a hiss, extinguishes the fire. The men – unflinching – watch the logs turn to embers and then to charred skeletons. Francis looks to Farmer, expecting a plucky comment which will lift them from this new misery, but none is forthcoming. He tries Hodgson, whose steadfast practicality has often made them laugh, but his eyes are cast down. They have nothing left to say in the face of death.

Instead, they nod their goodnights, and curl in on themselves as the next bombardment begins.

Shells whiz and drop and whirr, and thwap and clink and buzz, and the repeated thrub of them finding their targets is as relentless as the march of a corps newly stepped off a ship. Wrapped in his blanket, Francis presses his palms over his ears and waits for sleep, but he cannot silence the drumming. *Pah-pah-pah-pah-pah. Pah-pah-pah-pah-pah.* His own voice echoes the sound and spins it round his mind until he is a child on a merry-go-round, one arm outstretched, calling for his father.

Pa. Pa. Pa!

With each rotation, Frederick moves further away from his son, until, finally, he turns his back and disappears from sight.

Pa!

Francis gasps into waking, feeling himself covered with crawling vermin. Without a thought for his head, he leaps up, swiping at his shorts, his vest, his shoulders, his hair. Flitterbugs he and Lily used to call any insect with wings. But these are not flitterbugs. These are dirty red ants. He has made his bed atop their nest. The realisation springs tears to his eyes and he sweeps them away before they fall. Then, without lifting his sights to check if anyone is watching him, he settles himself in his blanket again and, for the shame of it, lets the ants scuttle across him in their neat, unbroken lines. What he sees then, in his exhaustion, are not small three-segmented bodies and busy legs and trembling antennae, but the letters contained on Lily's pages, marching over his skin.

He has not written her back since that night on Malta, with Berto. He does not possess the means to justify his misbehaviour, to fill a paragraph with *if only*, and *I didn't mean*, and *if it wasn't*, and *no one's to blame*, and *but I am to blame*, and *I will make amends*, and… He needs to explain it all, so that she will not think him anything like their father, but the words are inadequate. He struggles to find his breath. The muggy air is crawling into his mouth to suffocate him, and he wants the water, and his sister's unbreakable affection, and his father's admiration, and his oldest friend. But he knows he can have none, so he studies the ants. Beneath his blanket, he makes a ball of his fist and drives the knuckles into his own abdomen until he feels something within him might burst.

He had insisted he must come to Gallipoli to find Berto, but what has he done to locate the man except sit around fires and ask idle questions? He has not walked every inch of Anzac

Cove, stopping to look into the face of every huddled soldier; he has not checked every dead Anzac's pockets for some unknown evidence of his acquaintance; he has not interrogated Burrows or Patterson as to his whereabouts; he has not described each of his features to his new friends in turn in case they might recognise him from the oddly exaggerated protrusion of his Adam's apple, or the way he always winks after he has teased a little too much, or his perfectly kind soul.

Francis has not done everything he might. And perhaps, just perhaps, that is because, in truth, he is scared stiff by the thought of coming eye to eye with the man he has so badly betrayed.

War having been declared on Aug 4th with the Huns, we were all anxious to 'aim for glory'. Reuter started reporting stirring events in France, so we were all anxious to be there. Drafts were called for but although I persistently volunteered, I was always told I was of more use in Malta training Kitchener's men, who began to arrive. This naturally made me very dejected, especially as many of my mates were chosen. I soon discovered that my stripes were an obstruction, but though I tried to give them up, I was not allowed to. However, every dog has his day. By April I had two stripes and determined to be one of the next draft.

Nine

He is woken by the straying light of an enormous thunder moon. He lurches upright with a snort, panicked at having slept beyond nightfall, until, looking around himself, he sees that the other men continue to snore and twitch. They have been granted permission to dream. They had laboured straight through the previous night and day, digging a stubborn barren of mules from the sucking shallows and dragging them ashore only for them to wander forlornly back into the water. In the end, the breathless men, cramped and worn out before they started, had been forced to stand on the beach and watch the poor beasts go.

Francis tips back his head. Tonight, the moon's mottling is a deep, deep grey. There's a storm on the way, Lily would say, her superstitions and predictions based on nothing so much as invention. A thunder moon meant for a tempestuous turn. A strawberry moon meant for the birth of adventure.

He sees her as she had described herself, that first time she drank with her friends at The Three Lamps.

A strawberry moon still hung on the night when we tripped out of the pub, somewhere far beyond midnight.

'Nos da,' the others called as they drifted away. 'Welai di.' And the words were a strange poetry.

Then I lowered my head and strode off up Temple Street in a fit of determination. I'd had my excitement. I had spoken and been listened to. I had contributed to something other than my husband or the business or the children, and the fleeting selfishness of it fluttered at my chest. It's an unfortunate trait but always, it seems, I have to keep something for myself. I felt as happily muddled there, Francis, as I do when I lay pressed against Ernest and drop into sleep. It was breathless, and easy, and singular. I was my true self, but I was desperate to be home then, with Ernest, so that I could speak the Welsh I'd asked to be taught.

Caru ti, I whispered to him between his snores when I finally crept into our bedroom. I love you. Caru ti.

Francis can hardly imagine his sister a married woman, with a lanky ginger-haired husband, and two appley babies to raise. Norman and Violet both, he imagines, will look like Lily. And yet, he cannot imagine how this little family of four will hold her still. If Francis is of the sea, Lily has always been of the sky.

He touches the pocket containing her letter. Over the last few days, the tear at its folded seam has lengthened, furred. The paper is starting to deteriorate. He shall have to handle it less often. He resists the urge to look to it now and, steepling his hands in his lap instead, notices a lightning bolt crack jagging down the centre of his thumbnail, from tip to cuticle. He hadn't felt it happen, but it is deep and already blackened with muck. He holds it up under the moonlight to inspect it. It doesn't hurt. He flattens his fingers and angles his hand this way and that, considering the damage. And it is then that he notices, in the littered foreground, the figure of a man.

Beyond the strewn and bundled mounds of Francis' sleeping company, beyond the water barrels and the pale sag of the tent canvases, beyond the dark insistent jut of the six-incher, beyond the piled-up sandbags and the slanted roofs of the dug-outs, he moves delicately, stopping now and then, as though he is not a man but a hunting animal.

Francis stands to get a better view.

The man stops and snaps his head around, sensing himself seen, then, without any sign of acknowledgment, moves off again.

'Wait,' Francis says, but his voice is only a caught rasp. He brings his hand to his throat and measures its heat under his palm. He is flushed. His heart is bashing about his ribcage like a trapped rat.

'Wait,' he tries again, but his voice is lost. Just as it always was when his father wanted him most to speak, and it is that sensation which persuades Francis, all at once, that it must be him.

'Father,' he says, because he is certain, suddenly, that it is Frederick who is stealing towards the swollen cemetery. What he is doing on Gallipoli, Francis cannot imagine, but it must be him. No other figure could bring about such panic. Four years now, since he has seen his father. A voice set to paper is not the same. Words leaked from a pen-nib can never replace the physical presence of a person. One cannot learn, from a string of looped letters, that a raised eyebrow means quiet disappointment, that an ankle crossed over a knee means easy repose, that fidgeting fingers mean a want for conversation, that reddened ears mean amusement. There are too many gaps, too many assumptions.

Francis blunders around the sleeping bodies which lay between him and his father: past Whitman, curled tight as a kitten; over Drowning Edwards' legs, which stretch out from the sitting position he always rests in now. He has not troubled to pull on his boots, for they will only thud on the dried ground and frighten Frederick. As he goes, his socks slough down his feet so that the woollen toes flop emptily before him, but he does not stop to right them. He keeps his eyes on the man in front, for fear that if he looks away, he might disappear.

Around the water barrels, away from the dug-outs, past the cemetery he trails the figure in silence. Skirting the shallowest edge of the bluff, they begin a descent towards the waves. Francis' clumsy feet knock small stones loose and send them skittering downwards; he winces against their hail-fall echo but continues apace.

On the sand, they pass the new drop of water tanks, stacked up against the cliffs like a fleet of hulking ships, then scurry through the shadows of the mismatched huts, spotted, at intervals, by the moon.

When the man reaches a shell-torn sloop, he stops.

Some feet behind, Francis stops, too. His heart bunches like a fist. He still has not seen the man's face. Close by, though, he appears much smaller than Frederick House; skinny, even; and shorter by far than is Francis' father. It cannot be him. And yet, Francis knows that this is none of his men, for they are all sound asleep on the bluff. He knows, too, that it is not a Turk; no Turk would risk venturing so far over enemy lines.

Hidden under an over-large greatcoat and cloth hat, the figure breathes heavily. Francis watches the greatcoat rise and fall in even time.

'Christ,' he says finally. 'It's you, isn't it?'

The figure does not reply, does not move.

'Answer me,' Francis demands, his voice rising above a wisp for the first time since he woke.

But why should this man comfort Francis with a response. He owes Francis nothing. Francis is sure of that much now that he knows – perhaps, in truth, he knew from the first – who is standing before him.

'Please…'

A slip of cloud wreathes the moon, casting a net of darkness over the beach. The figure begins to rotate slowly. Francis looks to the sand, to avoid the immediate regard of the man standing beside the broken sloop and, where he expects to see a pair of scuffed boots, finds nothing. No boots. No feet. Nothing but the silvered air. And above that, no trousers, no belt, no vest. Francis' eyes move up and up, and fail with every inch, to meet expectation. A chill crawls the back of his neck. There is no man here. There is nothing but an empty greatcoat, and above the place where a man's head should be, a hollow peaked cloth hat.

•

Ten

'What is it with you and your letters, Sir?' Henley asks.

'What do you mean?' Francis replies absently. He does not take his eyes from the page. He concentrates on the small tear in the central fold. Now that he is returned to his dug-out and the greatcoat is gone from his sight, it might be dismissed as an apparition. He has let his mind wander too far into the past. But he knows that his letters exist – he can fold them between his fingers – and so he intends to hold tight to them. Surely he can fight off the imaginary, however frightening, with that which is real.

'Well, I mean, I've never seen a man reread a letter so many times. What can it say to have you so gripped?'

Francis lowers the letter onto his bent knees, but keeps the paper plucked firmly between thumb and forefinger. Some days ago, he lost a page to a sudden gust of wind on the cliff top and cried quietly as he watched it flap into freedom like some newly discovered genus of bird. He will not lose another. The letters are his only reassurance that he still has a somatic existence. They are addressed to him, after all; they are delivered to him on this sorry smudge of land; they are the proof that someone, somewhere, still knows where he is. The folded envelopes are pleasingly smooth against his roughened skin. He stacks them in a bundle beneath his makeshift pillow and, at night, runs a fingertip along their edges until he sleeps.

He cannot admit as much to Henley.

'They're from my sister,' he says. 'You know that.'

'I do, but... What else?'

'Isn't that enough?'

'No,' Henley insists. 'Sir.'

Francis looks from the words, to the eager chap crouched across the dug-out from him, then back to the words.

'They contain the truth,' he says.

'And yours don't?'

Francis shakes his head. 'Mine don't. Not always.'

Overhead, a shell scutters through a rare scarp of cloud. It leaves a smattering of puncture holes in the wilting whiteness. Francis looks again for the belly of a swooping gull, but is, as ever, disappointed. Birds wing only away from Gallipoli.

'What's she like, your sister?' Henley asks. Then, after a pause, he adds, 'You're turning her into a story, Sir, to amuse us. And it's good for the men. I understand that. But what is she really like?'

Francis knows that Henley is talking only to punctuate the rhythmic explosion of Bill's shells. It helps some of the men, to talk. It does not especially help Francis, but he is willing to play along, for Henley's sake.

'Short,' he says.

Henley laughs. 'What else?'

'Stubborn.'

'And?'

'Kind. Angry. Brave.'

'Angry, brave Lily,' Henley says, as though testing the sound of the name for the very first time. 'Do you miss her badly, Sir?'

Francis folds the letter back into its envelope and tucks it into his breast pocket. He will reread it later, when Henley has spoken himself into sleep. He needs to sleep. Bill has denied them even a minute's rest these past two days.

'I do,' he says. 'Very much. She always saw the best parts of me.'

It was a privilege she could afford, having never set foot inside Woodlands.

'As she should have, Sir.'

Francis raises his eyebrows, surprised by Henley's response. 'What makes you say that, Henley?'

Already, Henley is settling against the dug-out wall, letting his head loll back against the hacked away mud and stone. He hunches his shoulders as he knits his arms across his chest, comfying himself as best he can.

'Just that we all ought to try to see the best, Sir. I always do. We owe each other that, don't you think?'

Seeing Henley's eyes close, Francis lowers his voice to a whisper.

'Yes, I do,' he says. 'You're absolutely right.' And he vows there and then to endeavour, always, to try to see the best. In Tom Merton's fear, he will see the caution that might save them from attack. In Farrelly's occasional back chat, he will find the doggedness which might, at some important juncture, cause Francis to reassess and make a better decision. He owes that much to his men. He owes it to Lily, too. And Berto. Come to think on it, he might even owe it to the empty greatcoat, which might well have come to him out of need rather than menace. But why him? What could it possibly want with Francis? The thought sets him to shivering, and he closes his eyes and attempts to emulate Henley's softening slump, though he knows he will not sleep tonight.

In 1912 I met a lady – no names – and became so infatuated that I was soon engaged to her. I introduced Berto to her sister but though a more than close friendship was struck up, I could see it was not Mr or Miss Right. After this we would wait on the ladies every night at their home, and I must say we found much pleasure there.

Eleven

Rain trickles in one early August eve: the first Francis has felt in the longest while. It begins as a tapping on the dug-out roof. Then a pattering on his head, his shoulders, the rounded fronts of his boots. And soon it is jabbing directly groundward in the windless night, quick and silver and beautiful. Francis climbs up from his dug-out and into the makeshift cemetery, weaving between those offensively aslant crosses, his tin hat skew, his tunic loose and wing-beating, his boot laces untied.

'House!' someone hisses as he sways around and about the crosses. 'House! What are you doing?'

Francis lifts his arms, making a cross of himself, too, and tips back his head. Above, the clouds are deep and plum.

'You could plunge a spoon into those clouds,' he says. He recognises the words as the very same he'd spoken to Berto the day they'd found each other aboard the *H.M.T Sudan*. Quick as a lash, Berto had replied, 'I'll remember that sentiment, when we're looking at different skies.' But does he? Francis longs to ask him, but he hasn't the foggiest where to begin. Berto and Busty feel like characters he dreamt up after Dr Marks began administering the opium. They are too exuberant, too bright, too good. And he does not know where they are. They might be lying in the dark beneath a cheap cross of their own. They might have died side by side. They might have died alone.

'House!' another voice hisses. 'Get down man. You're going to get yourself killed.'

'Who by?' Francis calls, spinning now over the graves of so many men.

'A dirty bastard Turk,' Henley shouts. 'Now get down, Sir.'

Francis turns towards Henley's voice and, rocking on his heels like a drunkard, shakes his head as wildly as his neck will allow.

'Sir,' Henley goes on. 'Get down or I'll come and make you.'

Francis slings up his eyebrows. 'Oh, will you?'

'Have I got a choice?' he replies. And with that Henley – young, loyal Henley – is scrambling over the side of his dug-out, fresh mud thick on his hands and knees, and trudging towards his Corporal.

He grasps Francis by the shoulders. 'It's the opium, Sir,' he says. 'You've had too much of the opium.'

And Francis smiles at the beauty of the repeated word. It does not belong to the English language. Its sound, its rhythm, is too exotic. Opium. Op-i-um. He will write to his family of opium. But for that he will need the letters, the words. He needs to catch them before they take fright and flap away. He ducks away from Henley's grip and lunges about, plucking at the air above the six-inch, then above the dug-out roofs, then above the crosses of twenty of his twenty-five men. He looks, to those men watching on in silence, as though he is attempting the Maori war dance, but Francis' version is weak and disorganised. None can see the words he needs to gather up before he can explain himself to his superiors, to his sisters, to his father. The words, he knows, prinking themselves as resting birds will, are visible only to him, because the others have no need of them.

They have no excuses to make.

They have not lost twenty of their twenty-five men.

'Sir,' Henley insists, catching him by the collar of his tunic now. 'You need to sleep it off. Sir. House.' Henley whips Francis around, bringing them face to face, and for a moment Francis' eyes are filled with Henley's worried mask, but then, beyond that furthest headstone, he is sure... Yes... A man, crouching there... A high brow, a short twice-broken nose, boyishly round cheeks... A pair of pale blue eyes, peering out from behind the...

64

'Murley?' Francis asks.

Henley turns to consider the point in the darkness which has so captivated his Corporal, but he sees nothing. Francis brushes him aside and staggers away.

'Murley!' he calls. The peeping face disappears behind the wall of a headstone. Francis rushes forwards, towards the place where his pal is hiding, but his legs struggle to manage the weight of his tired body and he propels himself onwards at a difficult tilt. 'Come out, man,' he cries. 'It's me. You're safe here. I knew I'd find you. Christ, Berto, I've been looking everywhere for you. I should've known, here, under the plum clouds. I should have... Berto?'

A hand clamps itself over Francis' shoulder and spins him about on himself once more.

'Francis,' Henley insists through gritted teeth. 'There's no one there, Sir. No one at all. You're not well.'

Slowly, Francis nods. He wants to prove it. He wants to throw himself behind that cracked headstone and claw and heave and scratch up the dirt in case, somehow, Berto might be hidden beneath it. He'd seen him, after all, looking out. He'd known him on the instant. But he hasn't the strength to argue with the broad young chap who is holding him still. Henley is right. He is not well.

'No. I'm not,' he says. 'Not at all.' He notices the mapped vessels in Henley's eyes are popping. His breath slaps stale against Francis' face: masticated meat and cold tinned beans. The boy is panicked, and rightly so. They are standing in plain sight, and even at this darkling hour, the Turk guns could spot them by hinting moonlight. Francis has seen it happen. Raindrops squirm down each of Henley's temples and along his jaw bones before plummeting to the earth, and doesn't he look like Frederick tonight – wet and frightened and trying to bluff himself out of it by standing too tall. Exactly like Frederick, when he and Francis took to the Hoe in that January storm and could only watch as the woman who had surrendered to the waves was beaten, skirt billowing, against the rocks. She was carried from the beach the next morning – a heavy, misshapen rag – and father and son never spoke of her afterwards. They hadn't been able to help. That was Frederick's insistent thought as they struggled home, regretting rushing out into the rough night on a rare adventure. They would have tried, but they hadn't been able.

'Henley,' Francis says. 'I'm sorry. I shouldn't have. It was just –'

'You need to rest, Sir,' Henley assures him, patting his Corporal's narrowing shoulder.

'There's no time.'

'But you must,' Henley insists. 'Else you'll be no use to any of us. Now let's get you back.' He grips Francis' shoulder tighter and steers him towards his dug-out.

'Henley…?' Francis says.

'Yes, Sir?' Henley turns to await Francis' question, his eyebrows raised in anticipation. But Francis cannot recall the form of the question, fogged as it is by his increasing doses of opium. He opens his mouth to try again, and Henley stops to wait, and so it is from mere inches that Francis witnesses the emptying of that frightened lad's eyes.

One moment, he is there – Henley, thick-jawed and thick-bodied, as strong as his youth, the hazel halo around his pinprick pupils large and clear in the moonlight – and then, in half a breath, he is gone. It is like watching a lamp extinguished. Poof. Slowed by the rain, the crack of the bullet follows afterwards, and they fall to the ground together, House and Henley: one deranged with Dr Marks' opium, and the other bleeding out from the perfect hole punched through his neck.

Twelve

The rain sweeps away overnight, leaving the next morning clear for Henley's burial. Francis turns an ear to the wind, to listen for gulls on the sunrise. But, as ever, they do not visit Anzac Cove. The sky, though apparently gold dusted and flecked with two glowing parhelia, must in truth be blackened by the noise and intentions of all the men who have been deposited at Gallipoli and turned on each other like fighting dogs.

Notwithstanding the dead man's superior weight and height, Francis insists on rolling Henley into the soldier's blanket himself, careful, as he does, not to force the stiffening limbs, the wintered fingers, into unnatural positions. It occurs to him then how similar the process is to that the men employ to wash their clothes and thinks that perhaps he should rather toss Henley into the sea than the opened red earth. At least there he would not be trapped. At least there he would still know the sky above him.

He is about to ask what the others think to the idea when Burrows' voice interrupts proceedings.

'Ready the gun!' he calls, striding towards the congregation. 'We've new orders.' As Captain Burrows reaches the men, he begins passing out small, white, calico articles. He does not seem to note the gathered quiet. 'White band for the right arm,' he instructs. 'White diamond for the right shoulder. For identification. We're making a big push on the Turks... House!' He glances about himself, then snaps into business when he locates Francis in his hawkish sights. 'You're to fire the six-incher for twenty-four – hours – straight. First round at five p.m. Be – ready.'

Burrows spins on his heel, searching the face he will direct his next orders into.

'Ah, Merton, you're the rations man, aren't you? We need everything we can get our hands on. Take a few chaps with you and bring it all back up. All of it. Go.'

Tom does not move.

'Now, Merton!' Burrows urges.

But still Tom does not move. Gone is the boy Francis barely got to know, who dropped his head and scrubbed his knuckles through his hair when he made others laugh, whose smile travelled from left to right across his face, who used to sing gently into the spit of the fire and tap out a four-beat on his slender thigh. He has become one of those pale, classical statues one might see at a museum. Marbled. Nothing runs through his body now but fright. Tom, Francis is certain, will come apart eventually in enormous gobbets, which will not bleed or rot but only crumble to dust.

'Soldier!' Burrows barks.

'They shattered him to atoms,' Tom gabbles. 'They shattered him to atoms.'

'Jesus Christ.' Burrows lifts his arms then lets them fall against his sides with a slap, like a bird with cut primary feathers. 'This still. Jesus – *bloody* – Christ!'

'Sir,' Francis calls.

From the corner of his eye, he sees Tom's chest loosen a tad and is pleased. He has failed Henley in the most spectacular way, just as he promised himself he would not. He will not fail Tom, too. Dr Marks will have to find him some alternate treatment, for he will no longer consent to the opium.

'What's my target, Sir?'

Burrows steps closer and, leaning in, brings himself cheek to cheek with Francis. Francis feels him scrunch one eye shut before he lifts his arm and points into the middle distance. Mountain after mountain after mountain, rippling outwards and upwards until they disappear into hanging white mists.

With the ever-shifting sea to his other side, Francis has hardly deigned to look inland. If there is some distinguishing feature he is supposed to fix on now, he cannot discern it.

'Sari Bair,' Burrows says. 'Purportedly rammed to the hilt with Turks.'

Behind Captain Burrows, Tom continues to gabble, his fist bunched against his lips in an effort to keep the words within, but he cannot stop them.

'What does it mean, Sir?'

'What does what mean?'

'Sari Bair,' Francis repeats. 'What does it translate to?'

Burrows' face crumples. 'Yellow slope, I think,' he replies. 'What does it matter?'

Francis hadn't believed it would, particularly, but it transpires now that it does. In his sights is an elevated block of exposed yellow cliff face, topped by a narrow viridian ridge. 'Yellow slope' tells him exactly what he is to fire on. They are going to attempt to take the ridge.

The pain behind Francis' ribs starts up its plucking again. Some tendon or sinew he does not know the name or exact location of is being grasped and pulled and then released and left to vibrate, like a cello string stretched close to snapping. He presses a palm over his ribcage and tries not to wince.

'Five p.m., Sir,' Francis says.

Burrows nods. 'On the spot.'

'Very good, Sir.'

'Make certain of it, House,' Burrows warns. 'Yours is the signal for attack.'

As the older man turns and strides away, Francis considers the white shapes he has been handed: a band and a diamond, reminiscent of a moon and a star. The band would barely have fitted around Henley's bicep. Francis runs his eyes along the lumped figure which has lain wrapped at their feet all this time. Burrows did not ask who the body belonged to.

'Help me get him up,' Francis says. Farmer is at his side in an instant. A couple of the other men step forward. Even Tom Merton shambles closer. 'Help me get him up,' he says again. 'I need to lift him over my shoulders.'

'But, House…' Farmer starts.

'Over my shoulders,' Francis snaps. 'Help or stand away.'

Without another sound, the men shuffle around Henley's body and, easing their hands beneath him, lift him up and over Corporal House's back. The weight is tremendous. Francis buckles, staggers slightly, and, with a long heave, manages to bring himself back to full height.

'I have him,' he assures his men. 'I have him safe.' And then he turns away from the guns and Sari Bair and the complex of dug-outs and huts he has ratted around these past weeks, and he walks to the cliff's edge with his friend draped over his back, and he jumps.

Thirteen

Beneath is murk. Beneath is grit and blur. Beneath is endless space and none at all. Beneath is cold and colder still as Francis sinks, Henley's bulk thrown across his back and pressing him into the dark. Water swills into his ears and stings his eyes, but he opens them wide, wider, and tries to decipher which way is up and which is down. He flexes his legs and ripples out from underneath Henley's body, but keeps a grip on the edge of the man's shroud so that he does not lose him. Freed of his burden, Francis sways like a shed feather, letting the fluxing tide hold and carry him. He feels his hair lifted from against his scalp and wonders at how light it feels, at how light he feels. Here, Francis can float. Here, Francis is restored to the man who could rush through Dad Rymills' twenty-milers in order to sneak out and meet Lorenza come nightfall; the man who, for a lark, could hoist Berto over his shoulder and run about barracks with him, slapping his rump and making him weaken with laughter; the man who, at fifteen, could scoop his older sister up in his arms and dump her, squealing, into the shallows. Here, Francis is strong. He has no desire to resurface.

And yet, he feels his lungs contracting, failing him. They have squandered their air on the shock of the fall and they are shrinking in on themselves. Soon, they will resemble nothing so much as the shrivelled fruit in his pocket.

In a sudden fork of anger, he pulls the fruit from his pocket and casts it away. He is clad in only his shorts, vest, socks, and boots, but he cannot bear now to be touched by anything which might drag him deeper. Hooking the toe of one over the heel of the other and shunting, he kicks free of his right boot. He uses the woollen toe of his right foot to push down against the cuff of his left boot, then shakes that off, too. They helix downwards, laces trailing behind. Quickly, he tugs down his shorts and heaves them apart. Then his unpeels his vest and draws it over his head and rids himself of its clinging presence. It drifts eerily away, shaped as though a man remains within it still – a ghost of a man.

Fleetingly, relief spreads through Francis. Down, down, right to his middle, where that scrabbling pain promptly starts up again.

Is he ever to be surrounded by ghosts?

He opens his throat to a deadened scream. Little matter how bellowing and pitiful it sounds against the brackish shove of the sea into his mouth. No one hears him. And no one sees him as he makes round weights of his fists and drives them into his stomach, his jaw, his chest, his thighs, his temples until every inch of him throbs.

'Please!' he bawls. 'Please!' Though he hasn't a clue what he is begging for. Help, perhaps. Just that. Help. His face is a contortion of sobs, but the sea will not let loose his tears. He continues to pound at himself until the last of his energy abandons him, and then, shivering and spluttering, he tips onto his back and reaches out again for Henley.

Catching the end of the blanket between his fingertips, he thinks, *Forgive me for this. Please, forgive me.* And then, hoping that some part of Henley can sense his thoughts, he flattens a palm against the dead man's tucked form and rolls him out of his burial bonds. *Go now,* he thinks. *Go home.* Henley rotates gently loose. A spin. A second. Francis feels the grey scratch of blanket slackening in his grip, and with one final turn, he sees that the blanket is empty.

Terror jinks up the length of his spine, creeps over his shoulders and neck, hot cups his ears. He knows with a new and gut-wrenching certainty that when he looks around, he will come eye to eye with Henley's spirit. He knows, too, that he must face this man, as he did not face the first. Francis takes a long, deep breath and, making fins of his hands, spurs himself about. Nothing but the claggy jade-green insistence of the sea. Nothing but the cold expanse and the heat of Francis' pounding blood. Nothing but the drum in his head and the throb behind his eyes and the tightening of his lungs. And then, as expected, as dreaded... And then...

Henley.

Henley's expression is not animated. He does not narrow his eyes at Francis or open his mouth to a curse. He does not lunge towards the man who got him killed and lock his hands around his throat and attempt to strangle him. His body simply hangs there, as if he is a curiosity suspended in a jar for spectators to lift up and jiggle and peer into and wonder at. His eyes are wide and without focus. His lips are enough parted only to show the slimmest hyphen of blackness between. But Francis hears his voice as clearly as he did two days before: raw and sand-snicked and always a little too loud.

You won't find him, Henley warns. *You're looking the wrong way.*

Francis bites down on his lower lip and tries not the think the word, *Who?* If he asks the question, Henley might answer. Instead, he concentrates his mind on an apology.

I'm sorry. Truly I am.

But Henley's ghost has no concern for apologies or blame. Finally, his eyes find their direction and settle, unblinking, on Francis'.

We did what we could.

Yes, Francis thinks. *God knows we did.*

And then, because he cannot bear to watch Henley taken from him a second time, he closes his eyes and concentrates on the shifting blotches of burgundy red and bruised purple behind his lids until his thoughts are brought to silence.

Fourteen

Lily Carter is sitting in The Lighthouse Café on the Mumbles Road, resting her nose on the rim of her teacup so that the steam twists up to warm her skin. Outside, a shouldering wind thrusts wave after sooty wave into the crescent of Swansea Bay. Above, the sky mills out rows of smoky cloud. Lily sips her tea and watches, to the furthest right of her view, bouquets of spoondrift rise up to slap the white, octagonal sides of the Mumbles Head Lighthouse. Even on days as grey as this, the bay is beautiful. She has found her home. The power of the place fascinates her: how relentless the wind is; how loud the waves. If Jasper's Baby were to blast its warning into this dishevelled dawn, she would wonder at any man on any ship being able to hear it.

She listens for the rattle and chuff of the Mumbles loco-motive, for the footsteps of her friends as they chatter along the pavement…

But, no. This is not what Francis wants to see. He wants to glimpse his sister running or dancing or laughing or jaunting. He wants to remember how easy it once was, to rival around the beach together and later fall home into the cottage warmth, salty and exhausted. He wants to see her fighting, as she vowed in all those early letters she sent to Malta, to fight. If he cannot, then she must.

He rushes through the scenes she has painted for him until he finds her standing on the seafront with Geraldine, Doris, Evan, Crawford, Thomas, and Dean: her very own company of soldiers.

It has been less than a week since he spoke her words aloud to Farmer and the others.

We were buried in our deepest winter coats, but we kept our heads low under our hats and watched the wind rearranging the men's trouser legs over their shoelaces. Gales swept violently along the front, the gusts climbing and diving and dragging some wisp of the sky about. It clawed at our clothes, our hats, the rolled banners we were gripping. We shouted into each other's ears and tried to trap the escaping words in our gloved hands. The day was too rough for it, really, but we weren't about to abandon our plan for the sake of a bit of wind. No fight can be made so halfheartedly.

Evan was bawling, 'Everyone ready?' And we all nodded in messy unison because we were afraid of saying the wrong thing. I was thinking of Ernest, and how he never speaks the wrong words, and using the thought to keep my mouth clamped shut. Ernest weighs his discourse as carefully as he cuts his steaks. I should have been at the shop with him, but I had to find a way to fight, Francis. I had to do you proud. And I was enjoying myself, too, truth be told. We laughed as Crawford's flat cap was whipped off and went somersaulting along the tracks.

We heard the engine before we saw it, huffing towards us on the coming angry squalls.

'This is it,' Evan said. And before too long, the train was chugging into sight, straggling its black smut behind, its open toast-rack cars clattering through the weather, and even against that rowdy dawn, it was cacophonous.

'Ready?' Thomas called.

And I was, Francis. I am. Not just for that, but for whatever comes next. We have a cause, don't we? A good one.

Everyone is talking about the banners we've hung already. The morning after the train, the boys braved hanging two more from the High Street and Sketty tram. The same evening, three more appeared flapping against the walls of Swansea Castle. And by the week's end, between the seven of us, we managed to drape our words all over the

75

city: across the Albert Hall on Craddock Street; on the Grand Theatre's frontage; above the doors of Swansea Railway Station. Waiting Patiently Since 1906. *The police have been removing them the instant they spot them, calling them incendiary, but by then it's too late – the words have been read. And if they are read, so they will be spoken. And if they are spoken, so they might be felt.*

Something is changing. That's what people will say – we hope. Something is coming.

The hope was a chug deep in my belly, like a pounding heartbeat, as the tank engine pushed closer. And then it was upon us, passing us, and we were leaping, clasping hands, scrabbling onto the final car. We were smashing knees and twisting ankles. We were shouting then shushing each other. We were laughing and wincing in pain and checking we still had hold of our banners. It was madness, Francis. But, finally, we hauled ourselves safely aboard. The close grey sea cuffed the sea wall again and again, its rhythm playing against the workings of the straining engine, and the noise and the motion was too much, and I was giddy with it, but I swallowed hard and set about the task. The train was moving forwards. We had no choice but to go with it.

At that, the men had nodded and grumbled. They understood how that felt. They had no choice.

Fifteen

When next Francis lifts his face from the waves, he finds himself back on the Gallipoli coast. He gulps at the air, swallowing it into his shrunken lungs. He tilts himself upright and stretches for the sand beneath. He can reach it, just, and scrunches his toes into it to steady himself. The grains scratch at his sea-softened skin. The effect is anchoring. Chest heaving, he arcs one hand over his head and attempts to push the runnels of water from his eyes. Then he tips back his head and wails into the quiet.

The cliffs shove the sound back at him, and he imagines all the men on Walker's Ridge willing him to hush. He will draw Bill's attention. He will get them all shot. But Francis cannot help himself. The pain at his middle worsens breath on breath. And Henley's body continues to bob slowly away on the shallow rollers. And above, the clouds refuse to part for him so that he cannot bawl at the heavens. And he misses Lily. It was more than a year ago that she leapt aboard the Mumbles train with the others, banners at the ready. Or maybe it was two. It seems impossible, of late, to keep anything straight. A constriction at his throat alerts him to the fact that he is still crying, though he cannot feel his tears. The sea has diluted them. The sea has diluted him, washed great hunks of him away, eroded his certitude and his good sense. *Shush*, she says. *Shush*. And Francis listens to her, as he always has, closes his salt-chapped lips around his sorrow, and begins to wade towards the cliffs.

The wet sand gives out a throaty thwop each time he drags a foot free. The left and the right elicit a different emphasis and he discerns, in their lopsided pitch, the word which has most haunted him these past months.

Ber-to, the sand gurgles. Ber-to. Ber-to.

And because Francis cannot stand to let the water claim that precious name, he drops onto his hands and knees and crawls ashore.

At 4.30 p.m. he starts counting time away by the second. Somehow, in his absence, Tom Merton had gathered and reassembled enough fragments of himself to complete his ration runs and has since returned to his dug-out, to hug his knees and count the rat prints surrounding his boots. Bill Farmer blows smoke from his cigarette into Francis' face, and the bitter scent reminds him that Farmer shares Agnese's chosen brand.

'A Maltese brand,' he says, to break the silence. He is not the only man who has resorted to repeating himself.

Bill Farmer shrugs and, taking the cigarette from his mouth, turns it left and right in pointless contemplation, as though it might have Malta written along the side. 'Maybe,' he says. 'I wouldn't know. I picked them up from a fellow off your ship. I'll bet he's regretting giving them over now.'

Whether Bill is truly relaxed or acting at it, Francis cannot tell. He slumps next to Francis, however, like a man lately filled up on a Sunday roast: heavy and lazy and keen on idle conversation. It seems that everyone wants to talk this afternoon. Burrows is circuiting their little pock of land, giving the same orders over and over; Bill Farmer is prattling on about the various benefits of smoking cigarettes; Farrelly and Whitman lean over an upturned crate like matching bookends, playing a game of snap and shushing each other when it gets too competitive; Tom Merton is still in his dug-out, muttering; and Francis is saying nothing at all. Francis is concentrating the opium out of his system. Francis is counting his men into God knows what. And none of them is meeting his eye, because none wants to ask why he is dripping wet, or where he went when he plunged into the sea, or how he managed to vanish so entirely and then return in time to fulfil his orders, or what

Henley was doing amongst the graves. They are fixated on the seconds, and the rapidity with which they tick away, and they are desperately pretending not to be.

Francis mourns every last one. Each takes him further away from Berto and Lily and everything he knew to be certain, before ... this. A mere moment has passed since he was chasing about on St Elmo with Berto and Busty, waiting on his war, sneaking out after dark.

On the Sliema side of the harbour, waited the fifth – or perhaps she was the sixth – in a spate of secrets he had become all too skilled at keeping. While the men jerked back in the barrack room, Francis played patience and waited to hear the first snores start up from the bunks. Learning the workings of the cannon and transporting the great lumping thing about had proved exhausting, and fatigue throbbed through his limbs. He had to battle hard not to add his voice to the rumbling chorus. A lucky thing, then, that battle was a favourite pastime of his, for soon he was marching down towards the rumpled, moon-blenched water, glancing behind him here and there in that twitchy way which had become his habit after nightfall. He had learnt to keep his wits about him in Malta. He still carried the table leg he'd acquired in that scrap he and Berto had started with a drunken crowd last year.

They had been strolling along the harbour wall, studying the sounds and smells of the strange country in which they'd found themselves. Francis desperately wanted to wrap his tongue around the soft, lumpy phrases of the language, but the words slipped into each other so smoothly that he could not separate one from the next. He tried: he called 'bongu' instead of 'good morning' when he woke; he said 'iva' with a nod whenever the cooks asked if he wanted more food; he knew that 'le' meant 'no'. But his understanding was pitiful as yet.

There is no misunderstanding cries of violence, though, whichever language they happen to issue in. And before they knew it, Francis and Berto were running with all their might towards a mob of natives who were tightening around a single terrified British sailor.

'In?' Francis cried.

'In,' Berto called back, but his voice was distant, because already he was racing towards the man in need.

Francis grinned at the thought. They'd come out of that one badly – a split cheek requiring stitches, a snapped tooth, a bulbed eye – but they'd gained a reputation which had followed them around the island for a while.

He was too late for the launches. Tonight, he would have to risk a dghaisa.

Below, the dghaisa men sprawled slackly in their vessels, their hands and feet teasing the water. Some stared dolefully up at him. Some slept, as usual, with their hats pulled over their faces. Others smoked and chatted with their neighbour. Their skin had been made thick and leathery by so many hours spent in situ. As he scanned the water for a friendly face, Francis noticed that all the fishing boats moored below had painted on their prows sets of large, brightly coloured eyes. He had never felt so watched. Apart, perhaps, from when he made his first parade in blues at Woodlands. Apart, certainly, from that dread moment when their mother, reclining in bed, her ankles crossed and her attention trained on the book in her hands, had lifted her eyes and stared directly at him and Lily, caught in the crack in the door, and they had known themselves seen.

'Sliema, please, good men,' Francis called to the nearest pair of natives, who lifted themselves lazily upright and beckoned him aboard. His weight rocked the dghaisa immediately he put one foot to the wood, but he was braced for it. He was becoming familiar with the unpredictable shifting of these little vessels. After all, his restless urges obliged him to make this trip across the harbour every night he could spare.

'Eight pence half trip,' the smaller man said. 'The rest of way, waves harder.' He indicated rougher water by flipping a flattened hand from side to side.

Francis raised his eyebrows. 'Eight pence full trip. I have already involved the police once this week. I don't wish to do so again.' Francis gripped his stick and, lifting it an inch or two, said slowly, 'So, what is it to be?'

The natives, not understanding the larger part of his speech, turned to the pointed bow and started to row, and Francis took his seat and watched the muscles in their backs tightening and loosening in even time. Though short in stature, these boys had too much strength about them. It was the work; it toughened them. Francis breathed deep and kept his chest puffed. True, he still hadn't mastered the language but there were, he was learning, always other ways to communicate.

He glanced about himself. All around the dghaisa's flimsy shell, the black sea rolled and rippled into the harbour, unstoppable, and as each wave found its target so it folded back on itself and was thrust once more away into darkness. Francis listened to its repeated sigh of resignation. *Sssssh. Sssssh.* That one triumphant moment of arrival, the briefest meeting of water and land, and then it begun its endless journey over again, and even in this it quieted him. *Sssssh.* All life, he thought, knew this desperate pattern. It would forever be one long battle after the next, a series of struggles which culminated only in a fleeting rush of relief. But, God, those moments! He was nineteen years old and already he had known the scent of a thousand different dawns, the thrill of diving into the ocean, the simple pleasure of fresh cake crumbling on his tongue, the excitement of a fight, the indulgence of lying in bed watching rain bend the windowpane, the shape of too many girls' bodies, the happy worry of planning a future, the joy of running along a dozen beaches, the belly-ache of laughter amongst friends, the delight of lifting his arms and tipping back his head and letting the damp Welsh wind hit him, the sweet fall into sleep at a hard day's end, the perfect harmony of the choir at Pembroke Dock, the pure cadences of a compliment from his father, the anticipation of sighting his sisters when he stepped off a train, the release of soaking in a hot bath, the camaraderie of trooping uphill with a company of hurting men, the lonely satisfaction of reading in an empty room.

And there was so much more. If only he could erase that etching of his father's frown from his soul, then he would know what it was to be happy. But he had never quite managed it, however hard he laughed and fought and rutted his way from country to country. Berto alone knew how fiercely he had tried.

It was Berto who had hidden Francis when it was discovered that he had taken the so-called Lady of Sliema to bed, and her betrothed had stormed the barracks, demanding to have 'the boy House' brought out.

It was he who had made excuses when they were called from their bunks early and Francis was noted absent – swimming instead of sleeping – from one parade or another.

It was he who listened, when Francis admitted through bitter tears that he didn't know what it ought to feel like in the least, being a man, and that he was deathly frightened that he was going about it all wrong. He who realised, at Woodlands, that when the boys were granted leave, Francis was not going home but hiding out in the treeline behind the building until it was empty, then breaking in to resume his practice. He who thought to ask why.

'Because I have to be the best,' Francis replied, and Berto only nodded, picked up a pair of boxing gloves, and began lacing one on so that they could spar.

Perhaps it was because of all that that Berto voluntarily swore himself to secrecy when he discovered Francis behind the stables that night, his hands and face stained with someone else's blood.

'It was an accident,' he had said. And Berto had chosen to believe him.

Francis lifted his stick again and tapped it rhythmically against his opened palm. The dghaisa men did not turn to look at him. That was it, then: he wouldn't have to brawl for his passage this evening. He'd committed himself, though, to a fight. A fight which would make Frederick proud. Elation at the idea rattled along his veins and caused his head to pound. He'd just have to find it. He'd just have to nose his way around this country until he discovered the battle that must be here somewhere. There was no sense in the army sending him to Malta if there was no one to fight. He was briefly certain of it. But before too many minutes, he was stepping onto the quay and towards his latest waiting lady, and he lost every thought but those of her skin, her hands, her closing eyelids and their curved lashes.

That was where men buried themselves, wasn't it – in the bodies of women?

On the eventual dot of five, Francis stands to the immediate right of the six-inch, ready, with a swipe of his arm, to bring the devil's greeting down upon countless Turks he knows to be waiting beyond the shrubs, the ridges, the crags. He has not sighted a solitary one of them. But he need not. Their presence is made evident, every morning and noon and evening, by the accuracy with which they point Bill down at the beach and fire, fire, fire. Francis wonders at why the shelling doesn't continue under the lighthouse-beacon moon. But then, he supposes, they do not have an endless supply of shells. They must act when their stores will prove most effectual. The Turks, too, have their orders.

'And you had yours,' he wants to tell his father now. 'You had to follow yours.' If only Francis had found those words as they'd sat at either end of the breakfast table, glowering into their porridge bowls in search of something to say. The sentiment, he is certain now, would have drawn Frederick out of his silence and into the present.

Francis looks down at the five men crouched near his boots. Though he has lived amongst them these past weeks, he has suddenly lost their names. Whitman, Farrelly, Hodgson,

Farmer, Edwards. He knows the sounds well enough, but he is failing to attach them to their owners. Whitman and Farrelly, the accidental twins. Hodgson, low-browed and serious. Farmer, always ready with a quip. Edwards, scared and polite in equal measures. He knows these men. He does. But it seems to him now that they are no longer identifiable by their wholes. They are only a blood vessel forking angrily across the white bulb of an eye; prison bars of saliva blocking the entrance to a gaping mouth; a twitch in a taut cheek, flickering through the skin like a pulse; a row of knuckles, recently blistered and healing badly; a repeated sniff-sniff-sniffing through a stuffed nose. Each man eyes Francis' raised hand. They are poised to leap to their tasks: passing the shell, loading the shell, cranking the –

On the stroke of the hour, down comes his hand and quick as a whip, his men are tossing, feeding, sighting, pulling, firing. *Pop, pop, pop, pop, pop.* They are as seamless as a heartbeat. The six-inch jolts backwards as though in fright, the first shell growls and tears into freedom, and Francis, ears thundering, trails it as it climbs the parrot-feather sky like an airplane, rising, rising, until it finds its ambit and there seems to slow to a halt. Francis lifts his hand to his pocket and touches the little vial of red-brown liquid contained within, to ensure it remains safe; the glass is smooth beneath his snagged fingertips. Soon, he will hunch out of sight in the dug-out shadows and bring it to his lips, for, despite his intentions, he cannot do without it. The pain is too great. The pain in his stomach which Dr Marks has attributed to pleurisy. The pain in his heart which Francis has attributed to guilt. Soon, he will submit and, hunkered in mud and shame, throw back his head and pour the opium tincture down his throat and wait for the magic to take hold and return him to the timeless sea, where he can swim wildly into his past and away from his future until, eventually, he redis-covers that boy he can hardly remember now; that courageous boy who advanced across his parents' attic towards his adulthood, unafraid of anything that might be approaching in the opposite direction; that easy, loving boy, who swooped along the beach and yelled for his sister and longed to throw himself at the tides. Only in her cradling flows, Francis realises, will he find his sister and his friend. Only there, will he find himself. Because the sea has been his companion all along; she has witnessed his every fold and crease; she will carry him, when she is ready, off Gallipoli and into her shining depths, where he has always belonged.

At the gun's first pause, Francis closes his eyes and listens as she draws back, gathers up the chinking treasure of her shingle, and, tossing her mane like a spooked horse, rears, kicks her pale spume hooves, and drops into a surge for the shore. Ca-*cush*! He holds out his arms and braces his back as she roars towards him, and then over him, and he smiles as she bears him away. He has known, from the moment he followed Captain Burrows ashore and dripped on to the sand, that she would come.

The fire of my gun started a perfect hell, which I shall never forget. British cheers went up, then a moment's silence. Then I think every killing contrivance was brought into action.

Sixteen

In a blinked eternity, the first shell plunges nose-down into the far-off yellow dirt, and her brief soaring life comes to a dusty end. British and Anzac voices roar her home. They have just made their first dent in the Sari Bair mountains, and Francis is back in his position. Mouths pump out their excitement, eyes bulge in anticipation, fists shake, and chests are bumped, and shoulders shoved. Here we go, their bodies are saying. Here we come! Francis – though his arms are raised in celebration, too – witnesses it all as though at half-time. The pumping and shoving, the slow-issuing cheer, the silence which lumbers after it, cumbersome as a lame horse. The perfect hell that follows.

Because every man around him now wears Frederick's face.

Smiling, the time they passed a rugby ball around on the frosted back lawn and, Francis, just seven years of age, realised that his hands had grown big enough to catch it properly. Tearful, the day they stifled themselves into black suits and buried his mother. Hopeful, when Francis' acceptance letter from Woodlands dropped through the letterbox. Black, as night approached, and the daytime's distractions no longer saved him from his memories. Proud, as they posed for that photograph on the day Francis left for Malta.

Francis swings his regard from face to face to face, and there he always is. Waiting, desperately, for his son to do well and fearing, ever, that instead he will fall wrong. As he did.

The many faces of Frederick House close around Francis, and he can smell his father's breath – cigar smoke and sugared almonds. He can hear the crunch of the sweet casings between his square teeth. He can taste the sting of his cologne. He can feel his hot approaching bulk and the flinching of his own neck muscles as he awaits the drop of a fist that never was raised in his direction, but which he so oft expected all the same. He can sense, too, the stale sweep of newspaper prints over his fingertips. On good days, they read the newspapers together.

'They're for it now,' one of the men shouts, and Francis nods, not having listened to the words. All about him is fading, slowing, morphing. He does not recognise this new reality.

Though he has sworn against it more than once, he knows he will not manage to keep his men firing on the enemy for a solitary hour, let alone twenty-four, without another dose of his opium tincture. He touches his pocket, grips the vial between thumb and forefinger through the thinning fabric, and tips it up to feel the liquid spill from one end of the glass to the other. Its flow is rhythmic perfection. He tips it again. Ah, the endless back and forth. He has stolen the gravitational tug of the moon. He is creating his very own tides. He can choose when to suspend himself between fluted light above and the deep black below. And when to shuck off his skin, as readily as a blood-soaked greatcoat, and reveal his tail.

Lily's voice floats after him. 'You're no House,' she laughs.

> 'You're flotsam and jetsam.
> Lagan and
> derelict.
> You are a salt soul.
> A tide gypsy.
> A billow.'

Francis laughs.
That's it.

Francis House, Corporal. Francis House, sea god. Francis House, merman.

Seventeen

His first view of Albert Murley had been an unfortunate one. On entering his allocated number three room on his second night at Woodlands, Francis found that the lamp had been removed from its hook and replaced with a boy. Upside-down and stripped to the waist, he hung, trying not to whimper, whilst a much larger boy paraded around him, poker in hand. This larger boy Francis knew to be Hancox – Woodlands' chief bully. He'd been warned about Hancox on arrival.

'Sing,' Hancox ordered, circling his victim and waving the poker before his face. Apart from the flames of the fire, the poker, burning hot, provided the only light in the room.

Though Murley wasn't quite managing to supress the frightened animal yollops which insisted on rising from his heaving stomach, Francis saw that he was doing an admirable job of keeping his tears in. His tears and his song, for he was, thus far, refusing to sing. Francis threw his kit bag onto his bed. If Murley just kept quiet, he thought, kept quiet and waited out his fear, he wouldn't be troubled any longer. Francis would shake his hand later, tell him he'd been brave in facing off the threat of the poker. But then the fire flared and Francis saw that Murley was already injured – two white burns slashed across his stomach, one angled down towards the belt of his trousers, the other marking a straight line above his navel – and that was when he lost his temper.

'If you want to fight him, Hancox, pull him down and do it,' he growled.

Hancox spun around to find the voice in the darkness. Francis was the only boy standing. The others lay balled in their blankets, steadfastly ignoring Murley's predicament. Their eyes met and Francis saw that Hancox had the set of a bull about him: his face was scorched red; his eyes bulged; his nostrils pumped in, out, in, out. He was about to charge. Francis expanded his ribcage and tightened his fists in readiness.

'Perhaps, House,' he said through clenched teeth, 'you should fight. In his place.'

'Happily,' Francis returned and, because he didn't want to be seen shaking, he made a deliberate show of removing his new greatcoat.

Francis smiles now, remembering it. The greatcoat was too large by far. At fifteen, he'd thought he could take on the world with the right attitude and a willingness to fight. 'Never mind if you are beaten,' his father always told him. 'Just show 'em you are not afraid.' And he had long determined to keep the words close to his chest. But Francis had not slept a minute that night, because he'd known Hancox wasn't going to let himself be beaten, and he was waiting for the other boy to take his revenge.

'What are you grinning about, man?' Farmer asks, approaching Francis side on.

Francis turns just far enough for Farmer to see his left eye, winks, and taps his nose with a dirty index finger. *My business, not yours.*

'So be it,' Farmer replies, dumping the last box onto the pile and stepping into the queue. Orders are that every man is to bring two rations boxes from the beach up on to the bluff, then wait on a hot meal. They can tell by their weight that the boxes contain Maconochie tins, and can therefore deduce that the meal that will be ladled into a tin mug and thrust at them will consist of sliced vegetables, hopefully warmed until soft, and a dribble of transparent gravy. Francis is past caring, so long as it's hot. Often, his stomach balls like an empty fist. He is thinner than ever he has been. Now, when he watches his meals shelled and sunk off the coast, it is all he can do not to cry.

At home, he would have been ashamed of the inclination, but their camp on Walker's Ridge has become a nursery room full of cry-babies. So helpless are they. So hopeless are they. Anzac might just as well be a hospital ward, and the British Army's best rows of sleeping boys, swaddled tight in their cots.

Their mothers will die of it, Lily had said in her letter. And so they would, Francis thought, if only they knew. Even his own mother – so bound up in his father's moods and tempers, so frightened of the workings of her own mind – would have wept to see him thus. As he shuffles closer to the muddled-together field kitchen, he stares into the curve of a large cooking pot in search of his reflection. The steam dissipates to reveal something less than a man. He cannot decipher the outline of his face, the cut of his cheeks or jaw, the dome of his head. He cannot find the bristles of beard he has missed shaving by moonlight or the movement of his mouth as he talks to Farmer of everything and nothing at all. He sees only two dark hollows – which might be his eyes but might only be dents in the battered metal cooking pot – and the collar of his greatcoat.

Cradling their cups of stew, Francis and Farmer retire to their dug-out and slurp from their steaming mugs in silence: the bombardment of Sari Bair has left a mountain range of dirty yellow cloud between the Johnnies and the Jacks which nothing will pass through for hours. Farmer and Francis have learned the rhythms of Gallipoli together these weeks past – the chaos and the quiet, as regular and insistent as a pulse – and they know that today they have some time. So they sip and gulp at their leisure, and all they hear is the squelchy workings of their own throats and the drumming of days-old gunfire along their grimy ear canals. They are soon joined by Farrelly, who hunches forlornly over his vegetables. It is solely on account of Farrelly's fair hair that Francis has learnt to tell him apart from Whitman. F for Farrelly; f for fair. That's how he remembers it. Otherwise, the two lads might be one and the same, so young and peach-faced and spindly are they. It has become apparent, though, that Farrelly's moods are by far the more changeable. On occasion, he strops like a true brat.

Farrelly spends a minute swilling his stew around his mug, then, shoulders miserably slumped, he dips an erect forefinger into the concoction, stirs it around, removes it, pops it into his mouth and sucks the watery gravy off. Francis wants to slap his knuckles, for the filth of it. And for the sluggish attitude of his body. And because he has not been free to box or run or love these past months and his own body is aching for action without measure and intent.

'Shall we swim tonight?' he says quietly. It's not so much a question as a private thought. He does not expect anyone to answer him. 'Once Bill is asleep.'

'Sure,' Farmer nods, sucking a slice of carrot between his lips. 'I could do with a paddle.'

Farrelly nods, too. 'We've a long wait for nightfall, though.' He rolls his eyes upwards to indicate the trembling midday sun. 'Will you read us one of your letters first, Francis?' he asks.

And Francis, not wanting or needing to be asked twice, immediately sets down his tin mug, delves into his pocket for Lily's letter, and gently unfolds it.

'The parade was already in full swing when we got to Mansel Street,' he begins.

Men and women lined the pavements, their faces lit with excitement or crumpled by dread or rendered vacant by indecision. Young boys, wearing newsboys like their dads', raced hollering alongside the band of the 6th Battalion Welch Regiment, who marched the gentle incline in perfect four-four unity, their trumpets and tubas held high and pressed to their lips, the instruments glistening like the perspiration which wormed down their temples and around their ears. It was too hot for all that – marching and playing in brass buttons and stiff hats, swanky epaulettes and shone black boots. Their booming notes softened as they progressed uphill. Near the back, the drummer arched

his spine against the weight of his drum and, gritting his teeth,
pounded its skin with a left swing, a right, a left swing, a right. Boom,
boom, boom, boom. Like an elephant, I thought, tromping across a
scrubby savannah. Down the street, a tram clu-clunked after them, but
no one moved aside for it: not the band; not the children; not the
onlookers; not the men who, one by one, fell into line behind the 6th
Battalion Welch Regiment and, without a word, pledged themselves
to Asquith's war. One forward step and they were Kitchener's men,
bound for the continent and a fight no one much has yet troubled
themselves to question. And they didn't seem to think on it, Francis.
That's what I couldn't bear. That's why I dragged Geraldine and
Doris off with me and joined in with the procession.

I can't imagine what we must have looked like: Doris in her silky
black shirtwaist and Geraldine pursing her cherry lips. But we felt
like we were marching into battle, noses to the sky. And I'm sure we
would have joined up, there and then, if they'd have let us.

I sometimes think – if only I'd been born a boy. If only we'd been
the House brothers. Then, I'd have signed up to see the world and left
Ivy and Ethel behind to worry about me, too. It was all we wanted,
wasn't it, when we sat cross-legged under the house rafters and spun
that painted globe to decide which countries we'd visit? We weren't
playing, Francis. We were hoping. When we scuttled across the
floorboards, wielding broomsticks and cricket bats in place of swords,
and you said, 'I'm going to be a soldier, just like Father,' I was sure I'd
die of jealousy. To disappear into the rest of the world was the only
way to ensure my life would have any worth. That's what I thought.

And now you're so far away, and I'm sorry I thought it.

Do you want to come home, Francis?

There, Francis stops. The words have caught in his throat. He
looks to Farmer and Farrelly. Already, the yellow cloud is
drifting overhead, casting them in an otherworldly light.
Farmer is rolling a cigarette paper around and around on
itself, as if there is tobacco within. Farrelly's eyes are wide
and shining.

'I don't know,' he says. And this time, though he craves a response, neither man offers one.

'Sssh!' Francis hisses, slapping at Whitman's bicep as they sneak towards the shore. They have stripped most of their clothes off on Walker's Ridge and left them in bundles in their dug-outs. They must leave no evidence of their presence on the beach. Whitman and Farmer have opted to keep on their underwear and vests. Francis and Farrelly have shed the lot and strut over the sand as if they are weightlifters, demonstrating the dip and swell of their musculature rather than the increasing protrusion of their skeletons. Francis has retained some of the bulk all those training hours in Pembrokeshire and St Elmo built around his chest and shoulders, but day on day he feels himself weakening. Soon, his sternum will jut angrily through his skin. Farrelly hadn't much meat to begin with and appears much the worse for the rations.

'Johnnie Turk won't be listening out for us here,' Bill Farmer insists. 'Not at this time.'

None of the men believe him, but none will question him either.

It is the witching hour and every soul on Anzac has stilled. They have planned their jaunt carefully: after the bombardment; after dark. All those choreographed movements across the cove – shifting guns, digging in – have been executed, as requested, in good time for the breaking dawn. The other men rest or smoke or pleasure themselves under thin blankets or write home or scratch or drink weak tea and wait for morning, when they will at least be able to see their enemy approaching. As poor as it might be, this is their best chance at a moment of freedom and they cannot pass it up.

'Those Turks are sneaky bastards,' Whitman spits. 'They're probably crouched on the cliffs now, watching.'

'Let's give them a show then,' Farrelly laughs, and turning himself inland he raises his arms and shakes his hips like a belly dancer so that his cock waggles under the spotlight moon. Their laughter echoes off the cliff face and they fall back to shushing and slapping each other. Though they cannot admit it, even to themselves, they hunger for the touch of another person's flesh under their hands. Even if it is just another man's arm or back. They make excuses, to keep patting and gripping – a wrist, a stomach, an elbow. A hand.

As they pass the broken sloop where Francis encountered the empty greatcoat, he braces against a shiver. He disguises his unease by stepping closer to the rippling silver line the retreating sea has left on the sand and saying, too loudly, 'Here?'

The others shrug their agreement, trusting the avid swimmer amongst them. They have seen him, after all, sneaking off into the waves at the brim of the day and on the brink of dusky night and in the lulls between Burrows' barked orders. They have watched from the cliffs – Tom Merton wringing his hands in expectation of another tragedy – as Francis House traverses the currents, his hands pointed into paddles and his legs powering invisibly along beneath the peaking surface. He swims like a porpoise, his body rolling with the water rather than through it. For long moments, he disappears entirely.

At Francis' direction, the four men wade in together. When the water reaches their thighs, Whitman begins to prance, lifting himself onto his tiptoes and pinching his fingers into points. The others snigger and, cupping their hands in the water, splash it over his shuddering torso until he shrieks for mercy.

'It's not cold!' Francis laughs.

Farrelly doubles over for hooting at his mate. A couple of feet distant, Farmer folds his arms across his chest and smirks.

'You wouldn't be cold, House,' Farmer says. 'You spend more time in here than you do on dry land. You're a fish, through and through.'

With the accusation comes Lily's voice. Pearl Oyster, she'd called him. Flotsam. Barnacle. Clownfish. Manatee. Sea dragon.

She'd sit in her usual place atop the leather portmanteau in the attic, and dust off the compendium, and sing out the words: it was the best way to drown out the thumps and wails Frederick made as he rushed around the house, dragging open every drawer and cupboard door in search of his lost Lee-Metford.

Francis raises his eyebrows at Farmer and, turning, slinks into the shone black waves. Legs locked into a butterfly kick, he quickly circles Farmer then Whitman then Farrelly, plucking at their legs or pulling at their underpants, and resurfaces with his back to the beach.

'You're a menace,' Farmer cries, holding his bent leg with his left hand and flicking water at Francis with his right. 'That hurt.'

Francis winks and sinks below the waterline again. This time, they are not so easy to tease. They kick out at him as he steals by. They bob beneath and grasp his ankles. They use their hands to churn the water into miniature whirlpools. He surfaces again and, shoving and spraying and smacking, they plash each other until they are panting and spent, then lower themselves into the silt and kneel there so that the water laps around their necks. From the clifftops, they might be a plump of resting seals.

'Burrows will have our balls for this,' Farmer wheezes, pushing his hair back off his forehead. 'You know that don't you.'

'Not if he doesn't find out,' Farrelly answers, big-eyed with worry again.

'Of course he'll find out,' Farmer says. 'The man – knows – everything.'

The impression is good, and it sparks another fit of laughter. They are keen to find mirth. Soon, their cheeks ache from smiling and, god, the pain is welcome. Francis' stomach gurgles, and he wonders if the others can hear his hunger past his amusement.

They settle into silence, and Francis, looking from one floating face to the next, notes that the moon picks out only the scantest details of each man. Farmer's eye sockets. Farrelly's cheeks. Whitman's long-lamented 'strong nose'. The important parts – the colours of their stares, the curves of their lips, their stains and bumps and crevices – are hidden in darkness. These are no longer men, but collections of bones.

Not wishing to consider them any longer, Francis turns his regard on the shore. He will look to the ammunitions boxes and the sand bags and the rowed-up water barrels. He will look to the jetties and the moored boats. He will look to the huts and the gun wheels and the cannons. Anything but what his friends might become. Anything but what he…

Without warning, he lurches to his full height and stands to attention. He angles his hand across his brow, as though that will help him see something more than the bright spill of moonlight over the water. He makes to move forward, but he only manages to lift one foot before he stops.

'What is it?' Farmer asks, rising with him.

Francis can feel the smooth orb of Farmer's shoulder against his upper arm, and he wants to cling to it, for support, for assurance, but he knows that he will not. The empty plunging at his stomach he must bear alone. The plucking pain that stretches from his chest to his core, too, is his to silently endure. And the figure on the beach…

'Do you see him?' Francis whispers, pointing inland, past their stores and equipment, to the shadowed slats which mark the sand. Anzac Cove is a starlit ghost jetty, leading from cliff wall to cliff wall, from nowhere to nowhere, and at its middle, just beyond the shattered sloop, stands a man, or the shape of a man, in a greatcoat and cloth hat. Watching them.

Farmer squints along the length of Francis' arm.

'Behind the sloop,' Francis breathes.

He waits, heart thundering, while Whitman and Farrelly line up and peer in the direction he is signposting. He wills them to hurry up and speak. Something is pressing against his chest, constricting his rib cage. His breaths are shallow. He battles the urge to plunge into the water and propel himself away, back to Sliema, back to Pembrokeshire, back to Plymouth and his sister and his dreams. He might do a better job of chasing them, if he were just able to start over again. Given a second chance, he would not have heard his father say 'Just show 'em you are not afraid' and decided he ought to bring Hancox's bullying campaign to such a definite end. He would have not laid in wait for him. He would not have swung that poker into the dark.

'It's nothing,' Whitman announces finally.

'A trick of the light,' Farmer agrees.

'You can't see him?'

They shake their heads. 'No,' Farrelly confirms.

'Then he must have come for me,' Francis murmurs. He is cold, suddenly; trembling with it. The tide has turned, and it is rasping and too loud.

'Who?' Farmer wraps his fingers around Francis' raised wrist and pulls at him. 'Henley?' he asks quietly.

'No.' Francis shakes his head. 'No. *Him.* I was looking for him. I was pretending to. But he's troubled me out, and he's come for me instead.'

'Jesus Christ, House! Who?' Farmer calls as Francis strides away.

Without looking back, Francis sends his answer sailing over his shoulder. 'The man I killed.'

I soon made friends with one Bill Farmer, of
Gippsland, who for seven months supplied me with
clothing – I won't say it was all dead men's – and
always insisted on sharing his tobacco.

Eighteen

Naked and salt-drenched, Francis rushes around the sloop, searching the wedge of darkness beneath and lowering his face to the gaps in the hull, as if a man-sized figure could possibly be hiding there without his having witnessed it climb in. He paces back and forth on the stretch where he saw the greatcoat. He peers behind boxes and into the black depths of the caves beyond.

'Why would you hide?' Francis demands, his voice growing dangerously loud. He had tramped halfway up the beach only for the greatcoat to fold away into the shadows and disappear. 'I'm here. I've come. You can tell me what you want now. You can tell me the truth.'

He is answered by the careful beat of silence and, unable to tolerate it, he breaks into a run. He trips towards a pile of ration boxes and kicks at them, sending them tumbling noisily over the sand. He whips around and, crashing into the sloop's stern, propels a hollow, echoing bang up the cliff-face towards the ridge. His curses are loud enough to make the clouds shiver.

Stopping and throwing back his head finally, he roars, 'Tell me the truth, damn you!'

And that is when the hand, cold but strong, closes over his shoulder.

Immediately, Francis slumps down onto the sand, presses his balled fists to his ears, and listens for the rush of the sea around his cochleae. What he needs is to return to Lily. It was always she who steered him when he was lost. But he cannot reach her on these tides.

'I am coral,' he mutters. 'I am vampire squid.' The hand does not loosen its grip. 'I am frilled shark and seahorse and stargazer.' The grip only tightens. 'I am gulper eel and Columbus crab.'

He dares to look back towards the waves, where Farmer, Whitman, and Farrelly wait, the water poppling around their hips. Their inertia is a question. *What is it, House? How can we help?*

But he cannot begin to explain that what he wants is for them to splash out of the grey-glint shallows and lope after him over the dented sand. What he wants is for Farmer to lock hands with him for a fleet moment and reassure him that there is no one standing just behind him, breathing evenly against the nape of his neck. What he wants is to discover the hint of peace his father finds when he sits at the window to recite his poetry each Sunday morning. What he wants is to kick and haul into the sea and butterfly forever away from the tricksy phantom at his shoulder.

To calm himself, he closes his eyes and envisages himself taking a hiding place just off the Cefn Sidan sands and watching his sister walk there with her husband. *I am limpet. I am sea hare.* The lighthouse's shadow would be a quadrilateral of drear on top of deeper drear, the shades hardly distinguishable each from each, and Francis might linger unseen near the pile of rocks which support the structure's base. *I am rockling and sea scorpion.* Likely, he'd prop a bent arm up over the mossed granite and pull his shoulders out of the waves, gaining some height to better watch the two figures on the flat greyed page of the beach. Lily and Ernest. Mr and Mrs Carter.

It disturbs and fascinates him that, when she writes her name on the back of her letters, it does not match his.

Lily Carter, it reads. *28 Hopkins Street, Brynhyfryd, Swansea.* And he does not know the house, or the street, or the town, or the woman. And he wants to swim closer to his imagining of her and call out, 'Lily, I got lost on my way to nowhere. How did you find your way?' But he cannot. He is no longer able to simply slip ashore, as he would have when they were children and she waited for him on the sand. He is caught, part way between two realms. He is neither present nor absent. He is neither man nor sea creature. He is neither living nor dead.

We waited on a bleak day – light rain with a brisk wind – to say our goodbyes, she had written. *The beach was empty, but for the gulls, screaming about on their secret merry-go-round. Ernest asked if I thought there'd been many wrecks, and I said I hadn't the slightest idea. But he was taken by the notion all the same. 'Perhaps we'll see an old ship, with a cracked mast and a gappy deck,' he said. And it was because we were looking for a shipwreck that we didn't see the skeleton, doming up out of the sand ahead of us, until the toe of Ernest's boot knocked one trailing splinter of bone scooting away from the rest. We watched the splinter stop and settle back into the wind-rushed sand like it was a still-live animal, burying itself in its burrow. Beside was a ruined carcass. The ribcage rose on a curve, like the capsized ship's hull Ernest had hoped for. The bones were clean and sail white. Diagonally apart from the ribcage, two juts of jawbone were stacked neatly on top of one another, and, at the point where what had been the head widened into the neck and flanks, a thick swathe of brown-and-white-haired skin folded into itself like a dropped ribbon. Wind lifted the individual hairs, but not the whole, weighted down as it was by the sand grain which had worn all memory of flesh and blood and muscle away. The skeleton was unnaturally neat. It effused no smell beyond that of the salt water which washed it ashore. That poor creature, so readily tossed aside by the waves.*

Ernest swore it was a horse. Too narrow to be a cow, he said.

And we stood there a while, inspecting the chinks and rifts in the chalky bones, the marbled dips and bulges, the scratched in map lines, the hollows. Against the ghosting gull cries and the repeated smack of the withdrawing tide, I couldn't help but imagine it must surely have been a war horse, washed off the French shore and hauled and torn and tossed to a place it never knew, its service already forgotten.

I wondered if the lad who fed and watered it was out there somewhere, too, rolling under the waves, swilling into the afterlife.

'It probably just came across the estuary,' Ernest said, pointing to the low landmass which slunk into the mist a couple of miles across the flint sea. There was something criminal about that landscape, something sneaking, but perhaps it was only the feeling of having to say goodbye. Of knowing that Ernest would soon be on his way to France.

Desperate for the distraction of a sound, I said, 'Ernest, I'm cold.' And he unbuttoned his coat and wrapped me into himself, so I rested my chin on his chest and looked up at the flaming halo of his hair. Even there, Francis, under those glowering clouds, Ernest's hair shone like new copper. And that's what made me decide – there is nothing that can dim this man. Whatever happens in France, he will return to me, the very same brilliant tower of a husband I clung to on that beach. There isn't a soldier brave enough, or a bullet swift enough, or an aim straight enough to keep Ernest Carter from loving me – that's my truth. And here is your truth, Francis, as I know it to be. There isn't a soldier brave enough, or a bullet swift enough, or an aim straight enough to keep you from becoming that man you imagined you'd become when you swung a cricket bat around the attic for a sword.

Buried beneath those words, though, always, there are the others. Francis sees them in the gaps between the ink, catches them travelling towards him over fifteen years and the rolling weight of so much water.

'There's no way he'll forgive us all those tantrums and assumptions,' she says. 'Not now we've seen, Francis. He needs everyone to believe he's a threat. Do you see? It's his way of playing the hero; his way of pretending he made it back unchanged.'

'Francis?' says the figure at his back. 'House?'

The pounding in Francis' ears muffles the voice, but still, he is sure he recognises it. He nods his head. He is trembling despite the clammy heat on the cove, even at this hour. But the skin of his shoulder, where the hand grips him, remains cold. He lifts his own hand and clamps it over the other – hoping to recognise the bulge of the knuckles, the length of the fingers – and finding, to his despair, that he does.

'You're here,' he says softly. 'I was afraid you would be.'

All night long we worked at the gun, stopping now and again for repairs. I remember one shell bursting just as I was adjusting the clinometer. To do this I had climbed up the trail, and by all the laws of artillery should have been killed. But I bore a charmed life, for in the morning many bullets were found in the bank a few yards behind my position, and must have missed me by inches.

Nineteen

'They shattered him to atoms,' Tom Merton squeals and Francis rushes across the ridge towards him with the day's silver break. He is clad in only his flannel undershirt and his woollen pants and braces. His socks, his puttees, and his boots he has left on the rocks to dry. His leather jerkin, his greatcoat, his cloth cap, his webbing, and with it, his weaponry, he has left in a pile behind the guns. He cannot tolerate them in this heat, and in any case of late he seems to be blessed, or cursed, to escape every bullet Johnnie Turk rains down on him. It is as though the enemy cannot sight him anymore.

Still, he should not have left his post. He should not have left Tom.

Within minutes, he has resumed his lookout and balances beside the six-incher on the crown of Walker's Ridge. His men have spent the last two hours firing with painful regularity on the enemy, and for that he must applaud them. Consistency, Francis has found on Gallipoli, is invariably crueller than surprise. Steady shelling works its way into a man's nerves, beat by beat by beat. The transitory nature of a surprise attack offers a better chance at escape. Though Tom Merton, of course, did not escape – whatever the story his body is telling. Francis finds him with his hands clamped over his ears, rounding in on himself like an insect in the dark of his dug-out.

'They shattered him to atoms,' he wails.

Francis stands atop the dug-out wall, peering in and trying to decide whether or not to lower himself down and crouch alongside the boy whilst he garbles and screams. Just as he moves to do so, however, Bill Farmer claps a hand around his shoulder.

'I see you're back to yourself then, House,' he says, the words just pushing past the teeth he has closed over a wrinkle of tobacco. 'Thought we'd lost you, too, for a minute there.'

'I'm not sure...'

'Nah. Who is?' Farmer replies, though Francis hadn't known how he might end the sentence. I'm not sure where I am. I'm not sure what I'm doing. I'm not sure who I become when I pour back the opium tincture and it floods through my veins like fire water. I'm not sure time is moving as it did before. 'Look at that poor chap,' Farmer continues, nodding in Tom Merton's direction. 'He couldn't find his arse with the palm of his hand. He'll live in his imagination from now on, I'll wager. I've seen it before. Nothing to do but keep him from getting shot up and deliver him home.'

'And what about the rest of us?' Francis asks.

Farmer shrugs. 'I suppose,' he says, 'we just hold on.' Then he sucks the wilted string of tobacco into his mouth, swallows, and returns his attention to the Lee-Enfield he has claimed from amongst Henley's kit. Rather than look at it, Francis pushes up the sleeve of his sodden undershirt and studies his wristwatch. The glass has been badly sand-scratched and the numbers are visible now only through the milky opacity of the ruined face, but Francis can just make out the stutter of the minute hand towards the twelve. In seven strokes more, they will have passed another of their specified twenty-four hours' uninterrupted firing.

At the tick of the next obliterated o'clock, Tom Merton starts up again: 'They shattered him to atoms. They shattered him...'

And not one man urges him to stop. Because today, they long only to join him in his dug-out, where they will not see. They cannot possibly admit how damn thankful they are, in the endless minutes before the next attack, to belong to the artillery. They cannot confess to knowing that they might have volunteered to go with the Australians. They cannot stand to look inland, onto the plain below Walker's Ridge where, as arranged, the Australians emerge from the tunnels and, chased by a savage sun and their orders, start to run. Instead, they fidget with their boots, they tug at their moustaches, they pick flattened cigarettes apart and save the tobacco. And when they can no longer bear not to, they direct their eyes downwards.

'We're needed here just as much as they're needed there,' Francis murmurs.

Nobody answers.

'It wouldn't make sense,' he tries again, 'to put all our men in one location.'

This time, even he notes the upward whine of his voice. He is not sure whether it is the men he is trying to persuade or himself.

Without thinking, they form a line along the ridge, from where they can better watch. Francis suspects that they might look like football fans, positioned at the pitch boundary and ready to swear and fist-shake their boys to victory. There comes an unpleasant tightening at his throat. He wants to talk past it, but he has no more empty platitudes to offer. Down the line, someone rasps a match and holds the flaming head to a quivering cigarette end. Francis glances to his left. Legs dangle over the edge of the ridge. A solitary pair of boots swing a persistent one-two into the still air. A hand is lifted to a mouth to catch a cough. They are spies. Voyeurs. Burrows ought to shoot them where they sit – that's what Frederick would say.

'Stand up and fight, boy. Only a coward would do nothing.' Francis hears the words as a shudder down the back of his neck, as he did throughout his careful childhood. The voice Francis seeks to silence with gunfire does not belong to a Turk but to his father, and so Francis resists the urge to reach for his rifle. Frederick's imagined prompts have led him to reckless action too many times. But today, Francis will not blunder in attempting to help only to hinder. The sun has shone him from his moonlit frights and he understands that today, he must wait to discover his true course.

From the plain below, yells rise like winter mists – muted and haunting.

The sound is at odds with the sight of the Australians, frantically covering fifty feet. One hundred. They are small from this high on the ridge: toy soldiers. Francis counts them across the flatland. Two hundred feet, and their bayonets are raised. Three, and their strides are unsteady in mis-sized boots. A hundred feet more across scrubby ground they stumble. Over barb-wired defences. Around dusty, blasting craters. They scutter and leap and slink and tire. But they do not cease moving forward. They run with all their might, and Francis can only assume that they are advancing towards their deaths.

The Turk trenches are roofed with heavy pine logs, earth atop. The Australians do not pause. They cannot pause when the ground beneath them is being blown to bits. They cannot pause while their mates are taking bullets. They cannot pause because their hearts are pulsing out du-ty, du-ty. And that is the drumbeat they must rush in to – du-ty, du-ty – tearing and hauling at the odd gaps the artillery guns have made until, doubtless already exhausted, they pull back the trench coverings and drop into darkness. Du-ty, du-ty, du-

On the ridge, Francis closes his eyes over the noise and imagines himself dropping in with them.

All would be black. Close.

He raises his fists before blind eyes and braces himself, as ready as any man below for the forever that is thundering towards them. He does not want to descend into the Turk trenches – no man would – but he does want to fight. And it hardly feels like pretending as he listens and imagines the Australians' advance, because he has seen its like before. He has tasted it. He has trembled and vomited through it.

Beneath the earth, the Australians snarl and wail and throw their bombs, they find clubs and pound skulls, they hook fingers into eye sockets, they taste blood, they lick at screams, they bellow for help, they piss in their shorts, they touch heat and fear and the stiffened strength of their exposed flesh, they swallow bile, they stomp over dead men, they wade through piled-deep corpses, they try to envisage their women's faces, they try not to, they keep tramping onwards when their skin is cleaved open, they press their palms over last breaths, they drive their bayonets into soft bellies, they hear their own bones snap, they smell the excretion of their pals' shit, they tear hair from scalps and knock loose teeth, they grapple with Turks and kick themselves free, they gasp air into their crumpling lungs, they stop and thrust bloody shovels into the turned earth and lean on the handles and stare, they notice that the Turks wear white calico armbands to match their own, they lose their boots and see their helmets tipped away, they recall the last letter they wrote to their parents, they calculate how many miles they are from home, they elbow gaping faces and cracked jaws, they fall to their knees and allow other men to lift them again, they pray and curse, they curse and cry, they cry and howl.

And so loud is the following gunfire from their artillerymen that those howls will find no ear but their own.

They will die, too many of them, trapped in the enemy trenches, to the strange cadences of their own screams.

Repositioning themselves behind the guns now, Francis and his men are silenced by the clamour that rises from the Turkish trenches. That fracturing sound would leave a bloody gash on the heavens.

'They shattered him to atoms,' Tom Merton whispers, a thousand times over. And Francis closes his eyes to the thought that, this time, Tom is entirely correct.

Then he raises his hand to give the order, and they fire and fire until finally, out of the noise, come the dead.

Out of the roaring, come the wounded.

Out of the thunder, come the limping and the blinded, the stretcher cases, the bleeding and the deafened and the shaken, the unravelled and the mutton-chopped. Walking and carrying and rolling and crawling. A depleted officer heaving himself off his stretcher and commanding his men to pick up a dying Turk. A New Zealander with his arm hacked away by a maxim given a vertical movement only. A Maori, who until recently had possessed two eyes, cupping his arm around a buddy and easing him downhill. A private discharging his blood like a breadcrumb trail.

The clearing station is diagonally beyond and below Francis' gun position, just out of reach of the Turk artillery, and Francis watches that sorry procession of broken ghosts troop towards it just as he orders his men to create a line in their like on the enemy side.

'Fire!' Francis orders. 'Fire!'

And by the eleventh hour, nothing can stop him. The agony at his middle drives him demonically onwards. When the clinometer requires an adjustment, Francis pulls on his cloth hat, climbs up the trail, and makes it.

'Fire!' he bellows.

When the sights are being tweaked and a lucky shell clears them straight out of his gunner's hand, Francis calls for a strip of iron he had passed on the beach and makes do.

'Fire!' he bawls.

Darkness drips over them, and they bombard the weeping moon and everything in its silvered sights, and in each gunpowder flash is illuminated the square-shouldered shape of an empty greatcoat, advancing steadily in Francis' direction. Consigning it to the corner of his eye, Francis concentrates on the gun and shouts himself hoarse. 'Fire! Fire! Fire!' And never once do his men hesitate. He has trained them well. He is proud. He continues delivering his howled orders until morning peers over the horizon and he loses sight of the creeping artefact altogether.

Not yet, he thinks. I'm not ready to face you yet. We belong under plum clouds, you and I, spooning the future open and plunging in.

By the thirteenth hour, Francis knows he will have to partake again of the opium. Pain gnaws into the veils of viscous skin he imagines hang from rib to rib and digs-in for the long haul between his bones. Always in Turkey, it seems, somebody or something is tunnelling a way into deeper darkness. Is this purgatory, then? Is this loud, hot, dust-plain not the route to victory, but the route to hell? It is just past 6 a.m. and sweat already beads the nape of Francis' neck.

Bill Farmer pulls another cigarette from inside his tunic and twists it between his fingers. 'Morning again, then,' he says. 'And we've got company.'

'Company?' Francis enquires, without taking his eyes off his near-extirpated target.

'To your left, House.'

Francis allows himself a cursory glance. Why Farmer can't simply tell him what is happening, he cannot imagine. Irritation spreads through his body and he holds tight, waiting for Farmer to hock up a ball of spit and eject it, and hoping that, when the same happens, he can resist the urge to clock the man in the jaw. Only now, in the well of this interruption, has anger found the opportunity to possess him. The instant he turns his regard on Suvla Bay, though, it is replaced by relief. During the night, under cover of what will later be called the Battle of Lone Pine, that narrow crescent of sand has filled with hundreds of troops. The sea is black with ships. Help is sailing in. Hope is making anchor.

'Fire!' Francis orders, whipping about to fix Farmer with a

grin. And as he swivels round on his heel, he is lucky enough to catch sight of an angel flighting by. A true angel amongst the chaos. An angel so pearl-skinned and delicate and serenely purposeful in its movements that Francis stands rapt. Maybe, just maybe, they are destined not for hell but for heaven. Maybe he ought to follow the creature. But he cannot leave the gun.

'Farmer,' he breathes. 'Did you see that?'

Thankfully, home gunfire covers his words, for when he looks again he understands that the angel is none other than Tom Merton, rushing into the salvo of Turkish shells, his hat and boots and vest removed and his arms thrown out to mercy.

'Shit! Farmer, take over,' Francis barks. 'Farrelly, watch my back.'

Snatching up Farmer's rifle, he races after Tom Merton, his body held low and fast as his training in the Pembroke Dock mists taught him. Francis, being the larger and fitter of the two, has no trouble reaching the boy, and without a thought for what might follow, he launches himself forward and tackles poor Tom to the earth. Tom, perhaps believing himself hit, falls without struggle, and Francis finds himself lying nose to nose with his bombardier, staring into a face which longs with painful certainty only for an end.

The end.

Francis flicks his head from side to side. There is no one close by. 'Tom. Listen.' He speaks at a frantic whisper. 'I'm going to get you home. You're going to go home.'

Beneath him, Tom nods slowly. His grey eyes match the pallor of his skin. He is calm – calmer than he has been in weeks. There are no words on his lips, only the white pinpoint blisters brought on by too much heat and scant enough water. They look like lines of braille. *Help me*, Francis imagines they spell. *Help me, please.*

Francis checks left and right again. No one. He could do it, quickly, and there would be no witness. There would be no shame.

He reaches back into the leftmost pouch of his webbing and draws free his bayonet. He turns it in his hands, so that it points down towards Tom's right thigh. He counts himself into action: one, two, *three*, and with a jolt the blade pierces the muscle just above Tom's knee. It meets a spongy sort of resistance, and Francis pulls the weapon free and tosses it into the dirt. Tom does not flinch.

'Stretcher!' Francis leaps to his feet and waves his arms. 'Stretcher!'

But when he looks around, the ridge is empty. There are no stretch-bearers, no pointed guns, no crawling men or smoking fires, no shelled dug-out roofs, no bellowing sergeants. There is only the velvet drop of gold dawn light over the land and, silhouetted against the horizon, the empty greatcoat.

I left you on the beach, Francis thinks.

The dark shape of the cloth hat moves up and down, as though nodding.

Both times, I left you on the beach.

Again, the hat nods.

Are you here to punish me then?

At this, the right arm of the greatcoat rises and a handless arm beckons Francis.

Yes, of course.

Obedient now, he takes a step forward, and another, and –

'Watch it,' a voice warns. With its gruff intrusion, the noise and movement of the ridge is returned. The whirring shells, the thudding boots, the calamitous din of the new recruits marching onto the sand below.

Two men come scurrying forward to retrieve young Tom, and Francis manages to stutter, 'He's injured. Get him to the clearing station. I fear he's out of action.'

What he fears more, though, is the damage Anzac has done to Tom Merton's brain. The boy took a significant stab wound, and he did not flinch – not so much as a twitch of an eyelid or the swell of a tear – and that, Francis thinks terrifying. If he cannot even flinch in honest pain, Tom is lost. What then if Francis wanders entirely away from himself, too, into the fug of opium and hunger and guilt? What if he cannot find his way home?

He barges the idea from his mind and steps towards his gun. For the next twelve hours, he must attend to the shelling. But for that he will need to gather his strength. As he watches Tom Merton carried away, so he slips a vial from his pocket and turns the opium tides between his fingers.

Two stretcher bearers were carrying a man along the beach when 'Bill' was heard to fire. Without hesitation the man in the rear lowered his end and spread himself across the wounded man. His reward was five bullets in his thighs and the D.C.M.

Twenty

Above their heads, the corrugated dug-out roof creaks in the heat. In the headstone of shade below, Francis, Farmer, and Henley kneel in a circle, as though around a camp fire, and bring their faces together. They are sharing a cigarette, using their bent heads to hide the glow of it from the other men.

Having been denied it for perhaps a week, Francis, Farmer, and Henley are drunk on the tobacco. They grin idiotically and shush each other with raised fingers, though it is only Edwards who is making any noise, snorting through his nightmares behind the mud wall. It is past midday, but dusk is a long way off. A ribbon of perspiration progresses leisurely down the back of Francis' neck. He has removed his soaked socks and boots and the soles of his feet prickle as they dry. He wants to scratch them, but he does not want to loose the rotting skin and clog it under his fingernails. He scrunches his toes and concentrates through the itch by taking another drag on the cigarette, then passes it along to Henley. Henley's clear hazel eyes are bright with excitement.

'Where's Burrows?' Francis whispers.

Farmer pinches his thumb and forefinger together and mimes writing: he is at his diary again.

'Not like you to be secretive, House,' Farmer says.

'You don't think?' Francis replies.

Henley laughs silently.

'You don't remember, do you?' Farmer asks.

'What?'

'The other night. Clattering about on the dug-out roof, acting out all the parts.'

Francis feels his cheeks tingle into warmth. There's a hint of a recollection, but he cannot believe in it. 'You're larking.'

'I am not,' Farmer says, smiling. 'Marija! Agnese! Lorenza!' Farmer crosses his arms over his chest in imitation of Francis' performance. 'You should be on the stage, House. You gave us quite the turn.'

At the words, Francis is treated to a flash of himself, tiptoeing across the ridged roof as it creaked and bent under his weight, a torn Witney blanket thrown around his shoulders like a shawl, swinging his hips and flouncing about in imitation of Lorenza and her hideous demands. He begins to laugh through his blushes.

'I might fancy myself the pantomime dame!' he wheezes. The tobacco has hit the back of his throat and he needs to cough, but he does not want to draw Burrows' attention. The Captain will likely ask where they acquired the cigarette, and Francis cannot bear to have this hunched few minutes of pleasure ruined.

The shrinking cigarette completes a rotation and is returned to his lips. He draws greedily on its increasingly soggy butt.

'What shall we miss today?' he breathes, as he passes it on again.

To fill the time, they have developed a habit of describing those items they are most sorely lacking on Gallipoli. It is nothing but a way to tease themselves into homesickness, but there is an addictive quality to it which none of them resists.

'China teapots,' Henley says.

Francis eyes the hulking man hunched at his side. 'There is no way you have ever made use of a china teapot, Henley.'

'Course I have,' Henley replies, evidently affronted. 'It's the only way to drink tea, man. Boiling the water in these metal buckets ruins the flavour.'

Francis and Farmer laugh. Farmer rolls his eyes.

'Shall I tell you what I miss?' he offers.

'I think we're well aware,' Francis warns. They have heard Farmer's thoughts about his wife often enough that they might recite them from memory, were they inclined to speak about someone else's woman so crudely.

'Something different today,' Farmer promises.

Francis and Henley wait as Farmer takes his turn on the cigarette. The lit end dulls, then smokes, then dims. It is nearly finished.

'Today,' he continues, 'it's Martie's hair, when it's just washed and it's still dripping down her back and leaving little wet dots on the floorboards as she wanders about the house. I couldn't point out the flower if it meant escaping a Turk bullet, but I asked her once which it was, and she said, 'Jasmine, of course'. So that's what I miss – the smell of Martie's jasmine hair.'

He tosses the expired cigarette butt over his shoulder and twists his mouth into a smile which is shaped, the other men know, to stop his tears. Farmer cannot stand to be serious for more than a minute or two. Anything more and the yearning he feels for his wife, his children, starts him to trembling. Francis recognises the warning signs: he, too, begins to tremble when he has not had his tincture.

'Your turn,' Henley says, nodding in Francis' direction.

Francis makes a show of thinking about it, pointing his eyes towards the groaning roof and humming gently. He cannot bring himself to mention that midnight when he and his father stood outside the back door, Frederick showing thirteen-year-old Francis how to smoke a cigar, and the two of them dropping to the ground, shushing each other, when Eliza stepped past the window. In the glow from his cigar's lit end, Frederick's eyes were wrinkled into narrow dashes of delight.

'The cold,' he says. 'And the rain. And clouds that are grey, not white. And –'

'You know you only get one, House,' Farmer interrupts, sitting up straighter and resurrecting that forthright chap who knows just how to bear being separated from his family.

'Impossible,' Francis replies.

'You have to choose.'

Francis gives his friends a sad smile. There is so much to miss, so much to want, that he cannot find the words to encompass the loss that swells in his chest without sounding trite. It is something like grieving, perhaps. It is a deep sense of…

'Certainty,' he says.

That is what he misses most – the boy he had been when he and Berto stood at the ship's bow as the *Sudan* inched along the Point of Tigne and watched the country's approach.

Francis had angled his hand at his brow. At the water's edge, people moved about their business with the same silent synchronisation as a flock of birds. Atop the high walls which thrust up out of the waves towards the sky, rows of square houses sat like stringed jewels, each a different colour. Francis pushed the back of his hand across his upper lip but did not find the slick of sweat he had been expecting to discover there.

'I'll tell you something, Nellie,' Berto said. 'I'm more than keen to put my boots on solid ground.'

Francis shared his sentiment. Surely, nine days at sea were enough to put a man eternally off balance. But he was finally here, and he was too excited to complain.

'Quiet, will you?' he breathed. 'If I'm ever to escape that ridiculous name, you'll have to learn to stop using it.'

'I like it,' Berto replied, shoving his elbow into Francis' ribs. 'I don't think any name could ever suit you so well.'

Remembering then that it was Berto who had christened him so in the first place, he clipped the top of his friend's head, his fingers held stiff, and smiled at the thwacking sound the contact made. He really was glad to have found Berto again. And he was gladder still that they would step onto this new country together. Malta, he thought, looked like it just might be full of adventure.

'Come on,' Francis said, and the two turned to go below and collect their kit from their hammocks, jostling and punching at one another as they went.

Francis runs his tongue over his tobacco-furred teeth and shudders at the bitter tang. Yes, that is what he misses most – the certainty he knew as he alighted from that ship. And his friend.

But he refuses to let his sentimentality dampen the joy the cigarette has brought about.

'And Agnese,' he says.

'I thought it was Marija,' Farmer replies, rolling his eyes.

'Some days it is,' Francis smirks. 'But Agnese was a keeper. I was a fool to let Lorenza turn my head.'

Farmer shrugs. 'A chap your age,' he says.

'He's certainly had his fun,' Henley puts in, laughing.

But Francis does not treat them to the intimacies of the bedroom when he speaks of Agnese. Instead, he recalls one of their early meetings, when they'd sat in the stone pavilion behind her family manor and, looking out past her cigarette smoke at the ornamental gardens, talked of home.

'If we were in England now,' he begun, curling around her, 'we should have to sit this way, for the warmth. In February, it grows so cold that every surface is covered in a white frost, and my favourite thing to do then is pile on too many clothes and walk along the Plymouth Hoe, listening to the water storming against the sea wall.'

'Does it always storm, the water there?'

'Often,' Francis answered, 'in winter. But it's beautiful. One day, I'll walk you along the Hoe, all huddled inside a big coat and scarf and gloves, and we'll eat ice-cream cones, so you will know what real cold feels like, and everything will be grey and white and your nose will tingle with it.'

'I wouldn't like to be so cold,' Agnese mused.

'You would,' Francis assured her. He hadn't realised how much he'd missed it until now, but suddenly he was craving the quivering bite of British wintertime. If he could, he would transport Agnese home immediately, and stand her on the sea wall and watch all that pecan nut hair lifted and dragged and tangled by the wind. 'Everything is sharper when it's cold; everything is easier to feel and see. And then, when you return home, you rush to the fire and sit before it until your skin burns, and it might just be one of the greatest feelings, to be held warm inside when you know that just outside the window, the world is chilled to the bone.'

Agnese laughed. 'You are a strange man, Francis House,' she said. It was a peculiarity of her speech that she so often spoke his name at the close of a sentence, but Francis did not want to correct it. He enjoyed hearing himself on her tongue. Her voice, low and slow and even, poured from her lips like syrup. To be considered a man by her reduced Francis to his most boyish self.

'Why do you say that?'

'I've never known anyone to crave the cold so.'

Francis pressed his nose to her neck. 'You'll understand it one day,' he said.

'When I'm turned pale by the grey Ply-mouth sea,' she answered.

'Yes,' Francis agreed. 'When we're home.'

But going home was such a long time off. Though he couldn't say how, Francis knew it. A spot of swimming, some cannon training, and a love affair or two were not enough to return triumphant to Britain from. There must be something more. And there would be. Francis could feel it. Since the morning he'd arrived in Malta, he'd been dutifully watching that deflated blimp of a horizon, waiting for some fight or other to come pitching over it towards him. He'd been anticipating it his whole life.

But he hadn't known that it would look like crosses arranged small along a cliff top. Hadn't known it would smell like flesh scrubbed and bleached into the afterlife. Hadn't known it would taste like weak tea and rot. Hadn't known it would tear holes in his ambitions and his friends and his mind.

He stops and looks to Henley and Farmer. In attempting to

lighten the mood he has managed to sober them. Farmer swallows hard, trying to shove his love for his wife back down into the belly of himself.

'Why didn't you stick to her, House?' Henley says.

Francis shows them another smile, apologetic this time, and both men acknowledge that they would not have spoken like this – would not have thought like this – had they not landed on Gallipoli together. Henley lowers his head and rolls the extinguished cigarette stub between his fingers and… No, Francis realises with a jolt. Henley doesn't roll the cigarette stub between his fingers. Henley did not just laugh at the idea of House's shenanigans on Malta. Henley cannot do any of those things, because Henley is dead. That day was weeks ago.

When Francis dares to look to the fire again, he finds there only Farmer and the smoke.

Twenty-One

In the minute-beat of quiet which follows the fourteenth shelling hour, Francis offers the men another story. They shuffle close, as has become their habit, and huddle into a crescent formation, like a clutch of children in a school room. None mentions the fact that Whitman's eyes are puffed and red from crying – that, indeed, they heard him snivelling while they were trying to sleep – though they are all aware that it started up when he opened a recently delivered letter and they assume tragedy must have struck somewhere. Settling on a nearby sandbag, Francis draws his letter from his pocket and unfolds it, cautiously, fearful that the tear will finally reach across the middle of the page and split the spill of words in two.

He clears his throat and, accompanied by the far-off staccato of another company's gun, begins.

It's Lily slogging up to the top field he shows them this time, bucket swaying in her free hand, feet small inside Ernest's heavy boots, skirt gathered into a knot on one side to keep it from sagging into the dew-wet grass. She is bringing in Penelope – *short, grey, plump, and sassy* – ready to begin the morning deliveries. With Ernest gone, she is becoming self-sufficient, and Francis hopes sharing the fact might reassure his remaining men that their girls, their mothers, their daughters, will manage until they come home.

It was my first lone outing, he intones, *and I was sure I'd make a mess of it, that I'd let Ernest down, but then at the bottom of the street I saw two figures. Morning paled them both to gold, but I knew on the instant that it was Doris and Geraldine, come to help. So we trotted the empty streets together, the three of us crushed onto the little trap, and called the village out from between the snugged creases of their bedsheets and into the day, to laugh and breathe and live with us. That was the first good thing I did without him, Francis. That was my first step.*

There follows a pause.

'I liked the other one better,' Farrelly says eventually. 'The one about the skating lake.'

Francis lifts his head, confused, to question Farrelly with a wrinkled brow. His colour flares. What can the man mean, to say he liked the other one better? Lily's life isn't to be picked and chosen from. She is not theirs to shape and direct like a character in a play or a soldier under orders. She is free and brave and everything she announced she would be when she and Francis sat amongst the attic cobwebs and invented existences.

'Can we have that one next?' Farrelly continues.

'About the skating lake,' Francis says slowly.

'Yes,' Hodgson nods. 'I liked that one, too.'

'But, that's not...' Francis begins, fanning the letter before him. He does not finish the sentence. He does not know how. And besides, not one of the men who sit before him wants him to. They know, naturally, that it is the selfsame piece of paper Francis draws from his pocket each time he reads to them. Even if they could not see the tear, which lengthens with each unfolding, they would have known from the way he stutters, starts anew, changes his mind, moves Lily magically from one location to another, reinvents the trajectory of the tale.

They are not privy to the words which truly run across that creased and dirtied page, or even whose hand they belong to, and nor do they wish to be. Francis is inventing stories, and they are grateful to him for that. They have never known themselves so much in need of a heroine.

'If that's what you want,' Francis offers.

125

They nod as one and he clears his throat again, as if he is a preacher at a pulpit, delivering the most serious of sermons.

Our breath quills ahead of us as we step off the train and shuffle along with the other passengers, each following the hat and coat in front without question. Above, the clouds betray glimpses of peach and cornflower sky. The storm is forgotten...

Twenty-Two

Francis slouches beside his gun, his head low, and grouses at a mumble. Under most trying circumstances the men have existed these past months and now it is cold, and Francis is as heartily sick of being variously without shells, water, food, cigarettes, matches, or any means of writing home as any chap still perched behind the blasted six-incher. Seven months and they have made no advance.

Francis unfolds his creaking body and accordions back through the snow to his dug-out to retrieve his greatcoat, certain that should Johnnie Turk listen hard enough, they would hear his every scalic step.

Shrugging the item on, he measures the spaces his muscles used to fill. He is glad he has no mirror at Anzac. He must look an object, indeed. And a miserable one, too. As miserable as those sodden letters which less and less occasionally manage to find their way to him, having first been sent to General F. House of the 9th Battery R.G.A and opened and laughed or cried over. When he'd lain aboard the *Massilia* with too much time to think, he had fancied that his women would write to him often. He could practically hear the words Marija or Agnese would pen, skimming the sea spray like a congregation of little terns or storm petrels, desperate to reach him. More often than not, the letters he does receive are unreadable owing to having been partially submerged on a sinking barge, and none are from his women. He manages, though, to make out a few of his sister Ethel's pleas, a scattering of his sister Ivy's reassurances, a small collection of his father's neat endorsements.

It would be nice to tell your mother you've made Sergeant, Frederick had scribbled once.

Well, Francis has met that demand at least. Following the first night of the Lone Pine Battle, General Birdwood had visited the heavy gun and, impressed by its modified appearance, ensured Francis appeared in Australian orders from that point on as promoted to Sergeant. Francis is wise enough to know it won't stick – he doesn't belong to the Australians – but he is pleased, for the moment, to answer to the address.

He trundles back towards his position, his hand playing around a box he has discovered in his greatcoat's right pocket. He suspects it contains cigarettes, but he will not look yet. He knows not who has accidentally slipped them into his clothing. Still, he will claim them as his own and share them amongst the lads, to lift their spirits. They have all been dead weights of late.

An encroaching whirr snaps him to attention. Johnnie Turk is shelling again. As he runs back to the gun, he pulls the box free. Britannia cigarettes – perfect. Having no other light, he will have to return fire by their muted glow.

'Farrelly, Whitman.' He tosses them the box; one or other of them will catch it in the dark. 'I need you to smoke these. Who has a match?'

'Sir.'

Francis is already positioning himself behind the gun. 'Right, get those fags lit, boys,' he calls, 'then shuffle yourselves along to the aiming post. I need to see what I'm shooting at.'

'But, Sir –'

Francis nods, his hands speeding through their usual checks. He is almost ready to fire. 'Yes, Farrelly, you will be under a sheet of flying bullets. Do you want the cigarettes or not?'

'Yes, Sir.'

'Then the choice is yours.'

Farrelly glances at Whitman, who gives an affirmative dip of his chin, and away they sneak. It is no exaggeration to say they stand under a steady onslaught of bullets, but the illumination of the burning cigarettes shows Francis that they do so with mad grins on their faces. Without so much as a cough or a splutter, they smoke the entire pack.

That night, tucked shivering against the hardened muck of his dug-out wall, his greatcoat wrapped tight around him, Francis tastes the thick swirl of Britannia cigarette smoke on his dreams. As he does most every other night, he tries and fails to throw Henley to the ground before that fatal bullet finds its billet.

He grunts into waking at the sound of his name being called. Captain Burrows frowns down at him from above, his arms crossed, his eyebrows worked into deep canals. Beyond his bristling frame, morning conceals its apricot arrival in a breath of spinning mist, so that Burrows appears the calamitous result of a magic trick intended to reveal a beautiful woman in a sequined dress.

'You'll be glad to hear, House, that we're moving,' he says. 'Pack the gun and transport it to the beach, forthwith.'

Half caught in his dream still, Francis rises and climbs up from his dug-out. Dawn meets him with the chill touch of Marija's most disappointed glare, and he hunches in on himself, making a shield of his back, his shoulders, the crown of his head. What he must look like, he can't imagine. His father, perhaps. Certainly he laughs less readily now. His mother had warned him that war was apt to kick the laughter out of a man, but he hadn't realised it would also claim his optimism, his pride, his good sense, his perfectionism, perhaps even his ambition. Whether or not the Anzacs ever gain another sandy inch of Turkish ground, Francis longs to leave. And Burrows is explaining now that he will soon have his wish – 'You're to take the gun off Watson's Pier. You'll be first off. But – make – certain those bastard Turks don't see you go, House' – and

Francis cannot listen because forming up in the fog before him now are Henley and Carson and the twenty other souls he has so carelessly misplaced. They shape themselves, initially, like pencil drawings made by an invisible hand: rough lines sketched together to replicate a torso in a loose vest, a pair of scuffed boots, a sculpted upper arm, a thinning thigh. And as Francis peers closer, so the bodies are fleshed out by the wily movement of sunlight through the frosted air and plumped back into existence. Without delay, the restored soldiers return to their duty. They plead with their Corporal, their Sergeant, their friend. And they are led by that insistent greatcoat.

'What should I do, Sir?'

Francis closes his eyes. He does not want to acknowledge that amongst all those men he has spotted the slighter figure of a child.

'I haven't any boots, Sir.'

A child in the wrong place at the wrong time.

'Where should I go, Sir?'

Francis puts his hands over his ears and, pressing them down hard, listens for the low whoosh of the sea off the Plymouth Hoe. He might drown it all in the grey expanse of that sound. He might hurl his guilt into the retreating tide and watch it ebb away. There is no better choice. He will not spend the rest of this war surrounded by words he cannot say and men he cannot save.

He uncurls from his clamshell position only when he feels a gentle touch at his elbow. Slowly, he peels open his eyelids. It is gloaming. The first turquoise glints of night scatter the horizon, like the luminescent plankton Lily read about in her compendium four countries ago.

Burrows has gone, and though no one else will question Francis taking his rest, he is embarrassed by the depth and length of his slumber. He needs to know how long he has stolen from some other man who could have slept the day out.

'Not too long, Nellie,' a voice replies, and Francis darts up, slinging his greatcoat aside and knocking two emptied jam tins against each other so that they clang.

'Berto!' he breathes.

'The one and –' Berto pauses when he notes the horror on Francis' face. 'Christ, what is it?' he asks. He begins slapping at his cheeks, his forehead, his chin, his cranium, as though he is feeling his way around the mysteries of a crystal ball. 'You'd swear I was missing my head the way you're gawping.'

Berto's intent is to be comical, and Francis wants to smile, but his lips cannot find the correct shape. They have forgotten how.

'You were in my dream,' he says slowly.

'Was I now? Shall I tell Agnese? Or is it Marija again these days? You're some cad, House.'

Francis shakes his head. 'Not anymore.'

'Why ever not?' Berto asks, smirking. 'What are you doing now then?' He winks.

'Looking for you,' Francis replies.

Berto springs up from the dug-out floor and presents himself, hands and legs spread. 'Here I am. Wasn't I here all along, House?'

'No.' Francis shakes his head. 'No. I lost you. I...'

'Lost me?' Berto laughs. 'You couldn't lose me. Didn't we vow to it at Woodlands? Didn't we swear each other to trouble aboard the *Sudan*?'

'We did.'

'Right, so let's go after it then.' Francis watches as Berto swings his arms around his body and, knitting his fingers together behind his back, stretches out his spine. He can hardly believe that his old friend is standing in front of him, smiling and joking, his face slapped brown by the offshore winds and his irises paled further in contrast to his newly tanned skin. Berto, with his shocked round eyes and his skinny frame, has never looked so strong. Months Francis has spent looking for him – or talking about looking for him. Months and he has been able to discover only a passing hint of the man. And now here he is, appeared before Francis as if…

'Berto!' he says again, too loud this time, and throwing his arms wide he lunges towards his oldest friend, ready to rough him into an embrace, ready to draw him back and grab his hand for a shake, ready to punch his shoulder and admonish him for staying away so long. The corners of his lips tremble. He's ready to… He cannot imagine the mischief they'll get up to. Now that they're ready to…

But Berto is not ready. It is deep winter and Berto does not have his greatcoat. Or his boots. His cloth hat is missing.

Francis hits the sandy ground with a thud. His arms are empty.

To fool Johnnie Turk into believing the infantry are still in line, they set about fixing up rifles to fire out of the trenches automatically. This they achieve by the placement of shaking tins and burning candles: devices they presume they have invented. They have only to blow up a 4.7 incher and they are to take their leave. Francis' store of curios, which he has risked his life in collecting, is to be left behind, and he laments the idea of Johnnie enjoying it to an unreasonable degree. He has orders to fulfil, for God's sake. He has lives to preserve. To be so aggrieved at the loss of stocked up fags and biscuits is unseemly. And yet, they seem to have gathered an import, these worthless items, in the face of so much destruction.

They drag and grunt the six-inch towards and around Dead Man's Corner without too much trouble, and there, where the sand softens, receive sixteen horses and hook them in. By the time that fiddly task is complete, the wheels are already sunk deep in the sand, and much harness is broken in getting the gun moving again. Francis whispers the men into organised action.

'Heave!' he mouths, bulging his eyes and swiping his arm to compensate for the quiet on his lips.

The leathery slap of snapped harness sounds like gunshot. Over and over again it crack-cracks. But Francis' men are desperate to reach Watson's Pier, given the promise of being first off, and they rethread new leathers, they brace, they heave. *Crack-crack*, and the horses stumble backwards. *Crack-crack*. Despite the fallen temperatures, Francis' collar dampens with sweat and he resists the urge to pluck it away from his skin with his sandy fingers. He won't let his lads see his discomfort. Men do not fidget. Men do not fuss. Frederick's only demonstration of such weakness was to pinch at his trouser leg when his sat down and crossed an ankle over a knee to better arrange the newspaper. Francis tenses against the wet cling of cotton around his neck and, settling in alongside Drowning Edwards, brings his right shoulder and his left palm against a wheel spoke and begins to labour with the men as they whip and will and lever that gun across the beach like beings possessed of a supernatural strength. Strings of snot dangle from Whitman's nostrils as he cries and pushes and cries. Hodgson's wrist turns against the pressure of his efforts and, though they all hear the snap echo against the cliffs, he denies a fracture and carries on one-armed. Francis notices that Farrelly has one hand pressed to the six-inch and the other pressed to Whitman's shoulder. They must appear a demon army, 'Yah-ing' the horses on so and shoving the gun forwards with hands and shoulders and feet and fury. Their faces swell and redden. They trip over each other's bootlaces. They curse the man in front and the man behind and then they stop to lift the fallen to their feet again. They turn and spit into the sand.

But this is it. They've survived Gallipoli, and soon they will rest.

Upon locating Watson's Pier, Francis discerns immediately that the narrow, rickety structure has no chance of supporting the six-inch. Indicating that they should still the horses a while, he leaves the men to mill around and light their cigarettes while he steps closer to inspect the splitting wood. He stops and, putting one exploratory boot to it, shifts his weight downwards through one leg. The pier moans. It is held together by frost and memory.

What other option is there, though, but to heed Burrows' instruction? He will mention nothing to the men. Their new orders have been matched by a pronounced improvement in their mood, their health, even: the running of their blood has been overthrown by the thicker flow of promise. He cannot dishearten them yet. They will simply have to edge along the pier and pray the sea does not claim it.

'Bring her about, then,' he calls as he strides back up the beach. In their excitement, they have forgotten the need for quiet, and the men chatter loudly enough that Francis' shout would not be especially noticeable to any Turk who might be waiting to pick them off.

Shuffling the six-inch around by careful degrees, they line her up with the stretch of the pier and proceed forwards, feeling the sand grow harder beneath their boots as they approach the snow-cold sea. They fall silent again, until there is only the crunch of their footsteps and the huff of their breaths and the snorts of the horses.

They have wheeled the gun only partially onto the pier when the wood gives out an almighty groan.

'Pull back!' Francis orders, fearful of losing his trusty six-inch to the tide. And, slumped over their new disappointment, the men have no option but to obey.

A second pier they attempt with the same result.

Their third, and last, option is Walker's Pier, a good mile away and too busy by far to accept their approach today. It is agreed that the gun will be dragged to Walker's Pier after nightfall, and Francis and his ragged company settle themselves reluctantly on the snowflaked sand to wait out another shell-blasted Gallipoli day with the bitter Sea of Marmara teasing their toes.

'It gives us a chance to work through the biscuits, at least,' Bill Farmer offers with a snigger. Rumour has it that the biscuits are to be destroyed on their departure, and they can't very well allow that. 'I'll not let them go to waste.'

'Then you'll not leave here with your teeth,' Hodgson quips.

'I'm best off not to share, then,' Bill Farmer returns. As he speaks, though, he is shuffling amongst the gathered soldiers, offering out handfuls of the insipid Huntley and Palmers. Hodgson is right – they are beastly to get one's teeth through – but soaked in some tea a while, they weaken just enough. Francis shovels five of the round lumps into his palm and then, placing one between his lips, matches the tip of his canine tooth to the nearest puncture hole, ready to crack a section loose and suck on it.

'Killed by biscuit,' Farrelly mutters, 'on the brink of escape.'

And laughter drifts down the coast, gentle as a just shed feather. It will be the last Francis hears for the longest while.

Next morning, midst much confusion and hollering and the braying of grounded mules, they manage to forget their aching stomachs, persuade the six-inch along Walker's Pier, and board a recently shelled horse barge which has, upon inspection, been declared safe. The set of Old Sergeant Saunders' square jaw warns them against questioning the declaration.

Francis knew Saunders vaguely on Malta, and he shakes hands with the hoary gent as they go aboard, glad to look on a familiar face. After many stark months, he feels he is being returned to friends, and he wants to ask after Berto and Busty but he holds his tongue. The old man wouldn't know a whit of the sappers he fooled around with on St Elmo. Besides, Francis has his new rank to live up to. And, as it later transpires, it is better that Francis does not know where good old Busty Leonard is at that particular tipping point. Better to imagine, when the imagining might be kinder.

'Corporal House,' Sergeant Saunders grumbles. Francis has partly forgotten that deep voice – the way it hums through your bones. He sees Saunders in a crisp shirt and blazer, leading the baritone section of a vast male voice choir, but he cannot recall now whether the image has bloomed from information Saunders gave him or whether he invented it.

'Newly Sergeant House, Sir,' Francis replies.

Saunders nods. 'Very good.'

Francis smiles. He is leaving Anzac behind, and he is leaving as Sergeant, and he'll make certain to soon find his pals again – for Berto cannot be on Gallipoli if Francis cannot find him, and if he is not on Gallipoli then Francis must seek him out elsewhere – and such is the swelling joy at his middle that he considers he hardly needs the waves to carry him away from shore. He might capably propel himself, and his men, and the mules if it comes to that, damn it, all the way back to Malta with his gut alone.

He has not thought to ask Burrows, however, if that is indeed where they are bound.

They are towed towards open sea by steam pinnace, and there left to await their ship proper. The sky is a spray of pink carnations, reflected in the swell, and as Francis waits, the emergent sun bright on his face and the sulphuric stink of the currents in his nose, he knows that he would sacrifice every flushed dawn he might see till the end of his days if this barge would only transport him directly home to flat, grey Plymouth, where he could recline on plumped pillows, and read himself to sleep, and be coaxed into waking by the white cut of a winter dawn pitching in familiarly off the English Channel. Always, there is the sea. Francis is a merman. But these seas are no longer his. He has travelled into his boyhood fantasies on them, and now, on the 12th December 1915, the eighth anniversary of his enlistment in the Royal Garrison Artillery, Merman House is ready to swim back to reality.

'Sir, we've water streaming in!' comes a cry. Surprisingly – for the voice is lofty as a soprano's just then – it has issued from Stocky Hodgson, so named for his bovine set.

Sergeant Saunders eases his patient baritone into the rising panic. 'Look around, lad, and calm yourself. Your saviour is nearly upon you.'

Saunders is correct. Not so very far away is a large ship, nosing through the rollers. They wait for it to pull alongside the sinking barge, gathering their few belongings to them, buttoning their greatcoats, busying their hands in order to still their bodies.

'Make ready,' Saunders says.

As the ship and the barge line up, however, they hear – or surely mishear – a most ridiculous call.

'Mules and guns first!'

'Mules and guns?' Hodgson repeats. Farrelly, too, allows the words to escape his lips. Then Bill Farmer. Together, they form a dissonant chorus of disbelief. But they soon set to. As they must.

First, the struggling mules are dragged on stiffened legs onto the waiting ship. Francis watches their fubsy hinds disappear one by one, their rope tails whipping in terror. Having never had much cause to interact with animals, Francis hasn't a clue how to calm the beasts, but nonetheless he pities their screams. Even in the swivet, he pities them. They did not ask for this.

The mules safely aboard, they attend next to the guns. After much delay, tackles are lowered, and Francis, Hodgson, Farmer, Whitman, and Farrelly take turns diving into the gelid waters and attaching them to the submerged weapons. The barge, by then, is only the rim of a flowerpot on that carnation sea, and they work fast, whooping and punching the air when the guns are lifted out and the barge bobs a way back towards the sky. Now, however, they find themselves positioned directly below the swinging guns, and the men watch their measured arcs with breath held in fear of being crushed by the inevitable fall. The tackles are not securely attached. All is wet and weighty motion. One is sure to go.

'Jump!'

Who lets out the shout, Francis does not know. Nor does he care. He plunges in and swims for all he is worth, arm over arm over arm over arm. He dips below the surface, where the resistance is lessened, and, pressing his heavy boots together, flicks his body like the merman he has so recently declared himself. He eels away from that lost barge until his lungs tighten and force him back towards the air in the unstoppable manner of a balloon with a snapped string. Behind him, the barge is a fresh black gravestone, sticking vertically out of the cold, bruised water. It descends with all the stealth of a submarine, slow about it, and then, all at once, Francis is on the edge of swirling water. Always, he is returned to the water.

He throws up his arms and flails them about. 'Wait!' His neck and ears burn with the fear of being left behind. His stomach empties. His heart seems to shudder out of rhythm. He recognises the feeling from those candlelit nights he spent huddled in the attic with Lily, listening for the beat of his father's fists through the floorboards. He recognises it from that night at Woodlands, when he lay with his blankets untucked and waited for Hancox to sneak up in the dark and exact his revenge. And the time he dived into a high tide off the cliffs at Pembroke Dock and, having misjudged the footage, seemed to fall forever before the sea surged up to meet him. And the chaos of his first job in uniform outside of training barracks, when he panicked amongst the Llanelly rioters, trying desperately to move like a man. And that night on the beach, when he turned his back and ran away.

'Wait!' he bawls again. But the ship has disappeared. He has no sight, either, of the other men. He realises, too late, that he has not sighted Edwards since they departed land. He is alone again, as he seems destined to remain. He is being shoved back into the shallows, towards the sand, into the gold curve of Anzac Cove, and he pushes against it, but he is heavy and exhausted and it has the better of him, and even in the tumult he lowers a hand to his pocket and feels for the vial of tincture he has stowed there. He will need it, he realises, as he watches another roller rise towards him and braces himself for the downward bash of water, because he fears then that he will never leave Gallipoli. The cove is his own self-imposed purgatory. He cannot leave without his soul.

Twenty-Three

I'll set the scene for you, since you've never visited Swansea. All along Oxford Street, café and shop signs jutted out over the pavements, casting gloomy, geometric shadows. In the lamplight, white painted letters spelling out the names of the Sidney Palmer Café, the Empire Lounge, the Mansel Arms, Owen & Co, John S. Brown's Furnishings and Builders, and The Grand Theatre, were barely visible. Everything was murk and mystery, and honestly, I wasn't sure I should have listened to Geraldine and come out. I'm sure I even whispered something as cowardly as, 'These lamps really should have been set closer together.' What a scaredy-cat! Truly, Francis, I should be an embarrassment to you, bold as you are.

I couldn't let Geraldine see I was frightened, of course. She has managed to transform herself from slovenly and careless to one of Swansea's hardest working lady patrollers. Always she is dressed to perfection, and alert, and willing to steer giddy girls away from uniformed men twice their age. That's her job, you see, in a way – to keep young women safe. Often, she goes beyond the parameters of her obligations, checking in on haughty misses who have found themselves in unfortunate situations, tending shocked sweethearts who have felt the first crack of a fist against a cheekbone or a temple, measuring in her shrewd way whether those girls and lads who, being of a similar age, are embarking on genuine friendships. And she certainly wears purpose better than any shirtwaist or hobble skirt.

Eyes closed, Francis uses a flattened palm to tap at his chest pocket, feeling for the weight of letters within. Something is off. His hand finds skin in place of cotton. He sinks back into Lily's words.

I'd made the mistake of asking after Evan's hearing with the Military Service Tribunal, so we had fallen into silence. There was only the four-beat of our heels on the pavement then, until a clout of laughter issued from the kicked-open front door of the Mansel Arms. Spilling out onto the street were pairs of soldiers and girls, arms gripping waists and shoulders, palms in pockets, hands groping for hands and warmth and skin. Cigarette smoke swarmed around them. Laughter fogged the air.

We approached them. It's Geraldine's duty to do so. They eyed us cautiously, the partying soldiers, the hopeful girls.

Geraldine picked out the largest of the uniformed men and, leaning in close, murmured into the ends of his moustache. 'I'm patrolling ahead of the local constable,' she said. 'I'm to report anything untoward to him. Any improper behaviour. Anything considered undesirable. The police pay me to tattle it all back... It's a good position. It pays well. But I've no desire to get anyone into trouble un-necessarily, so I'd suggest you think about moving on before you're spotted with such ... enthusiastic young ladies. It's your choice, of course, but that's what I'd suggest.'

Their smiles drooped and fell into the dark. 'We'll be moving along now,' one of them said. 'Apologies for the noise.' And they slumped away. But here's what I haven't been able to shift from my mind since, Francis – the men's hobnail boots were still spattered with trench mud. Their puttees, their wool trousers, their tunics and greatcoats, even their stiffened peak caps – all bore morsels of French or Greek or Belgian dirt. They had not stopped to wash and change. They had stepped off their ships at Swansea docks and made straight for a cold pint and a warm woman, sweat still in their hair and down their necks, rain or puddle water still damping their socks, filth still clinging to their clothes, webbing sets still strapped about their shoulders. At close quarters, the romance of their uniforms could not hide that the men were shabby and skinny and far from sanitary. Their socks, when peeled off, would surely drag blistered skin away with them. Their lifted armpits would clog the girls' throats. I wondered if lice scuttered about their pubic regions. When I looked at their haggard faces, though, I saw two lost pairs of eyes looking back at me: yours and Ernest's. And that's when I decided that I would come and find you both. That I would rage into battle alongside either one of the two of you. That that was the only way I could do myself proud.

Francis nods his head. Frederick had taught him from the off that the path to pride ought always to be travelled at a steady rage. That a House man should stand tallest, strike first, work hardest, shout loudest, rush in. And Francis has tried to abide by those rules on Malta, on Gallipoli, in better ways than he had before. He will endeavour to abide by them on whatever mysterious crag of land he reaches next. But he is so bodily tired that, for the moment, he cannot open his eyelids, and so he lets them close around the memory of he and his father, standing side by side on the Plymouth Hoe, their bicycles propped against the sea wall. Francis stared out to sea, holding his arms wide and opening his mouth to lap at the salt spray. Frederick angled himself stubbornly inland. Francis can hardly remember why they were there – they took so few outings together – but he knows without doubt that he'd asked and asked Frederick to capitulate and watch the waves with him. He knows, too, that however hard he begged, Frederick would not turn around.

'He was frightened,' Francis mutters. 'All along, Lily, he was just frightened.'

But he is aware, somewhere beyond the edge of the delirium dream he is slipping out of, that Lily cannot hear him. It has been the longest time since she wrote. He cannot properly remember where she was going, or what she intended to do. He has been closing the gaps with his imaginings. He has been inventing. And his inventions are being steadily interrupted now by a rising voice, which, inexplicably, is saying, 'No rum, no food, no blankets.'

Francis opens his eyes to find himself surrounded by impenetrable light. He stops and listens to his stuttering breath: it comes fast and smells like exposed mudflats. Further apart from his stinking body – the long rake of the wind, and squawking sea birds, and the stench of fish scales dried in the sun.

Francis knows nothing yet of his shifting world, but he suspects it might just be glorious.

'No rum, no food, no blankets,' comes the call again.

An iron rack burns his body in thin, flaming bars, like a series of fire-heated pokers. He tosses from side to side but finds no relief. He is, he discerns, stripped to his underpants. The clothes laid over the iron rack beneath him are soaked: they offer little protection from the churning fire pit below. His ears throb against an engine's battle-bellow. He is aboard a ship.

'No rum, no food, no blankets.'

He closes his eyes. Listens to a man cough with the insistent regularity of a ticking grandfather clock.

'No rum, no food, no blankets.'

It is the voice of a stallholder, then, who has run short of his wares.

Francis sweats and shivers and splutters. He opens his eyes on star-strewn space and closes them again, giddied by the black-bellied emptiness he finds himself suspended within. Only the rack saves him from a fall into the depths. He opens his eyes to find himself looking up through a cut square into soft white space. His stomach claws at his insides. He rolls over his bent forearm and vomits into hell. He closes his eyes.

'We're aboard the *Akiah*, House. Six-and-a-half knots an hour towards a good rest.'

'No rum, no food, no blankets.'

Francis' skull splinters open at the reeling of his eyeballs, and he staggers upwards, scalding his palms as he pushes himself off the iron rack. The urge to urinate, too long ignored, floods through him, and he pitches forward, bursting out of the hot embrace of the engine room, and stumbling about until he finds his way on deck. Cold sea air slaps him upright, and he is forced to relieve himself there at the railings. His penis shrinks in on itself, like a snail into its shell; his chest and shoulders follow.

The *Akiah* carves through deep white clouds.

'No rum, no food, no blankets!'

He manages, fleetingly, to point his eyes at the man who is shouting him down. His is a square, saturnine face, set upon a creased neck, which protrudes from a bulky mass of shoulder. His lips split into a sudden, inexplicable grin.

'I tell you already – no rum, no food, no blankets. Do not ask for again.'

Francis shakes his head. 'No rum,' he agrees, 'no food, no blankets.' And then, without warning, he crumples downwards and sprawls unconscious across the deck. Before he submits to the quiet dark, he gives a single flick of his shimmering tail, meaning to propel himself overboard into waiting serenity, but he does not move. His tail is gone. It must, he thinks, have been hacked off.

He wakes next to the sway and pitch of the ship making anchor. Farmer, Whitman, and the others bustle about the engine room, gathering up their few remaining belongings: a boot with no laces, mismatched pairs of socks, dirty vests, snapped cigarettes which they push into pockets, intending to investigate later whether they are salvageable. Desperate as thieves, they take without a thought for necessity or utility. Sergeant Saunders remains on his back, fixing the ceiling with a glass-eyed glare.

Francis glances about, seeking a reassuring expression, but Hodgson only shakes his head.

'Exposure,' Hodgson says, cocking his tight mouth against the break in his voice. His dark eyes are hooded.

'No,' Francis replies. It is all he can think to say. There ought to be kindly reminiscences shared over cups of hot tea and condolences spoken into slumped shoulders at a rainy graveside. There ought to be clean shirts and black suits and washed faces. Francis had thought the war had already denied them everything it might, but that he cannot feel Saunders' loss, or pause to consider his family's grief, or mourn the sorry jettisoning of his body, galls him. He turns his wrist over and looks to his watch, meaning to count a minute away in the old man's honour, but he finds the second hand stuck trembling between the eleven and the twelve. It seems he has ceased to be able to think beyond the immediate now, because there is only now. His faith in the certainty of what might come next is in ruins. He knows that this ship will return him only to another beach, another gun, another graveyard.

He makes to lift Saunders, meaning to carry the old man on his back to wherever they are going, but that determined pain at his ribs flares up again and he is forced to return Saunders' body to its horizontal position atop the rack with a sudden clang. He blushes at his weakness.

'We can't take him,' Bill Farmer warns, noticing Francis' intentions now.

'Of course we can.'

'No. We can't.'

'Well, I'm going to, but tell me again afterwards that I can't if you'd like.'

Francis hooks his arms under Sergeant Saunders' once again and hoists him up, but even the slightest manoeuvre is a punishment and Francis is already struggling. It is as though the devil has whipped in and weighted Saunders' ankles with rocks, as though hell itself is beckoning him downwards. In life, Sergeant Saunders had been a lithe, stringy man, too tall for the even drop of his voice. Now, his body is heavier than death.

But Francis will not leave him. Of a sudden, Saunders wears his father's face, and then Henley's, and finally Berto's, and Francis cannot leave him.

They march above deck with Sergeant Saunders balanced on their shoulders: Francis, Hodgson, Farrelly, and Whitman. The last of Francis' men. Movement in this fashion is difficult enough, and coupled with the swaying of the settling ship, it becomes an operation in close concentration and harmony. They keep their feet low, shuffling like the exhausted mules they'd seen safe off that sunken barge. They time themselves to the rattle in Farrelly's wasted chest.

Having not viewed it by daylight on his first passing, Francis squints sideways at the dog-legs and oxbows of the cluttered coastline which curls into Mudros Harbour. Small sand buildings squat along the land's edge under a nebulous sun, connected each to each and dwarfed by the war ships which presently glide by. Lemnos, he knows, is a Greek island, but for all its sandy hillocks and crowded streets and dusty fort walls, it might just as equally be Malta. A little way inland, the peaks of so many tents sit like white thimbles arranged neatly in a sewing box. Farmer, who had been properly ashore here en route to the Dardanelles, tells them that the hospital abuts a French military wine-store; he points it out. From this distance, the rows of laid barrels show only a buff ripple to the naked eye.

On the harbour side, Saunders is removed from their charge

and conveyed away in the direction of the hospital. Francis bows his head in silent prayer for the old man, dead for … what? But before many moments have passed, he is forced to raise his chin to receive orders.

Francis, Hodgson, Farmer, Whitman, and Farrelly are to report immediately to the *H.M.A.T. Ulysses*, which will transport them all to Alexandria.

'But we're for Malta,' Francis protests. He makes mention that Farmer is the only Australian amongst them, but his words are not heeded. They are an inconvenience, this wretched clutch of five the Greeks pulled unconscious from the water only to starve. The other Anzacs bound for Alexandria had arrived three days previous and enjoyed the comfort of a sojourn at the field hospital, and a good meal, and fresh clothes, and were no doubt already aboard, claiming patch and swapping cigarettes and booze.

One hour hence, Francis and his chums would wave Lemnos away without so much as having dirtied their boots there.

Still, Francis tells himself as he troops up the gangway and aboard the huffing colossus which will bear them to Egypt, his eye on the ship's single funnel and his own foul stench clogging his throat, he will have Turkey at his back. Whatever happens next, he will have Turkey at his back.

He is hardly able to believe his luck, and, for fear of jinxing it, he determines not to turn and look back down the gangway at those who are boarding behind him. He does not want to admit what he has seen some way back there. He does not so much as want to glimpse, at the very end of the line, the sharp-threaded green shape of the empty greatcoat, following him.

For some unknown reason, our passage was delayed and consequently we were starved for three days, till we reached Lemnos. Here Sergt Saunders died of exposure. An old man, he died for the sake of duty and example.

Twenty-Four

They dine like kings aboard the *Ulysses*, and then the other men sleep. They sleep as better-rested men play cards and drink wine and smoke pilfered cigarettes. They sleep as submarines chase them stealthily across the Levant. They sleep as the sun crests the horizon, then slumps below it again, crests and slumps, crests and slumps. In and out, their breaths go, in perfect slumberous rhythm. And every time Francis drops below a nap and into the depths of true rest, his nightmares show him Berto, standing alone on the cove and bawling for them as they steam away, and he snaps awake. His shame at having pretended to believe that he would not find his friend on Gallipoli cannot be expunged from his dreams.

He closes his mind to it, and stays awake.

When, finally, they arrive at Alexandria, and civilisation, Francis is sagging in his hammock and drowsily calculating that it has been six – no, seven – long, weary months since he has clapped eyes on a woman. He considers the skinny length of himself. His outfit consists of one long sock and one short, an undershirt relieved of its sleeves, someone else's riding breeches torn off at the knee, a good pair of boots, and a new hat he lifted when they were aboard the *Akiah*. He cannot say where or when he lost the rest of his kit. He'd known himself to be an object on Anzac, but he hadn't thought the situation this dire. His bared knees are hardened to crusted bone. His eyes are gritty with sand. His arms are sinewy and tanned to caramel: the ordinarily brown hairs shine gold. Unwieldy, too-big hands protrude from feeble wrists. His hips obtrude against the scratchy fabric of the breeches. His broken health has worn him almost to nothing, but he is determined to at least dress that almost-nothing well. A Sergeant must present himself properly, however poor the internal situation. If Frederick had taught his son anything it was that a man, however broken, however injured, however low, was to show the world only strength.

The man who had ghosted about Francis' childhood home, dead-eyed and flinching from shadows, became a giant when he stepped outside the front door.

Francis finds scant opportunity to attend to his uniform, however, as no sooner have they disembarked at Alexandria than they are shoved like cattle aboard a train. They are denied the time even to take a glug of water. But so fragmented has Francis' existence become since he swilled off Gallipoli that he does not wonder that, whenever he opens his eyes, he is sitting amongst cigarette-cloud conversation aboard a new transport. With each blink, he is being shoved towards an unknown somewhere else, and he is too ashamed to voice his fear to the other men. Instead, he obeys the heavy persuasion of his eyelids and returns to the torturous black sleep which had bumped him across the Levant. He wakes only fleetingly, to hazed murmurings and griping pain. He fails to focus and closes his eyes again.

The train huffs forwards without delay, its wheels rattling through his bones, its smoke fogging his eyes, its whistle deafening him, and Francis does not ask where it is going. He only waits, and prepares, and naps and dozes. He is dreaming his way back to himself. He is dreaming of Malta.

On the slip of beach that moated St Elmo, Francis had stripped to his shorts, then nodded for Berto to do the same. Berto, settled already on a slab of rock, leaned back and rested on his palms.

'Do we have to?' he moaned. 'I haven't the energy, Nellie. Really, I haven't.'

'A boxing match, then,' Francis returned, pacing the over-

shadowed sand. His footsteps made round dents in the
greyness. Above them, the star fort menaced the coast.

'You want us to box? You and I? I can't hit you, Francis. And
besides, what would be the purpose?'

Francis rolled back his shoulders. 'To prove ourselves.'

'To who?' Berto snorted, smiling just a little and sitting
forward.

'Everyone,' Francis replied. His answers were coming too
fast. He was not giving them a jot of consideration. He was
only reacting, as swiftly as he could, to keep himself moving,
to drive out his fury, to swallow the urge he'd had to lift
Lorenza from her bedsheets and shake her and tell her how
careless and stupid she was.

'Everyone,' Berto said, shaking his head. 'And what exactly
are we going to prove to everyone by beating lumps out of each
other?'

'That we're men!' Francis replied.

At this, Berto allowed himself to laugh. The hooting sound
echoed up the walls of St Elmo, hollow as an owl's hungry cry.
'And that's the mark of a man, is it? How well he can hurt
another.'

'Shut up!' Francis strode suddenly towards him, gripped the
neck of his vest, and dragged him upright. 'For Christ's sake,
Murley. Fight me!'

Berto wrapped both hands around Francis' one and tried to
prize it loose, but he could not budge his friend's straining
knuckles, his whitened fingers. Berto's eyes were blue globes
of shock; the pupils, specks of bottomless black.

'House!' he hissed. 'Stop it now. You'll regret this come the
morning. What's come over you?'

He couldn't say it. He couldn't give voice to what Lorenza
had asked of him, but if he did, he wouldn't need to explain
why it had so angered him. Berto would know.

From the start, Lorenza had drawn promises and
acquiescence from Francis with her body alone. Her words were

a melody he answered with matching notes, unable to focus beyond the rising treble of a bucked back or the flattening minor descent of her lowered lids to discover the meaning. But with repetition, the effect had lessened, and tonight, the melody had not sounded anywhere near so sweet. She wanted him at war, not here. She wanted him writing to her from France or Turkey or Belgium about all those men he had killed, tallying them, fetching them to her feet as if they were shot birds and he was a working dog with delicate jowls and a pleasing tail. She told him so without even a trace of shame. Her amusement, when he questioned her on the assumption, had brought him close to repulsion, and he had pulled free of her, his arousal withering in the changed air. It excited her, to think of him taking a life. She wanted him not to fight honourably or fairly, but brutally. She wanted him to bring back bloodied scalps they could count from between her bedsheets, as though he were not a trained and uniformed soldier but a marauder.

'Killing is not so easy,' he had said. 'I'm not that kind of man.'

But he was no man to her at all. He was a plaything. And she wanted him to become his father. As Frederick did. Just that morning, Francis had received his father's letter and realised that he knew. Frederick knew. And only Berto could have told him.

Francis had gone to Lorenza thinking to calm himself, so that he might confront Berto with a level head. But she had said exactly the wrong thing, and now here he was, spitting and swallowing tears and scared of his own fury. Was there nobody who would not betray him?

He spoke through gritted teeth. 'We're going to box.' He flung Berto aside and turned away as his friend sprawled backwards onto his rump with a softened thud. 'Ready yourself.'

And at that growled instruction, Berto finally succumbed to his anger. Shooting upwards, he hurled himself at Francis. Head down, he collided with the larger man's core and wrapped his arms about him in a rugby tackle. He propelled Francis back a pace or two, and they grappled for a few awful seconds, then Berto released him and stepped back, fists raised, ready, as his oldest friend had demanded he be, to fight.

They did not circle each other and skip around. They did not waste the time. They both knew that this, whatever it was, would be short lived.

Francis advanced and swung a right hook into Berto's cheekbone. There was no crack, only a sickening whump – as though Francis had merely plumped a pillow. Berto countered it with a jab to Francis' stomach followed by an upper cut to his lowering jaw. Francis felt the second blow smartly. He pulled himself upright.

'That's it,' he shrieked. 'That's it! Hurt me, damn it.'

Berto obliged and winded Francis with another punch to the stomach. Francis buckled and dropped to his knees. There, he waited, face screwed shut, for the thrust knee Berto ought to bring up to his nose. It did not arrive.

'Stand up, you bastard coward,' Berto spat. 'If you want to fight so badly, stand up and do it.'

Nodding, Francis lifted his right foot and set it firmly in the sand. He echoed the movement with his left and drew himself upright again. A swung right, an answering left, a hook, a cut, a jab, a trailing one-two, and finally the two men stood apart, heaving over their spread feet for breath.

'You...' Berto began, pointing an accusatory index finger at Francis. 'What the hell ... has gone wrong ... with you?'

'With me,' Francis breathed.

'Yes.'

'It was you!' Francis shouted, puffing his chest and throwing open his arms to the reinforced walls of St Elmo on his left and the muttering sea on his right. 'You told him.'

'Told who?' Berto shouted back.

Francis glanced about himself, as though he was truly seeing the island for the first time. 'My father. He knows, and you're the only person who could have told him.'

'Your father?' Berto pressed a hand to his cheekbone and frowned. 'Christ, Francis. How many times do we have to go over this? You don't have anything to prove to your bloody father.'

'If I didn't before, then I certainly do now.'

Berto turned away with a huff. 'Riddles, House. I don't know what you're talking about, or why you had to crack my bloody cheekbone over it. Talk sense or I'm going.' He made to walk away.

'No!' Francis strode after him and, grasping his shoulder, flung him again to the ground. Berto struggled to push himself back up out of the mounded sand. 'Don't pretend, Albert, you fucking coward. You told my father about Woodlands.'

At that, Berto stopped. Francis listened as his breathing slowed. When he spoke, it was at a whisper. 'Never,' he said. 'Not a soul, Francis. You know I wouldn't.'

Francis took a pace backwards and allowed Berto to stand, brush himself down. They'd been friends for such a long time. Perhaps he'd had good reason to tell Frederick. Francis needed to slow down, listen through an explanation. He concentrated on the empty thud echoing inside him. It seemed to him that a hole had opened up where his heart should be, and God did it hurt. He stared down at his own chest: the dip between his pectoral muscles; the covering of near-black hair, which had thickened of late and stood half an inch shy of his flesh; the flickering of his skin as he fought to stand still and give Berto a chance.

'Tell me why you did it,' he said quietly.

'We swore against it, Francis,' Berto replied.

'Then why break the promise?'

'I wouldn't.'

Francis lifted his head, unable to moderate his words any longer. 'How else would he know?' The question built to a crescendo and crashed off the fort walls.

'Jesus Christ. Listen, House. I don't know! He doesn't. He can't. Fuck – I thought you were a better man than him.'

At the comparison, at its hideous implication, Francis' anger rose again. Stupid. Unreasonable, given that Berto had proven without doubt that he believed Francis a better man than his father. But Francis could not think past his rage, his shame. Charging over the rutted sand like a mindless beast, he threw one last punch. Loathsome. Cowardly. Because this one Berto wasn't braced for, and it threw the shorter man's head violently backwards, and his neck made a singular clapping sound which Francis recognised from all those years before. That sound had never left his nightmares. He knew then, deep in his gut, that it had happened again. It was unbelievable, that one man could make such a mistake twice, but there it was. Again. Francis could only watch as Berto swung backwards, blinded, then flopped to his side, tucked like a seashell on the sand. Vomit rose from his stomach, and he angled himself apart, so that it would not spatter over Berto. And once he had done that, he could not bear to look back and bend down to touch the place where Berto's pulse ought to beat and confirm it. He could not endure the sound of the lapping rollers: speechless witnesses to his crime. He could not tolerate the disgusting shove of his truncated breaths and their two-syllabled insistence: Ber-to, Ber-to. So he turned, and he ran.

At Cairo, the men are shoved inside a rattling ambulance wagon and transported, without explanation, four or five miles into the bitter heart of a black Egyptian night. They sit shoulder to shoulder, misting the window glass with their empty words. Francis does not dare wipe a porthole in the steam and look out. He is bilious, giddy. He is struggling to hold himself together and to stare out at the passing country would undo him. Especially as he had thought he'd seen... He was sure, as they'd left the flaring city lights at their backs and driven into darkness... The shadows and the sand had made the shape of Walker's Ridge beneath the moon.

He sits in silence as the vehicle slows, then chugs, then finally gurgles to a stop. He waits away a minute or two and, deciding that it will not move off again, grasps the handle and pushes against the door's stiffened hinges. It opens with a whine, shedding some flakes of rust. He hooks a leg out and, grinding his heel down to ensure he won't fall if his weight is too much for his weakened limbs, ducks free of the wagon. As the others file out behind him, he only gawps wordlessly upwards.

'Heliopolis Palace,' Farmer remarks.

A thousand electric bulbs light the night as the men clamber out of the three convoy wagons onto the landscaped gardens, nursing their various injuries and gaping at their new situation. The palace extends to left and right and beyond the periphery of their immediate vision. Its stone is the same pale shade as the sand-swept dawn which will, a few short hours hence, melt through the pressing darkness. Its frontage is crowned by battlements, below which four stories of windows shaped like keyholes reveal the expensive lighting within, and from somewhere at its middle emerges a vast copper green dome, adorned with a topmost point which surely needles the belly of the moon.

Why or how, Francis cannot imagine, but the Australians have housed their hospital in the grandest royal palace he has ever laid eyes on.

The men stand at the centre of a web of white, tepee style tents – small and neglected and boyish and lost. They watch white-winged nurses flit along the corridors through the windows.

'Jesus Christ,' Farmer whispers.

Whitman nods slowly. 'And we've been scratching around in the dirt like… like…'

'Like –'

'Jesus Christ,' Hodgson puts in. 'I've a mind to turf every last chap out of there and claim an entire floor for myself.'

Francis smiles. 'And how long do you expect that would take?'

'I don't know,' Hodgson answers, his mouth hanging open long after his words have escaped it. 'But I want to run along the corridors and drop to my knees and slide the floors like a little lad.' It's the most they've ever heard him speak in one go.

'You want to run!' Bill Farmer replies, slapping at Hodgson's shoulder. 'What's the matter with you, man? I want to take a long soak, then sleep till someone shakes me to tell me this blasted war's over.'

Hodgson nods. His face is solemn, contemplative. 'Or we could do that.'

And that, Francis finally realises, is why they have been brought here. They are no longer fit to fight. They are hospital patients. They are ill. Perhaps they are dying. He can hardly tell.

They are traipsed up the marble stairs by a short nurse with a gentle tongue. 'Please,' she says, rather than 'Come this way,' or 'Hurry along'. How she might have spoken to them in a rowdy pub off the Plymouth Hoe, Francis cannot suppose, but here she restricts herself to pleases and thank yous. It is her way of showing them that she appreciates them for the creatures they have become. They follow her obediently through imperial ballrooms, where they are stared at by portraits held in gilded frames. Their softened boots pad after her clipped heels past the doorways of bedrooms dressed with finest cottons and silks. They shuffle between tables occupied by soldiers bent over their own folded arms and their memories, and soldiers who steam out of hot baths towards their bunks, and soldiers bandaged into sleep. And, by degrees, it becomes apparent that they are destined not for a night in the wards, but for the next arrangement of tents. None hides the weight of his disappointment as they leave the palace by a rear entrance and are overwhelmed by the checkerboard gardens, where white tent after white tent is laid out in diagonal precision.

'Might we still enjoy the baths?' Farmer asks.

The nurse nods gravely. The men do not respond. Francis

wonders if they, like him, had believed that they were to lord into their recoveries inside the palace walls. Likely they had thought they deserved as much. Likely they had thought that someone, after all this time, had recognised their efforts and was keen to reward them. The poor fools. Francis is aware that his head has been muddled on occasion these past months, but to think he would now be tended in a prince's bedroom, surrounded by electric lights and stoked fires and alabaster. He truly has lost track of himself.

The idea sets his throat to tightening and his eyes to brimming, and he concentrates the urge to sob away with thoughts of the bottled opium tincture he has stashed about his person. Soon, he will submit to another measure, and in losing himself, he will plunder his soul for the soldier who can forsake his search for his friend in favour of his duty, for the soldier who might make Frederick proud. He is, after all, becoming a man.

Who he had been before, he cannot imagine. He considers now that perhaps he had been no one at all. He had possessed only the various parts of a person, and it is the war, not his juvenile loves or his plucky attitude, which have wrenched and screwed and hammered him into a convincing whole. It is the war. He is the war. And somehow he can touch and smell and hear every part of it. Francis is built from lice infestations and sleepless nights, from the vibrating earth and the blasted guns, from the coppery stink of blood and the rain pattering on his dug-out roof, and the calming flow of his tincture. If Francis House were blown apart tomorrow, all the juttering screams he has closed his ears to these past months would spill from his body and, rising in a desperate scramble for heaven, turn the sky forever black.

That's what Francis is. He is the memory of other men's pain.

He closes his eyes and drops into a faint.

Later, when he starts to rouse, he finds himself being laid on a blanket inside one of the tents.

'Who do we have here?' asks an unfamiliar voice. Judging by its calm and authority, Francis supposes it must belong to a doctor. Or his father. Regardless of what Frederick might have felt, when he spoke to his son, he always did so with perfect authority. *Just show them… There's a need to… Listen… If you don't… This is how real men…*

'Not sure, Sir,' comes the reply. 'A Sergeant, but I haven't got his name.'

And that is fitting, Francis thinks, because his name was forgotten some time ago. He is only Sergeant now. He is just a uniform.

Twenty-Five

'Fran-cis.' The voice sing-songs into his ear and he flinches but does not wake.

He is back at Woodlands, and standing in the trees behind barracks, the very same poker Hancox had used to abuse Berto clenched in his aching fists. He has been fixed to the spot for upwards of twenty minutes, waiting. It is a black, moonless night, and the trees are dribbled ink stains between which Francis peers but sees nothing. It has been three weeks since Francis pulled Berto down from that lamp hook in number three room, and, rather than turning his attentions to Francis, as Francis had supposed he would, Hancox has only intensified the cruel tricks he plays on Berto. Well, Francis will stand for it no longer.

He's left a note folded on Hancox's pillow. *Midnight. Behind the stables.* A boy so thick-headed as Hancox would not be able to resist such an invitation. Even if he suspects it is a trap, Francis knows he will come. Bully Hancox thinks himself too tough to be bested, even if caught by surprise.

The chatter and laughter of boys who are supposed to have bunked down for the night drifts through windows propped ajar to allow the smoke of their contraband cigarettes its escape. The undergrowth rustles as mice or voles or shrews scutter through it. The trees whine in the light wind. And Francis listens past it all for the regularity of falling footsteps.

It is half past midnight before they come, slow and cautious in their approach, but unmistakably human in comparison to all those fleeting sounds Francis has grown familiar with over the last hour. Nature does not announce its arrival so clumsily.

He grips the poker tighter, tracking Hancox's weaving movement between the trees. He closes his eyes, to better listen, and envisages the boy clumping heavily along, his forehead furrowed angrily over his eyebrows as it so often is. He even imagines he can hear the wet suck and spit of Hancox's slack-mouthed breathing. The boy is giving his position away perfectly. Francis' stomach gurgles as he draws the poker back like a golf iron and readies himself to swing. He is scared, naturally. He does not really want to fight Hancox, but his father's words reverberate endlessly through his mind.

Never mind if you are beaten. Just show 'em you are not afraid.

The only way, it seems, to convince Hancox of the same is to wallop a few bruises into him. But he is sturdier than Francis by far, and Francis needs to lead with a shock. A firm blow to the stomach with the poker should suffice, just to take him down and give Francis the first advantage. He keeps his eyes closed, nodding his head in time with the approaching footsteps, and counts himself into action. Five...

'Fran-cis,' the voice calls again. Sweet as treacle. A girl's voice. And Francis is sure he ought to recognise it but however far he reaches into his memory, he cannot place it.

Four...

His eyelids are welded shut now. He needs to open them, to better aim his swing, but they are weighted and gluey. They will not part.

Three...

He will have to swing blind, then. There is nothing else for it. Wherever the blow lands, Hancox will deserve the damage. The puckering white burns on Berto's stomach prove that; the welts across his buttocks from Hancox's whipped belt; the handprint bruises which mottle his arms.

Two...

The footsteps grow louder. Francis' breath stutters.

One...

And he swings, with all of his might, and as he does so he

snorts into waking. He is prone beneath the pale canvas roof of a tent. The light glares, and for a moment he cannot make out what it is which pins him to his hospital cot. He blinks and blinks, searching lines of detail in the dark shape before him, and then he sees her.

Hovering, an inch from his nose-tip, is the face of a girl. She is no more than fourteen years of age. She has thick, ash-blonde hair which hangs over her face, partially hiding it; a small, straight nose; a thin-lipped mouth, cocked at one side in consideration of him. She is small inside a borrowed greatcoat. And her eyes… Oh, her eyes. Round and grey and eternally wide open, they spark with such rage that Francis fancies they could light up the desert without.

'Who –' he gasps.

But before he can go any further, the girl clamps a cold hand over his mouth.

'Estelle,' she hisses.

When Francis next comes properly to, he is surprised to hear a gentle rendering of *God Rest You Merry, Gentlemen* echoing spookily from beyond the tent canvas. It is a chill, white dawn. Christmas Day.

'Here's the chap now,' Farmer says, and his voice is full of such jollity that Francis jolts upright, expecting to see Berto loping towards him with his funny, stiff gait. 'And just in time for his turkey dinner. Slow down, now.' Farmer puts a palm to Francis' shoulder and persuades him to recline again. 'You need to rest.'

Francis keeps his eyes trained on the tent flap, but no one steps through it. No one is coming. Farmer must only have been talking about him.

'Where is she?' Francis croaks.

Farmer frowns. 'Who?'

But Francis doesn't know how to explain and he is embarrassed by his mistaking what must have been another dream for reality. It is, he is frightened to realise, becoming harder and harder to tell the difference.

'Where are they?' Francis says, pretending at a slip of the tongue. 'The others?'

'Well,' Farmer begins, 'the bloody Australians, having money, disappeared into town last night and haven't been seen since.'

With the arrival of each man in turn, Francis learns that Farrelly, Whitman, and Hodgson, having no money, have been forced to remain in camp. Accompanied and entertained by an unexpectedly loyal Farmer – here, Farmer bows as though to royalty and grins madly – they have laughed and relaxed and worn this new disappointment well. When, however, for their Christmas breakfast, Francis finds that their only fare is to be a cup of weak tea, he rouses himself from his sick bed and marches off on trembling legs in the direction of the Australian General to demand pay for himself and his men. This, the others laugh at, but Francis is indignant. Christmas Day isn't supposed to blow in on a dry, rasping wind. Christmas Day isn't supposed to leave sand on your lips.

In Plymouth, they had idled into hoar frost mornings, cradling cups of cocoa and holding the steaming heat to their faces, then celebrated with fat birds and good wine and tuneless carols. The Houses were always on top form for Christmas. Frederick's moods were forgotten and Eliza's nerves were mellowed by a single glass of sherry and the four children, even as they grew into adulthood, promised faithfully that they would not argue over trivialities until Boxing Day dawned. Christmas Day was conducted with kindness and smiles and, long after the cold silvered sun had tumbled into sleep, they would sit, the six of them, to a bedtime reading of Ethel's choosing, she being the fondest of books. One by one, they would drop heavy into dreams distorted by an excess of rich food, and later be woken by the cold absence of the fire against their skin and shuffle to bed, ready to wake late again the next morning.

And Francis will – he determines as he traverses the camp, hobbling against the festering blister on his right heel, his vision blurred – have something of comfort in Egypt, too.

When, twenty minutes later, he marches back to his tent with flushed cheeks, a woozy head, and five Great British pounds for each man, the other chaps cease their laughter: with such a gift, they will be kings for the night. And as darkness falls, their cheers carry them out of camp and back towards the city faster than those grumbling ambulance wagons carried them in.

Francis' recollections, when he awakes on Boxing Day morn, stumble and fall away. However far he reaches, he fails to retrieve them. Only two hazy flashes remain.

In the first, he is horribly mixed up on French wine and standing on a table top, waving a rifle in solemn declaration that he will visit all the shooting galleries and shoot the Kaiser straight between the eyes.

In the second, he is presenting a bundle of won handkerchiefs to a veiled Egyptian lady in the middle of a tree-guarded street. They stand face-to-face, as though to duel, he holding out the handkerchiefs and she shrinking him with her full penny-brown stare. Her head and face veils, connected by a beaded column which travels down the bridge of a strong nose, reveal little more than her eyes and a narrow wedge of bronzed cheek, but Francis can see indecision shuddering through her. She twitches, hesitates, then snatches the handkerchiefs from him and makes off down the road as fast as her lengthy legs can carry her. And isn't she a vision, racing away from him so, the moon casting tree branch shadows over her blue zircon veils as they ripple behind her, like the discarded garments of a figure on one of those erotic cards the men trade, or the abandoned attire of a vanished magician's assistant, or the loosened wisps of her spirited soul.

Francis thinks that perhaps he has never seen such a beautiful sight as that lady rushing away down the street, her step lighter than his exhaled breath, her body cooled by her flowing veils and the moon-shone dark. She is a hallucination. She is a blue jay, swooping hope through the Egyptian dust. She is a bird or a goddess or a phantasm, imitating human form to make a poorly soldier smile. Francis is certain he will never meet her again – and moreover, that he will never know whether she is real or not – but little matter. She is a passing reminder of his youth and his strength. She is the prompt he needs to recall that those assets are not lost, but only misplaced, and can be discovered again.

In Egypt, he decides, he will recover himself. Here, he will locate that soldier who had longed to leave Malta and fight his war, and the instant he does, he will send him straight back to the front. What was he thinking, to want to escape Gallipoli? There, he had purpose. There, he could be the man he dreamt up as he scuttered along the beach with Lily, kicking at rocks and encouraging crabs to climb onto his flattened palm and hoping. There, he could search out his best friend, as he had sworn to. Since leaving Anzac, he has succumbed to an ugly dereliction, and what has that led him to except drunkenness and delusion?

Well, he will countenance no more of it. The midst of the fight – his country's and his own – is where he belongs.

Twenty-Six

Late the following week, they shift to Tel-el-Kebir — a grubby, six-mile tent city, situated on the desert proper. It is populated, Francis has heard rumour, by some forty thousand Australians. It is plagued, he soon finds, by twice as many flies. As they trail through camp, nodding at clutches of torpid, bandaged Aussies, Francis considers that their movement here must have been intended as a cure for the dysentery which afflicts them still, and makes up his mind that it will have the desired effect, and very soon indeed, for he will not stay here, amongst the injured and the empty, with a stench like stagnant pond water in his nose and no means of reaching the rolling sea. Already, he feels so much the better. Rest, good food, and a thorough wash have near restored him to himself: excepting the fact that his legs are dry and flaking and they long not to stride but to butterfly kick; excepting his disbelief in the fiction that he is a man called Francis House and not simply a uniform labelled Sergeant; excepting the unpredictable appearance and disappearance, first in the hospital and then in camp, of a slight young girl named Estelle. But he need not speak of those matters. He can swallow them down and trap them in the pit of his belly. He will do whatever it takes to ensure that he does not sit out his war, constantly turning away from the empty greatcoat he snatches sight of now and then at the corner of his eye. Always just out of reach. Waiting.

He fully intends to have his promotion validated, and vows to set about persuading a man to do it the instant the early morrow stretches across the desert. But no sooner does he lay his head back than he plummets into a sleep so black that his intentions are completely forgotten. 'Wait,' cries the familiar voice in his dreams. 'Wait!'

He is woken next day not by his ready attitude but by the landing thud of a string-tied lump of letters at the foot of his blanket. His Christmas mail. He stirs himself and sits up to investigate it by the beaming sunlight pervading the tent's interior. Thirty-five letters and twelve parcels, most months overdue and all variously stamped *Missing, Hospital, Try Australians, Try Hellas, Killed*. Being with the Australians, it transpires, Francis and his men have been firstly forgotten and then thoroughly lost.

'What do you think to this?' he says, waving an envelope decorated with an unsympathetic *Killed* at Bill Farmer, the only other man yet awake.

Farmer shrugs. 'You might just as well stick with us, then, and call yourself an Australian.'

Francis frowns over the prospect. Is it possible that he could leave Egypt an Australian? Could he see this war through, then go home to a place he has never visited, even in his reveries? That would be some adventure. But it would not be his.

'Will you have me?' he jokes, winking at Bill Farmer. 'Honorary?'

'Sure,' Farmer replies. 'You could rattle home with me if you liked, bunk up for a while, till you found yourself somewhere. Nobody'd notice an extra body amongst five kiddos anyway.'

'You have five children?'

Bill pauses to lean forward, put a finger to one nostril, and shoot a sphere of snot out through the tent flap and onto the sand. The dirty habit is deeply ingrained, and Francis has grown accustomed to it, though he will not stoop to it.

'Five,' Bill nods.

'Christ,' Francis replies. 'I didn't realise.'

Bill shrugs. 'Maybe six by now. We were getting suspicious just before I left.' He raises his hands before his chest and cups the air, indicating a growing weight.

'Suspicious.' Francis laughs at the choice of word.

Bill laughs with him. 'Suspicious six. Who needs six gutsy ladies to turf out into the world, hey?'

'All girls?'

'So far. I always fancied myself a little fella, you know, but I'm glad now that they're all girls.'

Francis rummages around in his blanket for the stolen cigarettes he has stowed there and, locating them, tosses one to Bill. Bill catches it and turns it between two fingers like a baton.

'Why?'

Bill presses his lips together and huffs. 'In case this happens again,' he explains, turning both palms to the heavens in a prayer of his own design.

Francis never questioned Bill Farmer's exact age during their months at Anzac, but suddenly, held here at the pleasantly chill break of an unknowable day, he feels himself in the company of a man by far his senior, both in years and wisdom.

'Do you think…' Francis begins.

When he and Berto had huddled in a store cupboard in the swaying belly of the *Sudan* and, sitting on a creaking pair of upturned buckets, whispered about their plans for the future, they had not come close to imagining this.

'I'll do my time, and then I'll have myself a family,' Berto had said. 'At least ten kiddies. That'll suit. And a good round wife. None of your turmoils for me, House. I know what I'm about.'

He reached forward and plucked the cigarette they had pilfered from between Francis' lips and, when Francis inhaled in readiness for a complaint, flicked the tip of Francis' nose with a straightened forefinger.

Francis winced and attempted to return the assault, but Berto's dodge was too quick.

'What about you, House?' he prompted. 'What will you do when you've worn out your new boots?' He cast a grin at Francis' polished boots.

'Look for a house by the sea,' Francis answered slowly.

And that answer, he thinks, remains as true now as it was then. The war will not change everything.

'Do you think it could?' he continues. 'Happen again?'

'Yes, I do,' Bill replies. 'I think anything that's happened once can happen again.'

Francis studies the sad lines which leak from the corners of Bill Farmer's eyes: his skin is weeping. Then he clamps his mouth around his cigarette and nods. Anything that has happened once might happen again. Yes. He is inclined to agree.

Though the thought that he might one day have a son of his own to worry over as Bill has described does not strike him. Having so readily broken his attachment to one woman after another, having never permitted himself to fall into the depths of love, when Francis looks to his future, he sees only himself occupying it. He cannot imagine anything other than himself and his house by the sea. He cannot possibly entertain loving a brand-new boy well enough to fill a notebook purely with advice and wishes for his happiness. Nor that that same notebook might find its way from an unknown attic into the hands of Lily's great granddaughter. Nor that she, studying her great-granduncle's words, would find something of herself on the page and, lifting a pen, open up a notebook of her own.

No man can see so far. And Francis, it seems, can see no further than Gallipoli, for more often than not when he looks out into the desert, what he discerns are not the empty plains of Egypt but the tightened curves and juts of Walker's Ridge.

'Don't you think...' he begins. He isn't sure how to frame the sentiment. What he wants to say is that he does not trust the landscape outside his tent, that the world shifts before his eyes now in ways it could not possibly have done before, that he is not entirely sure that he and Farmer and the others ever left the Dardanelles.

But when he turns back towards Farmer, to search the words

on his face, the older man's head has slumped onto his shoulder and he is starting to snore.

Dropping forward onto his stomach so that his legs might flail freely behind him, Francis shuffles through his bundled letters again, spreading them over his blanket and searching out the familiar slant of Lily's hand. There is his father's oversized address, Ethel's delicate copperplate, Marija's childlike letter-making. None belongs to Lily.

He touches the pocket containing the tattered remains of the letter he has carried around Gallipoli all this time. Though there had been more to begin with, on Malta, for such a long while now there has been only this one. This most important one. He can hardly stand to look on it and see what has been written there since the first. Truly, he had not been able to see the words for the longest while. His own mind had hidden them from him, for safekeeping. It had put inventions in their place. But now he has remembered the truth of them. And here, he knows, while he feels rested and well and does not swim through waves of pain, he will be able to read them anew.

As Bill Farmer continues to snore, he draws the letter forth, unfolds it, and flattens it onto his blanket. His heart pitter-patters too fast, noisy as rain driven against a windowpane. The letter is filthy against the newly pressed white cotton of his cot. It is torn almost entirely across its middle. Its corners are rounded and muddied. It is specked with tobacco stains. It is perhaps the most precious item Francis has ever owned and he knows that he shall never lose it. Whatever the cost, he will hold tight to this, the last he can reach of his friend.

He takes a deep breath and lowers his head to the words, praying they will be the ones he expects.

I've met a girl, Francis. Her name is Carina and, well, I've only asked her to marry me, haven't I? This very night, in fact. And she and I only acquainted this past fortnight. Sorry for keeping secrets, old chap. Soon as you're back from Sliema, get yourself down to

the harbour. We're waiting to start the celebrations and we can't
very well do that without my best man. Quick about it now.
Your Old Pal,
B.

Francis closes his eyes and brings the paper up to touch his
nose. Yes, of course. He could not admit to it before. He could
not face it. He was not brave enough. But this is the reason he
has stored it against his heart for so many months.

The letter has always been from Berto.

Twenty-Seven

They soon take to sleeping on the sand, the better to spot the desert dogs which sniff continuously around camp. The animals approach with heads low and haunches high, noses twitching in anticipation of the wounded, the unconscious, the weak. Their approach is quiet but desperate: a blind man could see that they are starving. But even those men minded to do so cannot throw them scraps. They have none to spare, and besides, they know it will only encourage the beasts. Instead, following Stocky Hodgson's clumsy lead, they chase them off, shouting and clattering and banging anything to hand until the pack turns, tails tucked, and yelp back into the coffin-black tract of their home. Each retreat is guided by the cackle of a laughing hyena.

The persistent ritual drives the men slowly mad. While he sleeps, Whitman throws up his arms and clangs invisible pans together.

Sniff, sneak, clatter, yelp, retreat.

Sniff, sneak, clatter, yelp, retreat.

Hooo-ho-ho-ho-ho-ho-ho-ho goes the hyena.

Hooo-ho-ho-ho-ho-ho-ho-ho!

Sometimes, under the moon, the dogs lift their noses and sing out long, sorrowful howls. Francis wakes and listens to their chorus and thinks that perhaps he knows that sound; that perhaps some part of him is howling with them.

While Farmer and the others sleep, he stands and steps between their curled bodies in the direction of open desert.

With the vast ripple of camp tents at his back, he might just as well be on the moon, or back in Gallipoli, or nowhere at all. The world is only a pale slab of sand being steadily flattened by a black stack of sky. The horizon is a perfectly straight line. The stars are thrown salt. Though he can hear the dogs, he cannot see them. All that stands before him, some distance away and silhouetted under the moon's splayed light, is the greatcoat. He resists its summon, knowing that it will return tomorrow night, and the night after, and that soon enough he will find the courage to go with it.

So deep do the yips and whines of the dogs gnaw into the men's minds that one rose-bloom dawn, as he stands stiff on parade, Whitman lifts his rifle, takes aim, and shoots one of those poor lingering hounds straight through the skull. A pop, a hiss, and it dies with a silent slump, never having suspected a thing. Still, Francis feels for the beast. He committed no crime beyond an attempt at existence. The other men seem equally troubled – Whitman included. None speaks or sighs or complains as the rest of the pack make their usual yelping departure. None lifts a pan and chases them off.

Death, even that of a mangy desert dog, is ever met now with a spell of silence, or a prayer, or a nod of acknowledgement. The men have taken to offering it their respect. Just in case.

'Whitman,' Francis whispers, when they have recovered themselves a tad and turned their watch from the hunk of flea-thinned fur collapsed, too close, on the sand. They will hear the flies devour it from this distance. 'Whitman?'

'Sir?' Whitman does not glance back at Francis. He speaks from one twisted corner of his mouth. His pale-lashed eyes are large with unshed regret. Francis can see his Adam's apple juddering.

'I'm making it my business to return to the front. I'm posting my application for transfer. Are you for it?'

He nods. 'Yes, Sir.'

'You're certain?'

'Yes, Sir.'

'Good,' Francis says, locking his hands behind his back and stretching out his spine with a groan. 'I'd hoped so. I'd no intention of going ahead without the bunch I almost drowned alongside to save a barge of soggy mules.'

A smile flickers across Whitman's face. Along the line, Francis hears Hodgson snort: 'Bloody mules'. Francis directs his grin at his feet. He still wears those mismatched socks – one long, one short – but he is no longer ashamed of his ragged appearance. Ragged or otherwise, he will fulfil his duty as Sergeant. For as long as it is feasible, he will keep his remaining men together. He will do it with kindness, as Berto would have.

He steals a last glance at the dog. The yowls of his mates echo over the desert flats, conveyed on approaching girders of broad, swan-white daylight. Here it comes, Francis thinks: my fortune, good or bad. And then he closes his eyes – to measure its warmth on his face, and because already the flies are clustering over that damned dog, and he does not wish to see a meal made of one so recently fallen. He pushes his hands over his face, rubbing at his sun-cracked skin, and determines not to look in that direction again until tomorrow.

The flies hum into a swirling black column and descend towards the dog.

Soon, all evidence of its existence will be destroyed.

Soon, he will be gone.

That night, the greatcoat ventures closer than it has in weeks. Francis wakes to the wing-flap of its hems on the wind. A laughing dove chuckles overhead and he lifts his eyes to follow it towards the rim of the moon's light. There, it disappears into the glow. To avoid looking across to the place where the greatcoat waits, Francis sets about gathering up his belongings, scant as they are. In less than a minute, he is dressed and can dally no longer. He drapes his own greatcoat over his shoulders and, with a deep inhalation, lifts his eyes to the apparition.

He steps towards it as though under hypnosis, without questioning what it wants. It has been trailing him all this time. It has waited so patiently. He feels duty bound to do as it bids.

What exactly it is bidding, though, he is not sure. He paces steadily forward, travelling further into the void of desert and further away from Tel-el-Kebir, and as he does, so the greatcoat seems to grow smaller. It is moving apart from him, drawing him into the deeper darkness beyond the tent city, and though Francis is jittery and trembling, he finds he is willing to follow.

A sudden rush of wind scuds across the plain, dragging an eerie moan behind it, and Francis starts as something touches his cheek. He halts, heart drubbing heavily, and brings his hand up to investigate what it is. He almost laughs when he realises that it is only the collar of his greatcoat, lifted on the wind so that the hemmed edge strokes his skin. He pushes it back down against his shoulder and continues. The dogs howl. The wind gusts. Francis' boots crunch over the shivering white sand. And eventually, after many minutes of walking, he advances upon the greatcoat and stops before it.

'You wanted me to come,' he says foolishly. His voice is small and gritty, as though it is formed from the sand which surrounds him.

After a pause, the empty hat dips up and down in imitation of a nod.

'Why?' Francis asks. Naturally, he knows there will come no answer. A being made of serge and stitching and burnished button will have no voice. He wonders stupidly for a moment whether he is supposed to wear it – whether taking off his own greatcoat and shrugging this one on will enable him to become the man he ought to be – but deep down he knows that is not why the ghost has appeared to him. What it is showing him, he supposes, is the hollow man he has been. The hollow man he might continue to be. The hollow man he became that night on the beach with Berto, when he turned and ran away.

'You're going to have to help me,' he says.

He waits while the greatcoat seems to deliberate on this and then, slowly, lifts its left arm and points directly at Francis. Francis echoes the movement and brings his hand up to his chest.

'Me?' he asks.

Again, the dip of the hat. An affirmative.

'Yes,' Francis replies. He is becoming exasperated. 'Yes, me. But what about me? What should I do?' He closes his eyes, seeking patience in the pulsing dark behind his lids. He feels a rushing sensation and, when he opens his eyes again, the greatcoat is mere inches apart from him. The buttoned chest rises and falls, as though it is breathing. In, out, in, out. Francis' own breath quickens in response.

The arms of the greatcoat rise again and, moving towards its collar, begin working their way from button to button. Francis watches in awe as, one by one, the untouched buttons pop loose. When the greatcoat flaps open on the passing wind, Francis does as he has been ordered and, working from the neck down, undoes each of his own buttons. What this must look like, Francis cannot think. A man in a greatcoat, standing opposite an empty greatcoat, mirroring its movements as though he is a boy taking lessons from his father in dressing or shaving or manners. He is glad that only the dogs are awake to witness such a spectacle.

When Francis' greatcoat, too, is opened on the wind, so the arms of the other rise again to its breast and, shifting as if a body truly does reside within, shrugs the item off its invisible shoulders. It drops to the ground, chased by the hat, and the two articles settle there as neatly as they might at the foot of a bunk, folded carefully by their owner.

'You're telling me to take it off?' Francis offers.

From atop its pile, the hat lifts and dips. Yes.

'But why?'

And even to Francis' own ears, the question sounds meaningless. He knows now what the greatcoat is telling him. You cannot make yourself a man with serge and stripes. You cannot shape a person from a uniform. You cannot claim an identity with a title. And yet, Sergeant House is the only man Francis knows how to be. Wearing a uniform, leading men, charging into battle, swallowing his fears, being alone, silencing his doubts, fighting with his fists, acting autarkically – this is what being a man has always meant.

But Berto was warm and funny and unguarded and generous, and he was a far better man than Francis. He was the very best of men. He had proved that time and time again.

'Berto,' Francis whispers past the tightening at his throat. The hat tilts; a cocked head. Francis' next words flood out on his grief. 'I'll try,' he says. 'I promise.'

The greatcoat resurrects itself and, looking for all the world as though there is a man within again, hangs on the air. For a terrible moment, Francis thinks it is going to envelop him. Perhaps that is its purpose – to lure men from their companies and swallow them up. Perhaps it consumes souls and it is their restless energy which sends it wandering over the continent. Perhaps it is the form death takes when it comes for soldiers. Perhaps, if Francis were to put it on, it would wrap him safely in the darkness of eternity…

He closes his eyes and waits again for that rush of movement. Almost immediately, the greatcoat whips around him – a cold draught plays over his neck, his shoulders – and then it is gone.

He glances about and spots it gliding away across the sand.

'Wait!' Francis finds himself shouting again. His voice is hoarse, barely more than a crackle. The greatcoat will not hear him. He starts to run, but his legs only churn in slow motion, as though he is floating in deep water. The greatcoat grows smaller and smaller, and Francis reaches out a hand, as though he might pluck the item off the skyline and hold it between his thumb and forefinger – a model soldier's garment. His pinches his digits together. Misses. He tries again. Finds nothing but empty air.

'Please wait,' he cries. 'I can't do it without you.'

But the greatcoat does not listen or does not care to, and Francis can only slog after it, calling out now and then, desperate to keep it within his sights. The moon dips into a pile of plum clouds and emerges again to spotlight Francis when the cramp in his thighs has hardened them to stone. He has been walking forever. There is sand inside his boots. It has torn his skin and the tears burn but they do not bleed. He had thought Tom Merton a statue on Gallipoli, but it is he who is carved from marble. He does not bleed anymore. He does not cry. He does not crave or ache or tease or laugh. He is only someone else's vision, trapped atop a plinth. He is only an idea. He has no will of his own. He is hardly even surprised when those familiar brushwood cliffs rise out of the sand before him and he finds himself back on Anzac Cove, with all the weight of the sea behind him and a hopeless upward scramble before him and nothing whatsoever in his empty, cowardly gut.

In November 1917, I was taken ill and was forced to report sick with a pain in my side. I was reported 'fit' though I fainted in the Doctor's arms (many similar stories I could tell of the despised Salonica Army). Naturally, I was much hurt by this treatment and started unsteadily for my dug out. Snow was on the ground and I was freezing cold, having stood stripped in the doctor's tent for a considerable time with the flap open. I fainted halfway back and here I was found and kind hands carried me to hospital. When passing the S. Major he gave his usual shout, 'Make him walk', but I was unconscious.

Twenty-Eight

Francis glances about for the broken sloop and, sighting it, begins stumbling at a long diagonal across the beach. His shorts, vest, and mismatched socks drip from his bones. His greatcoat he drags over the sand behind him like a dead body. With every step, it grows heavier. Something is filling it. Someone is filling it. He dare not turn around in case he finds a body within. He does not know whose it might be. He fears it might be his own, and that it is only his phantom struggling up the beach towards the sloop. He'll find shelter there, in the narrow bowl of the boat. He'll lie flat, his eyes on the speckled stars, and wait while Turks and Brits and Aussies and Maoris sneak ignorantly past, too intent on killing each other to notice that the dead man in the sloop is still breathing. He hadn't understood how Tom Merton could have been dead but still breathing for such a long while on Gallipoli. He does now.

At last, he reaches the little boat and, gripping its rim with a shaking hand, attempts to roll himself over and in. The transition is too difficult. His feet will not lift off the sand. Two, three, four times he attempts to hoist himself upwards before he clatters in, setting the sloop to rocking.

Crossing his arms over his chest, he waits for his cradle – or his coffin – to still. It creaks and creaks and finally slows into silence. Francis sifts relief out through his clenched teeth. His breath is rancid. He can smell it, lingering on the dry Turkish air. It is staled by empty stomach acids. He cannot remember the last time he ate. Aboard the *Ulysses*. That was it. But that was before he arrived on Anzac. It must have been. For he remains trapped here. He has not swum away. Everything that's happened since the push off Walker's Pier was … a fancy, then? Self-deception? Just another trick of the opium? Farmer was posted to Egypt. Perhaps Francis has stolen those stories, as he has stolen so many before – to impress his family with, to comfort his friends with, to construct himself out of.

'But it felt real,' he mutters.

'If it felt real then it surely was,' comes the response. 'You have to trust yourself, House.'

Francis opens his eyes to find Bill Farmer sitting on the sloop's one intact bench, his boots set wide apart, his elbows on his knees. His sand-scruffed hair stands out in every direction. There is a cut just above his lip, not deep, which lends him a sneer. He squints over a cigarette he is rolling. Francis concentrates on the end of his untied lace: draped, unmoving and wet-heavy, over the vessel's nailed slats, it leaks out a shadow.

He shakes his head, feels the ungiving wood rattle against the curve of his skull.

'There's nothing worth trusting,' he decides. 'Least of all ourselves.' Farmer is quiet. 'Least of all our perceptions,' Francis continues.

'Bosh!' Farmer sniffs.

'The truth,' Francis argues. 'I don't even know what I am.'

Farmer steals a long drag of his cigarette and exhales with relish, tipping back his head and rounding his lips so that he looks to be howling at the moon. Just like those Egyptian dogs.

'I am white anemone,' Francis begins, slurring and dropping his words. 'I am leatherback turtle. I am sea star and lantern fish and stingray. I am stonefish. I am shingle.'

Yes. That is exactly what he has become: a pile of bashed-round cobbles, smoothed by the tides until they no longer fit together, but still trying, desperately, to re-form themselves into a whole. He is that same rasp and tumble and grating. He is that same confused effort.

Farmer is smiling, laughing at him. He lights a matchstick

and holds the glowing flame to his cigarette end. It illuminates his face, accentuating the dints and slants Francis had thought himself familiar with in strange new ways. He shakes the matchstick out and flicks it over the side of the sloop into the sand, where it *tisses* itself out. Farmer's movements are easy, loose. He is Francis' opposite in almost every detail.

'Why not read us one of your letters,' he suggests. 'Get yourself back on track after the … swim.'

Francis considers the suggestion for more than a minute. Then, his limbs impossibly heavy, he manages to shove a hand into his shorts pocket and draw forth a single piece of sodden paper. The letter has twisted itself into a ragged bow tie. Fingers trembling with cold, Francis attempts to ease it open, slowly, slower still. Gently now, he chides himself. He needs the words. He needs the reassurance. But his movements are too jerky and unpredictable. He gasps as the letter tears in two in his hands.

Tears lurch from his eyes, sudden and unstoppable. He jolts into a sitting position, sending a strange guttural cry from between his lips. 'Oh!' he roars. 'Oh!' And then he realises that, could he close his mouth to properly form the sound, he would be shouting Berto's name.

Immediately, there is a hand on his shoulder.

'You know the words,' Farmer insists. He is whispering now, and Francis cannot imagine why. There has been no shelling since they came ashore. The Turks are asleep or dead. Farmer and House are alone on the beach. 'You don't need to see them. You have them in your mind.'

Farmer is right. Francis squeezes his eyes closed and concentrates past the galloping in his chest. If he can calm himself, slow down his thoughts, he will see the loops and lines of ink in front of him. He will see them as clearly as though they were restored to the ruined paper. They belong to him, after all. They cannot be lost.

'She was leaving,' he says.

'Lily?' Farmer prompts, though they both know that Francis is talking about Lily. Francis has only ever talked about Lily. She is his constant. His core. His heartbeat. The idea of Lily House – brave and forthright as he always knew her to be – has kept her brother alive all these months. He cannot name the man who is part of his soul, so he names the woman instead.

In the dark behind his eyelids, Francis begins to recite the words she once wrote.

The air in the children's bedroom danced with the sweet dew of their sleeping breaths and the fading scent of Johnson's baby powder when I went in to press one last kiss to their foreheads. The room was soft, its edges blurred by Norman and Violet's nursery rhyme dreams. I hummed an invented tune as I tiptoed over the creaking floorboards, hoping the children would not wake. Hoping they would.

I wanted to say goodbye, but I could not admit that I was leaving. That I wanted to. I would not have admitted as much to anyone but you, Francis. I would not have burdened Ernest's heart with it.

I ought to have snuck out quickly, before they stirred, but I couldn't resist the smell of them, the gentle huff-huff of their breathing, the fluttering of their eyelids in the dark, so instead I perched at the foot of Norman's bed a while and cried for the sombre moon. I watched it spill over the docklands, four or five miles distant, and thought that perhaps it was crying with me – for men like you and Ernest, for women like me, for all of us.

I wasn't certain then that I could do it, but there was no better option. I could not be present in two places at once. I had to choose.

'I'm going to be a canary,' I told the children. I told myself. 'I'm going to flitter away, and then, as soon as I can, I'm going to flitter all the way back. I promise. Where could my wings ever take me but home to you?'

I said goodbye to Elaine quickly, both of us trying to avoid descending into snivels. Then I stood on my own doorstep, listening to Elaine's stocking feet on the stairs, inhaling the star-shone cold, recalling the time I stood just yards down the street and said to Ernest,

'We're going to have our babies here.' The memory caused something deep in my stomach to rise up – a wail or a scream – but I clamped my lips around it, pushed my right hand into my pocket, and plucked at the corner of the envelope there.

I'm coming, I thought. I closed my eyes and counted myself into bravery.

Then, breath held, I strode off along the shadowed route to the tram stop, towards all that adventure we had craved, and away from my life and my home and my babies, my way lit by nothing more than the Miles Road lamps and my promises.

'Did she make it?' Farmer whispers.

'I don't know… I can't remember. I… I didn't write back. I came to find my friend. That's what I…'

Francis curses at the number of times he has uttered the word 'I'. He must not think on himself. He had forced Berto to fight on the beach that night. He'd knocked the dear man clean out. He'd run off and hidden instead of waiting to help. He'd lain in his bunk, wide-eyed, through the dawn hours when he knew Berto was to sail for Turkey, because he was too frightened to go down to the harbour and see if his friend had made it aboard ship. He'd followed a possibility to Gallipoli and pretended to seek it out. But he'd considered only himself, himself, himself. And it will not do. Little wonder the cove has ensnared him in her forsaken curve. It is Berto he must not leave here without. Not his soul, then, but his guilt. He is here to reclaim his guilt.

Dropping the two sodden halves of his letter back into his pocket, he springs upright and hurdles the rim of the sloop.

'Where are you going?' Farmer calls.

'Home.'

'Home?'

'Yes,' Francis answers. He lifts a stiffened hand into a salute, uses the forefinger of the saluting hand to prod at his temple, stomps his right foot, then turns and makes away across the sand towards Walker's Ridge. All these months, he'd chosen to believe simply stumbling around Gallipoli was enough, but he has discovered an understanding in the washes and swells of the last misshapen days and he wants to weep or crow or sing in celebration of it. He must stop pretending. He must put on the greatcoat again. He must fill its empty seams. He must accept that he is no longer simply a man or a sea creature or a lover or a soldier or a surging salt tide. Not he. Francis House used to be many beautiful things. He had written love letters, just for the satisfaction of folding pretty words into an envelope and sending them off to be torn open and blushed over. He had tried to make amends for the terrible assumptions he'd made about his father with offers of bicycle rides and sea swims and pints of bitter – almost always refused and taken up by Francis alone. He had met Lily at the passing points of their lives, at smoky train stations, and clasped her to him and smiled and smiled into her same violet and soap scent and recalled what it had been to be a hopeful child. Now, he is stagnant water pooling around badly dug graves, and the flinches that follow gunshot, and promises broken by bravery, and hollow eyes, and dirty feet, and sobs which fall out between snores or screams. He is rotten. He is spoiling. He is the war. He had forgotten that for a while, in the welter. But he remembers now. He remembers everything. Every snatched breath. Every glance of admiration or hatred thrown his way. Every lofty dream. Every snigger. The moment that plucking pain started up inside him. The first time he wrapped his father's watch around his wrist and slotted the leather strap through the buckle. Every dance. Every early morning rising. Every landed blow of every boxing match. The sulphurous stink of rain. The softening of his bowels the day he arrived at Woodlands. His first kiss. The desperate open-mouthed kiss he later claimed as his first kiss. Every blissful fall into the steel and silk sea. And he knows what he must do to put matters right again. He must allow himself to look straight into the eye of the truth. It is as simple and horrifying as that. The word he needs most to speak is not, after all, sorry.

He stops, still in the shadow of the cliffs, and turns back towards the sloop.

'Farmer,' he says. 'Who's inside that greatcoat?' He nods to the body he abandoned in a hunch on the sand.

'Farrelly,' Farmer answers, without moving to check.

'I didn't know his first name. Did you?'

Farmer replies through another tobacco-thick exhalation. 'Alec,' he says, and the two short sounds slip into the smoke and rise with it towards the moon and, all too soon, disappear.

Twenty-Nine

Francis is running along the ridge. Beneath his feet, the land pitches, drops, tilts. The soles of his boots are salt-softened, split, pliant enough to absorb the sudden changes of terrain. One is laced tighter than the other, but Francis cannot stop to rectify it. He does not look down. He does not need to. He is this place. Eyes on the marble sky with its burst of telescope moonlight, he rushes towards the cliff edge. Far offshore, rain spears over the sea, grey and gleaming, and Francis tries to run faster, eager to meet it sooner, for it to hit his skin, run him wet, streak off the grime of all these months, wash him away.

Headstones appear on the skyline: a motley congregation of crosses and granite lumps, gathered as though in muttered complaint. The pulse in Francis' neck quickens. His legs are loose, heavy as mud, but he pounds on, baring his ground teeth against the incoming weather front and willing it to butt heads with him. He cannot do what he must do next under swathes of velvet sky. He needs shrieking wind, stabbing rain, gusts which shove him off his feet. Twenty-two of his twenty-five men are lost. Hell ought to open over him and disgorge its worst. But the sky does only enough to silence him as he weaves amongst the gravestones and screams for Berto.

'Murley!'

First, he needs to tell his old friend that last childhood secret – of how they had watched through the crack in the door, Lily and Francis, as Frederick House stood before the gilt-framed dressing table mirror in their parents' bedroom, illuminated by a low plank of lamplight, his shoulders straight, his slippered feet flat to the floorboards, and swung a hammer he had retrieved from their mother's stocking drawer into the barrel of his ribs, the reddening sides of his neck, the thick but still-flat board of his stomach, his puffed chest, his tensed thighs. His broken and broken again jaw. They understood then, from his posture, that it had always been himself that he hurt. The muffled thud of gathered knuckle against skin they had imagined they'd heard through their pulled-up bedsheets, was in fact caused by a bronze hammer head twice wrapped in silk.

'We can't stay here,' Lily had told him. 'We can't live like two tightrope walkers, always trying to balance the truths and the lies.'

Francis had known then that he would find a way to follow his father to war. He'd known that he would make sense of it all with his sweat and his aching muscles. It was the sight of his father, punishing himself for his imagined failings, which had taken Francis to Malta – to make himself a man worthy of his father's forgiveness.

And it was the thought of Frederick knowing the very worst about his son, and the pain of Berto's betrayal, which had caused him to pick that fight. But he knows now that Berto did not tell Frederick that, at fifteen, his only son had swung a fire poker so hard into a passing little girl's neck that he snapped it outright. He knows, too, that Berto didn't tell Lorenza. It was only an unfortunate coincidence that Frederick and Lorenza had spoken to encourage Francis to kill that same day: Lorenza for her vanity, because she wanted 'the strongest soldier on the island' to call her own; and Frederick in fear for his son's safety. Concern – that was what had led Francis to betray Berto in a greater way than Berto ever had Francis. Frederick's concern and Francis' disbelief in it and the ridiculous conclusion it had led him to.

Seeing death at close hand changes a man, Frederick had written. *That's the truest thing I could ever say to you, Francis. Whether it's a soldier in battle or a girl in the wrong place at the wrong time, it changes you. And you will be asked to kill and kill again, so what I have to say, before you sail, is this – you are already forgiven. Don't let guilt take a hold of you, Francis. You are not at fault. You are already forgiven.*

It was not until two days after the ship Berto was destined to board had sailed for Gallipoli that Francis realised – in a short, breathless instant – that Frederick had been referring not to the girl Francis had mistaken for Hancox at Woodlands, but the young woman they had seen drowned in that awful January storm so many years before. Where Francis, a boy, had seen a woman, Frederick, a man in his forties, had seen the loss of a mere girl.

The realisation hit Francis with all the impact of a bullet. He had been referring to the woman in the waves. He knew nothing. Berto, as ever, had been true.

'Murley!' he screams again.

It is Henley who rises to meet him, clambering out of his dug-out and scratching his hair back into shape. 'Jesus wept, Sir – the racket! Who have I got to knock out to get some rest about here?'

The poor man thinks he has woken from sleep, then. He thinks he is more than a glancing spirit. He thinks he truly stands before his sergeant, complaining of the noise. And Francis will not ruin the illusion for him. He will not kill him twice.

'Sorry, James,' he says. 'I'll keep it down. Go back to sleep.'

He waits for Henley to trundle back towards his dug-out and resumes his search. Head low, he prowls from gravestone to gravestone, looking for the names. Some bear none. Others show letters hacked crudely into the wood, mismatched as teeth. He searches one that reads Albert Murley. Only Francis or Busty would call him Berto. On his grave, it will be Albert. Francis discovers a Cedric North and a Daniel Hughes; he rushes around the huddled stones to a solitary Jim, a B. White, a Nathaniel Grange. But he locates no Albert Murley. He opts for an unmarked cross, strangled by a fray of rope, and flinging himself down onto his knees before it, begins to dig. Being without a shovel, or even a rifle, he uses his hands, shaping them into letter Cs and scooping the earth away between his legs in a scattered arc.

He is two feet deep in someone else's grave when the rain hits, but he does not slow as water streams over his forehead and into his eyes. Backside to the clouds, head to the deep, he digs and digs. He does not notice the frost sting across his shoulders or the blueing of his wet legs. He does not notice the swelling and splitting of his hands. They had been delicate once, those hands: they had folded and unfolded torn paper without worsening the damage; they had fingertipped across ready lips. Now, they are weapons. He is an automaton, with shovels for arms, and gun wheels for a ribcage, and bullets for eyes, and an empty billy can for a heart. Whenever he moves, his parts scream. If they ever sail him home, his metal components will sink the ship. He is, he realises, a being newly brought into existence. Nothing of his sort existed before 1914. He is a battlefield invention, made for purpose, and when the war ends, what will become of him then?

Thunder spools across the sea and Francis braces himself for the glowing vein of lightning which will surely spark off his curved cannon back. None follows. He listens to the thunder as it charges for the shore, issuing its throaty warning growl. He enjoys the echo of it in his hollow water barrel belly. Momentarily, it eases that picking pain at his middle, which has not ceased now in many months.

When he uncovers a pale bone, bright in the sodden earth, he redoubles his efforts, grunting and shovelling until he exposes two skeletal feet. These he grasps by the ankles and pulls on – harder, harder – until their owner slips out of his grey blanket shroud and lands with a clatter on top of Francis.

'That's the way,' Francis says, righting himself. 'Ready to re-join the fight. Good man.'

He moves along to the next headstone and repeats the process of excavation. This soldier was more recently buried, and still has thick blue-white flesh on his bones, but Francis does not register the pulpy feel of it under his palms. He props the man up against his headstone, moves three yards to his right, and begins again. His breath comes in agonising heaves. He is both hot and cold with sweat. His limbs are sagging into exhaustion. But still he continues, until he has unearthed the first row of bodies from the Walker's Ridge graveyard and lined them up ready to defend their patch.

Francis flops down onto his backside, his chest shuddering desperately.

'Shall I ... tell you a story ... while we ... wait?' he gasps.

He gropes around in his pocket for a letter – any of Lily's letters. Retrieving a gathered lump of paper, he carefully unfolds it and, as fat blots of rain thwup onto the page and the ink begins to run, he reads. His sister's words. His words.

I might have passed minutes and lifetimes, standing in the splayed light of the lamp beside the tram stop, my hands white-knuckled around the handle of my suitcase, refusing to cry. I was nervous and guilty and all those things. But – a call from the Ministry of Munitions. It sounded like some sort of secret organisation. I couldn't have refused it in favour of going out as a nurse. Not since I'd heard the reports on the wireless about girls being taken out to France, to work in factories closer to the front, nearer the men. I was sure then that that was the way to find Ernest. I'd sooner have my hands blown off by a badly packed shell than chance stepping into a hospital tent and bloodying my whites trying to put the blown apart pieces of my husband back together. That's the truth of it. Better my hands than my sanity.

And the Ministry of Munitions is willing to give to me, Mrs Lily Carter – cook, wife, mother, butcher's shop girl – a position as a munitionette.

So, I'm writing you from the train, Francis. First thing tomorrow morning, I'm to report to ROF Rotherwas, Lower Bullingham, Herefordshire. The letters, I have discovered, stand for Royal Ordnance Factory. Ordnance; artillery. I am to follow you into war after all. In a certain fashion. Imagine this: when you give your men the order to fire, the shells that burst from their cannons might well be the very same shells into which I have inserted the explosives. Because that is what the women do at ROF Rotherwas: day after day, they take up the shells, pack them with a substance called trinitrotoluene – did you know that was its name? – place the detonator on the top, tap the detonator into place, and begin again.

I might not be able to sign up to fight, but I might still make myself q soldier yet. Ernest will only love me the more for it. How could he do otherwise, when I finally reach France? All across Swansea, other women are continuing to bring up their children, and waiting patiently on letters from their men, and rolling into sleep in empty beds, and not once considering following their husbands across the English Channel, and there's no reason I should be any different, except that I feel it. And it scares me to think that maybe, somewhere in the ugly deep of myself, I'm still chasing my own adventure. That perhaps I am travelling not towards Ernest Carter, but towards Lily House. That maybe I'll never be free of that pesky, stubborn girl, who decided what she would become in an attic surrounded by story books and daydreams.

Still, as I stood at the stop, there came the sudden trundle and clank of the slowing tram, and I got on it. I had to. It seems a foolish thing to admit, but I thought it might carry me all the way to my true self.

Francis reaches the end of the page and turns it over to find that the words have petered out. There is only the blank paper.

He tries to hold to that picture of Lily, caught in the long reach of the umbrellaed lamplight, but she is dimming. First her wild curly hair and her straight-bridged nose; then her small bowed lips with their wide-open smile; next her berry red skirt and the small hands which protrude from the arms of her coat; her matching round-toed shoes; and finally, her short, proud stance. Within moments, she is but a shimmering movement under a guttering gas lamp. A loosed thread that might be snatched up on the wind and carried off. One careless exhalation and she will be blown away.

Francis turns the paper over again and finds both sides devoid of script.

'No,' he mumbles. 'No, no, no.'

Not Lily. He cannot lose Lily, too. In his terror, he tears the paper in two again and inspects its new edges – as though he might discover her hidden between the atoms of the page. Finding nothing, he tears the halves again, into quarters. Not a trace. Again and again he tears, until he left with a hundred impossibly small scraps, which he casts into the air. As they fall, he rises and steps amongst them like a man caught in a sudden disturbance of snow. They settle on the ground, the grave-stones, the seated men. They drift out to sea. They eddy around Francis' head and shoulders.

'I'm sorry to call you back to action,' Francis says finally. It is the tone he has always used to speak to his men: warm, slightly clipped, deeper than is strictly natural. 'I know you need to rest. And I swear it's just this one last order I'll ask of you. After that, I'll have you sent home. I'll make sure of it. I know you want to go home.'

There comes no answer, and Francis ploughs on. He can hear the pleading note in his voice. He is not ashamed of it. He needs his men; their knowing it is no impediment.

'Here's the directive. I need you to find a sapper by the name of Albert Murley. He was to come ashore off the Dardanelles, some months ago, and we cannot – leave – here – without – him. Do you understand? There's not one of us stepping off Gallipoli without Albert Murley.'

He waits for the nods of assent, the muttered 'sirs'. They are slow to follow, but eventually, from below the dug-out wall, he hears Henley's voice – gruff and curt and glorious.

'Sir,' he says. Francis manages a tight-lipped smile.

And then, cautiously, comes Tom Merton's voice. 'S-s-sir.'

It is echoed by Drowning Edwards', Farrelly's, Stocky Hodgson's, Whitman's, Goskirk's, Carson's.

'Sir.'

He listens for Farmer's – for the man has surely followed him up to the ridge – but he cannot hear it among the chorus. Francis pushes on, striding through the snowflake spin of the obliterated letter.

'I should have realised sooner,' he says. 'I should have known what needed to be done from the beginning.' His men wait, not daring to nod their agreement now. 'But will you help me find him anyhow? Will you help me find Berto? I came to find him, you understand. That's why I came. That's why…'

He loses track of his words and stumbles to a stop. But the ghosts of his thrown-together company nod eagerly and Francis' confidence balloons again. He straightens up, puffs his chest. He takes longer steps. He folds his hands behind his back, the way Cruikshank always did, in a show of strength.

'We'll wait for Johnnie Turk to shell himself into exhaustion,' he begins, though he is not entirely sure of the orders he will issue next. *Just find him*, he wants to say, and thereafter watch them all leap into action. For he knows now, perhaps more definitely than he has ever known anything, that once he finds Berto and says what he must say, some spell will be broken that will release them from this nightmare place.

But first, they must distract those waiting Turks.

'And once Bill quiets…'

Francis stops. Without explanation, he moves away from the men and towards the furthermost cross in their stopgap cemetery. He lowers his head and squints at it, hoping wretchedly that he has mistaken the name etched into the thinning wood, though in truth he knows he has not. He falls in front of it, knees sinking into the deepening mud. He lifts a hand and traces the curls and lines of the letters. He swallows the familiar bulge of his grief. And, when he can fool himself no more, he speaks the name.

'William Farmer.'

Twenty-three of his twenty-five men.

Thirty

Countless emptied opium vials ago, Francis had stepped off the cliff's edge with Henley heavy across his back. Tonight, he steps towards the cliff's edge with his good friend Farmer on his tongue: he does not know how to honour the man other than to plunge into the depths of the black midnight sea and swim until he cramps to a stop. He toes the collapsing lip of the land and feels around in his pockets. He is hoping for another full vial, or a letter, but he finds nothing. He closes his eyes and lets go.

He hits the water with a slurping smack and immediately disappears below. From the ridge, he is only a shivering moonspun ring on the tide's inward tilt. Beneath the surface, he is, at first, a chaotic intrusion: all awkward limbs and heavy fabric and grief. But the rhythmic churning of the waves conspires to remind him of himself – of his salt heart and his bladderwrack veins – and soon his arms are a compass needle, pointing into the dark, and his legs are a thickly muscled tail, driving him downwards, and he feels he has never left the sea. That he has been under her ink and iron surface for the longest time. All that rushing about in the dust of Malta and Turkey and Egypt skulks around his mind like some strange, patchy dream. And there is more to come. Or there might be. He does not know how long he can keep swimming the opium. He knows, though, that he is not finished yet.

He has not yet sailed past Mount Olympus – the *S.S. Caledonia* small and clanking and bell-clanging in her cuspidate shadow – and been deposited at Solomon Harbour on a shining April Fool's Day.

He has not packed vial after vial into his pockets and his kit bag and pretended that he does not need them, despite the determined scritch-scratching of the pleuritic creature causing such pain at his middle.

But he sees himself doing these very things. He feels himself doing them. And he wonders if this working loose from the linearity of a life is the way people come to understand their path, or whether it is only a symptom of the fact that he is dying.

He cannot say, yet.

All he knows is that should he survive long enough, he will discover that Salonica's streets are paved with pebble-stones. That transport wagons, clattering over them, cause a frightful noise which sends sea birds scrawking back to the sky. That mules lose their footing there and trip. That soldiers' boots clomp as noisily as hooves over them. That soldiers' feet rise away from the pulses of pain which push through their thinning soles. That the pavements are slippery as glass, and Francis cannot imagine why.

Should he survive … he will, he will, he will. And yet, at any given point along his new path, in a singular ordinary second, he might cease to be. And he might not even know it.

That awareness sharpens every colour he sees, every scent he inhales, every sound he discerns. His nerves jangle with the possibility that, if he makes it…

That first day, they will be formed up and marched to Karissa Camp, about half a mile outside town. Should he last longer, he will settle in and retire to his tent to rest with the other men, and they will hear the transport wagons clattering over the pebble-stones. Every sound then is a constant grinding – the motor lorries, the men's bones, the wind, the moans, the tent pegs, the war. They struggle into sleep to the rumble of its relentless machinations.

And should he survive that, he will find his army peopled by Greeks and Turks and Britishers and Australians. Discernible too, here and there, are the flat brim hats of the Indo-Chinese. The hats remind Francis of the tents at Tel-el-Kebir. He does not extend his friendship to any of the Indo-Chinese until, wandering Karissa in the soot dark one aimless midnight, he sees one man start from his nightmares. They all slip on the same pavements. They all dream of transport wagon wheels clattering over pebble-stones.

They all dream that they are anywhere but here.

And they are all cold: previous, they had wilted in the Egyptian heat; in the Balkans, they each have a single blanket. They roll into them and grind themselves to sleep. Francis shivers until he cramps. And the greatcoat watches from a distance as he trips through time.

Always, the greatcoat watches.

One peeking sunrise, a motor lorry transports eighty-four siege men and their baggage to 9 Kilo, Serres Post, where Francis and the others have recently been entrenched in the hills surrounding the knot of Salonica. These are the rest of their number. Their eyes are hungry. Gawp, gawp, gawp go their mouths, but no sound falls out, only hunger. They are baby birds. Their uniforms have had the dead laundered out of them.

The pain flares at Francis' side. Scritch-scratch, scritch-scratch. He presses it still with a palm.

H.M.S Exmouth steams by and sends ashore four six-inch naval guns. The men dig them in and adjust them with heaves and cracks. *Heave, crack, heave, crack.* Their shovels are musical instruments; they sing in time to them. They are transformed, all, into owls: only two thin circles around their eyes escape the settling of the pumpkin-coloured dust. They dig in and adjust. *Heave, crack.* A Major Garwood inspects them with approving nods. They dig in and adjust. They do not attempt to wash off the dust. They have made house in it. It keeps them warm.

A lifetime past, held in the familiar chill of a faraway attic, two children point their forefingers and draw their dreams in the dust. On old table tops and the globe's equator, on book covers and chair backs and a locked violin case, on broken pots and pans. Pictures spell out the adventures they will one day have. They are there still, buried beneath the grey dust which inhabits forgotten rooms.

'Do you have a woman at home?' someone asks, and everyone answers with silent nods or head shakes. Their women's names do not belong here, in the excavated earth above Salonica. Nor do their own.

'House,' Francis says, when his name is enquired after.

'House!' his mind hisses when he reprimands himself for falling asleep or failing to execute an order promptly.

And he does fail to be prompt, repeatedly, because he can no longer trace the direction of time. Once, he knows, he studied the crank handles of his men's guns as they leapt forward and flipped back; once he had thrilled at the rippling dance of shells into their feed block; once he had enjoyed the eerie wheeze of a steam engine's whistle, and the breathy stutter of its chug, and wondered at the orbit of its rods around their crankpins. Once he had dealt in minutiae. Now his brain processes only the loudest details. Weeks condense into a single mud-shot artillery exchange. Days are only a swathe of grey dawn, or a lit cigarette, or a streaking memory of Pembrokeshire sky.

And Francis takes to the sea.

Time and again, he lowers his rifle, unlaces his boots, and barefoots silently down from the hills, through the narrow streets, between the wedged-together houses with their burnt umber roofs, towards the ships' masts and their stretching shadows, and into the shallows. There, he lingers a while, turning onto his back and floating with his face to the stars. And only when he has found the rhythm of the tides beneath him, and matched his breathing to the soothe and hush of the waves, does he ripple below the surface and start to swim: to Plymouth,
   to Swansea,
      to Malta,
         to Gallipoli, to Gallipoli, to Gallipoli...

'Fire!' Sergeant House cries. 'Fire!' And Farrelly obeys, and Whitman obeys, and Hodgson obeys. And the six-incher pounds out shell after shell. And Tom Merton says, 'They shattered him to atoms.'

Francis slumps against the wheel of the six-incher and drips words onto the paper he will fold into an envelope and post to his sister.
   Dear Lily,
      Dear Lily...
         Lily... Lily...
         This war is all the wrong shape. I am all the wrong shape.
         I am missing my scales.

And before he can write another word, Francis stands, clambers up into the graveyard above his dug-out, rushes through the mismatched crosses at a gathering sprint and, reaching the cliff edge, clamps his hands together, takes a great heaving breath, and dives.

He needs to reach his sister. He needs to tell her to stop. To wait. To look around and realise how much beauty there is in the fact that she is home. There is nothing on the continent for her. Adventure! What fools they were. Glimpsing Frederick beating adventure out of his very own bones hadn't taught them a damn thing. They'd been too young, too certain, too stubborn to realise that they had it all wrong, curled up as they were in the cradled warmth of their attic. They chose to get it wrong. Their ideas were hooked on passing winds and dragging tides, and they were waiting only to be carried away. Christ – what Francis would give now to swim back to those hope-lit days and show Lily what adventure has meant for her little brother.

And then Francis is at home, walking the Hoe, a charcoal wind combing his hair and watering his eyes. When the Plymouth air calls upon him to cry, he obeys. He always has. The Hoe knows more of his secrets than any woman ever has.

The creature burrows deeper. Scritch-scratch, scritch-scratch, it goes. Scritch-scratch. Francis attempts to silence it with gunshots and dreams. But soon, he fears, it will reach his core.

The weather warms and the men turn into zombies then drop down dead. First come the sweats, then the chills; headaches and vomiting lurk close behind; they defecate where they sit; flies feast around them; they grow weak and drowsy. Inevitably, they slide into the long sleep. Those who fight, though, fight hard with the demons claiming their skins. They shake and froth and flail and kick. A doctor calls it malaria. At night, the men whisper their belief that it is more likely a curse.

Rarely the Bulgars worry Francis and his new men, and when they do it is with airplanes, which the men duly bring down or give thrill-chase to. It is a game, to see those humming black dots approach and, having lain in wait, launch into attack, ferocious as starved hyenas. Aaaaa*oush*! Aaaaa*oush*! And then the dirt-rain. It is their only excitement, that game. Aaaaa*oush*! They laugh when they make a hit.

Scritch-scratch. Scritch-

A zeppelin visits Salonica. They finish it with one well-placed shot. A crack and a whir and – *boom*! – it falls towards the Varda Marshes in flames, crumpling as it goes, a black sack draped over a twisting metal skeleton. It burns long after it falls. The men inhale the rubber and gas stench. Its scorched grave becomes their reference point on the Marshes.

Francis writes to Lily, reminding her of all those mythical creatures they populated their childhood with and secretly ticking off how many he's encountered since the war's beginning. Ghouls, zombies, a merman. Finally, his attic room adventures have come true. They are not what he anticipated. He does not mention the merman.

He learns to ride a horse. The mobile forces are to move forward and establish a line in the Struma Valley, and soon Francis will have miles to cover. He receives instruction in how to navigate the animal's varied strides: how to pull down through his spine into a comfortable canter, how to embrace the transition to gallop, how to ease the beast back down into a bumping trot. He grits his teeth and manages it, but it only worsens the pain at his side. He takes another swig of opium.

And another.

And another.

Finally, the creature ruptures some deep blood place and takes new territory. It curls in, settles to stay. Perhaps it is nothing more than his merman's heart, consuming his old, weaker, man's heart.

'Are you alright, Sir? Did you hear me, Sir?'

Yes, yes, yes, says the stranded merman. His throat is dry. He is unsure if his voice finds the air.

Blistered backs bend again and again into the sun and, by means of picquets, the Struma Valley line is extended all the way to Albania. It is scowled at by ragged mountain ranges and rutted ravines — the Bulgars' natural defences — and Francis longs to be put to work in that angry shadow. He is ordered to remain at 9 Kilo. He volunteers for a heavy battery.

The creature in his ribcage gnaws at him with its persistent scritch-scratch.

May collapses in in a sweaty heap, and Francis joins 20 Heavy Artillery Troop at 69 Kilo. They shift, across difficult country and without road to carry them, some eighteen miles to the west. The land, blasted by shells, battered by bodies, dances beneath their feet. They proceed at an eternal off-balance. They are desert dogs, or hyenas, or equines. They follow the river's flow. They hunt the stars. They are learning to be their own ancestors.

Somewhere,

later,

they go into action behind Venizelos' Greeks. They fight amongst scrubby bushes and dirt tracks, sandbag walls and scrawny trees, rattling wagon wheels and triple beat hooves and gullies and hillocks and dust storms. All, the same shade of dirty. And Francis thirsts for the sea. She is so far distant now. Unreachable. The Struma runs only towards blood.

Pap-pap-pap-pap-pap. Urine stains the air. *Pap-pap-pap-pap-pap.*

Francis hunkers behind a stack of sandbags, closes his eyes, and cusses the creature nesting in his ribcage. He slurps at his opium and falls out of time.

'How do you know you killed him?' Farmer asks. 'For sure.'
'Some days I do,' Francis answers. 'Some days I don't.'
'Well, on those days you think you do, then?'
'It was the crack,' Francis admits. 'It was the way he fell.'

A bicycle patrol glides past. The bicycles are black whirrs across an unknown indigo backdrop. The spinning wheels sound like freedom. Francis watches them rush away, lifts his rifle, takes aim at the final departing back. He does not shoot. These are his men.

His men now are English, Scots, Welsh, Irish, Russian, Greek, Serbian, Indian, Senegalese, French, Indo-Chinese, Italian, Australian. The painted globe from his parents' attic spins before his gun. The world against … who? He has lost track. Strange tongues swoop about him, bats on a calm summer dusk. He has forgotten all his Maltese. He has forgotten all his Welsh. He has forgotten…

The creature at his middle makes a ladder of his spine and scrabbles up, clawing bone chunks away in its desperate climb. It gives off a curious heat. He knows it is making for his brain.

Pap-pap-pap-pap-pap. Aaaaa*oush*!

The rifles are woodpeckers; the six-inchers are lions.

And men fever away. Men wither away. Men are bulleted and hacked and blown away. Men curl away in midnight privacy. Men dive away before breakfast assaults. Men ride and yell and run away. Men drown and crouch and tumble away. Men smash away over stony drops. Men flatten away under turned wheels and fallen horses. Men fracture away like pickaxed ice. Men trickle away through puncture holes in their legs and shoulders and chests and hearts. Men fade away into ghosts who rise to take another hit, another two, before submitting to the afterlife.

Close-by, a lad who has had his legs freshly severed loses all sense and goes running off on the spurting stumps. He travels twenty feet, maybe more, then topples onto his front and dies with a single gurgling scream his chums might have mocked him for once. No one flips him over to attach a name to his face. When they march past, they tread in his puddled blood.

And Francis refuses to look into any more of the faces that fall. They might all be Berto. They might all be Busty. They might all be him.

'They shattered him to atoms,' Tom Merton had said, over and over again, and Francis realises finally that he hadn't a clue who the boy had been talking about. He hadn't wondered. He hadn't asked.

Summer dips away sudden one berry blue twilight, and Francis canters over darkening ground, then frosted ground, then snow-fell ground. The nights are as protracted as the months, the days extend to years, and Francis blunders through misshapen time, reaching for an end, his fingertips brushing up against nothing. He dreams of clock hands rotating in the wrong direction.

The creature wraps itself about his neck and clings on. Francis is being strangled so slowly that no one has yet noticed. Privately, he grasps at his neck, tries to ease the tightening noose, but he cannot get a purchase on the crafty animal. The creature's name is Guilt, perhaps. Guilt. Perhaps.

Somebody writes him but he cannot read the words. The pages are gibberish, lines and lines of it. Lines and lines of little ink blobs that look like men, forming up and marching off the paper's edge and dropping into oblivion. They have names, Francis is sure of it, but he cannot recall them. They have disappeared.

November's country is a white shirt, splattered with spilled red wine. They have withdrawn to the Struma's south side, fearful of being cut off by her noted winter flow. There they've discovered a farmhouse and claimed it. Francis' last three day's sustenance has consisted of one mouldy biscuit and a cup of tea. Tom Merton's voice drags him from sleep, though he is certain the boy has been returned to England. 'Who?' Francis cries as he wakes. 'Who?' And he half expects Tom to appear before him and say, 'You, of course.'

Francis has been shattered to atoms.

Francis is being shattered to atoms.

Francis is being…

Francis is…

F r

a

n c

i

s

… shoots up over the rim of someone else's dug-out, glimpses the black gleam of enemy artillery in the middle-distance, then thuds back against the sandbag wall. The impact winds him. 'The Greeks have orders to advance. We're to provide cover from the heavy artillery on − the − far − left,' he explains, stressing the words as Burrows always did. 'Have you had sight of your target?' The boys hunkered around him nod. Those who are destined to chase the Greeks into purgatory grip their rifles to their hearts. Francis sighs: they will not make adequate shields.

A solitary shrieking shell, a hundred pounder at least, and Francis watches another batch of boys wade and slog over the bursting earth. *Pooogh! Pooogh-pooogh! Pooogh!* Soil explodes upwards then hails down over them, asserting its new ownership.

Earth and death conspire and strike a deal.

Death drops red and white flecks of men on the snow and fails to return to collect them: chunks of thigh, dollops of muscle, shreds of flayed skin, splinters of bone and gobbets of opened heart, dashes of bravery, lumps of limb and shards of fear, inches of intestine, morsels of who-knows-what, and strands of hair, and crumbs from exploded stomachs, and, scattered through the stinking mess, scintillas of soul.

The stretcher-bearers bring back a lad with his face peeled clean; his naked tongue laps open air as he searches a new way to say, 'It's dark. I'm still here, but it's dark.'

The stretcher-bearers bring back a head on a spine, like a balloon on a string. The mouth in the head does not gape as Francis expects, but is clamped firmly shut. The spine is red-ribboned.

The stretcher-bearers go blind and bring back a clod of rotting horse flesh.

Francis prays, then – to the sea, not to God – that it will swell up over the land and surge towards him. Whether it carries him away or drowns him, he doesn't much care. So long as he is never mistaken for a clod of rotting horse flesh. So long as he is never mangled thus. When he dies, he is determined to do so in one whole piece.

The day Francis shoots his horse, he stares her square in the eye. Of all the shells and madmen and river crossings she has survived, it is ice that lames that horse. A patch of invisible ice, a slip, a crack, and the poor brave beast only snickered as her foreleg snapped. Francis stares her square in the eye, strokes her bristly muzzle, and, holding his face to the smooth, dun hair, murmurs, 'Well done, Sir. You did yourself proud. I'll be along to join you soon.'

The pop of his gun starts the nearby injured off moaning and ranting again. *Let go of me, you crazy bastard. I'll kill you, I will. I'll murder you while you sleep. I'll hack you into bits.* Francis does not peek at those twitching, broken bodies. They are all of them dead, to some degree. His army has become an asylum.

The creature eases loose from around his neck and crawls up the back of his skull. It gnaws as it goes, chomping out chunks of this or that and spitting them to the ground. Francis is being chomped to atoms. His head is a ball of searing rage.

A cigarette or a boiling billy can, a knocked lamp or a drip of pure hatred – whatever the cause, the farmhouse catches fire. Men charge for the exit and, assembling at the narrow doorway, tumble and cascade over each other and out. Vests rip. Boots fly free. Curses split. Trousers tear. They stand in a clutch on the cold, packed earth and watch it burn. Silence, but for the scuttle-hiss, the crackling, the whumph of escaping air. Francis, still bone-tired, clambers up atop a hayrick and finishes his sleep, the blazing house warming his back and his dreams and his loyal cleaving creature.

It is better, when he sleeps. He feels whole, when he sleeps.

He wakes only to grip another glass vial between his trembling fingers and toss it back. He used to think there was medicine contained within. Now, he knows that all the vials offer is enough hydration to keep him going.

Lily unfolds a fan and disturbs the heavy attic air with it. 'Death is going to be most predictable adventure,' she breathes.

'It's spreading!' a voice yells. 'Come on, House! It's spreading fast!' He stirs to find men on the run again. The fire has hurdled the patchy snow and ignited the nearest hayrick. It will take the lot. He drops to the ground, realises he hasn't his boots, and takes off without them. His feet might blacken but his soul will not.

The dark is a blindfold. They race towards nothing but instinct, rolling ankles, grazing shins, breaking toes. The flames, meanwhile, growing wild. The fire has found an accelerant. The men chase their own noses and, vacillating like weather vanes, scatter, covering too much ground or none.

The crackle of fire; the thunder of footsteps.

Francis finds himself ahead of the pack and charges on, on, on…

And back into the flaming blast of Walker's Ridge.
    'Fire!' he cries. 'Fire!'
    His men, stiffening and tiring, move from weapon to weapon.

Presently, four swift chaps – some of his best – relinquish the six-inch, throw themselves to the ground, and crawl into position before their maxims, hands reaching for the grips, fingers tickling the triggers. Farrelly, Whitman, Hodgson, and Henley lie lopsidedly, left eyes closed, right eyes peering through the foresight. Francis pauses whilst they settle and then, channelling his father as best he can, he asks, 'Target in sight, men?'

'Yes, Sir,' come the prompt replies.

'On three, then,' he says, 'we go again'. It is the twenty-second hour. They have but two hours of continuous firing left to see out.

He swings his arm downwards with each count, as though swatting the numbers into the air. 'One. Two. Three.'

Without a jiffy's hesitation, they batter the opposing ridge. And the world spins a fraction slower as Francis watches the crank handle of the gun nearest him leap forward and flip back, and wonders at the rippling dance of the shells into the feed block, and listens to the high-pitched *tsk-tsk-tsk* of the shells piercing the night. Hodgson's strongly sculpted face is crushed in concentration as he fires shot after shot after shot. *Tsk-tsk, tsk-tsk.* He squeezes again. *Tsk-tsk, tsk-tsk.* Steam puffs from the muzzle, water drips from the drain plug, *crack-crack* goes the crank handle. Against the moonlit quiet, they are raising hell. Sergeant House's men fire on the Turks, and the Turks fire back on Sergeant House's men, and along the coast, as organised by Captain Burrows, the next battery stands poised to continue the assault they have started.

Francis looks to that familiar black spill of sea.

And he cannot resist turning from the guns and stepping towards its deep brackish scent, closer to the cliff edge, closer still, until he can feel the salt spit on his skin, and he closes his eyes and breathes in the vaporous spray of all that pitching water, and he lets himself fall.

Arms held wide as wings, he drops.

Feet clamped together in anticipation of his alteration, he drops.

Hair raked by a gravitational wind, clothes torn at, cloth hat lost, he drops
    directly into the tips of a thousand waiting daggers.

And collapses downward. The Struma, in deep winter. She stabs him into stillness and he sits, legs splayed like a toddling child, on her stony bed, staring at his bare feet and awaiting the transformation from skin to scale. It will come; he has never been more certain of anything. Should it not be quick enough, shock or frostbite might take him first, but he cannot allow such thoughts to occupy his closing mind. He has to think of the scales: of their shimmer into existence; of their cool, glassy touch; of their fern and teal gleam beneath the moonshone Struma's waters. He has to tell himself the story. His tail is manifold shades of green-blue. Here is his truest form. He should have submitted to the sea when he was on Malta, or in those first hours on Gallipoli, or when he'd been abandoned to the sea off Anzac. If only he had yielded then, he would already be swimming the sepulchral depths he so bodily recognises. Well, he is yielding now. There can be no doubt. Berto is lost. Lily is determined to find her way to France. The empty greatcoat cannot be shaken. But Francis begged the water to come and collect him, and she has obliged, and, for the first time in his twenty-three fighting years, it is time to surrender.
    'I'm ready,' he declares. 'It's killed me.'

He steals a final glance at his blueing feet, then he lowers his eyelids, and presses himself up against all that black infinitude, and he waits. The last of his men.

Thirty-One

He awakes to that familiar silt suck around his ankles. He is upright. Trooping. Without looking around for the broken sloop, the water barrels, the stacked-box ammunition, he drops his head into the slog up the beach towards Walker's Ridge. Beside him, the empty greatcoat glides silently over the sand, just out of reach. Francis speaks gently to it, as one might a young dog or a flitting bird.

'If you're on this peninsula, I'll find you,' he promises. And this time, he means it. To seek the man out is the only way to discover whether or not he killed Berto Murley. He will not pretend at searching again. He will conduct himself honestly. Because, despite his worst fears, he truly does not know how much damage he did that night at St Elmo. He was too craven to stick around and find out. He was too scared to enquire.

Francis re-joins his men by the halfway strike of the twenty-third hour of the bombardment of Sari Bair. The men's movements are stilted, their limbs and backs weakened, their reactions dulled. The crack of the gun no longer throbs through their ears. They have ceased cheering when they find their target and the bright turmeric earth explodes upwards then skitters down in imitation of an elaborate water fountain. They suck at the blisters on their fingers and thumbs with dry mouths, craving tea or tobacco or bully or beans and tasting only blood, pus, and dirt. Their tongues are bandages. Their share their bodies with scarecrows. They are numb.

And yet, in thirty minutes more, they will believe this shelling their greatest triumph.

'One of your letters, Sir,' Drowning Edwards suggests quietly. 'Before we begin again.'

'If that's what you want.'

Edwards nods and the others gather closer, waiting for the voice of their Sergeant to transport them off Gallipoli and into a story.

'She was at Rotherwas,' he begins.

The man seemed to leak out of the shadows, as though he had been conjured on that very spot. He was tall, as grey as anything else inside the factory. Light never does penetrate such places, does it. We were bent over the metallic din of our labour, paying him not the slightest attention. But soon he leaned close over my shoulder, to make himself heard, and said, 'Mrs Carter?' I knew then that he held news of Ernest between his fingers. He passed the Western Union telegram back and forth from hand to hand, fidgeting as he waited for me to put out my own hand and accept it. But I wouldn't. I refused. I left him standing there, until he had to ask again. 'Mrs Ernest Carter?'

The factory clock ticked and ticked. Six minutes. Seven. I stared at its bent minute hand, stuttering forwards, forwards, and mourned the fact that I could not stop it. How such a large, rowdy factory could have grown so quiet, I couldn't understand, but quiet it was. Every goggled eye was fixed upon me. The girl next along was saying, 'Is he killed? Open it, Lily. Is he killed?'

I did as instructed and, trembling, tore open the telegram. I ripped the right topmost corner and I remember thinking how unforgivable that was as I flattened it out to scan its neatly typed words.

I read them. I reread them. And then a strangled cry twisted free of my body that I would not even have recognised as my own, had I not been able to feel my mouth opening. It echoed louder than a hundred tapped shells under the tin roofs. Louder than any we'd heard before. Louder than any we'd lately leaned over. But not half so loud as the one that was not meant to be tapped at all. It was a flinch, nothing more – perhaps in expectation, perhaps in response to my stupid wail – but it was enough to cause a twenty-year-old canary called Amy Singer, reaching mindlessly over her shell, to shove down against her detonator.

It was enough to shatter her throat and jaw and chin. Enough to shred her lips. Enough to turn her dainty nose into a mined pit of missing flesh. Amy, when she was stretchered past by a garland of frantic women, had only her eyes left to speak with, and she was using every speck of olive iris, every pitch of black pupil, every brightly bulging vessel, to shriek. Silently.

And so was I, Francis, because though my eyes had trailed over those military-straight lines of letters, I could not believe I had read them correctly. I could trust my sight then as little as I could trust my weakening body. I could not so much as coax my lips to pucker around words, because a telegram had arrived, addressed to Mrs E. Carter. A telegram had arrived for me. And I'd thought, for the very first time in truth, that he might be dead. I had believed, for a breathless trice, that my brilliant man was gone. I had felt myself pushed from a cliff-edge and known that hopeless final plunge. They had sent a sheet of paper to inform me of whether my husband was alive or dead: not a fellow conscript bearing generous words, or the nurse who had eased him through his injuries, but a sheet of paper I might easily rip into pieces and scatter to the wind, should the words prove too much to bear.

Eventually, after they'd conveyed Amy to the hospital I would imagine, someone came back to check on me.

'Is he killed?' they asked again. And I responded with the only words which seemed willing to form on my thick, dry tongue. They came away gummy and slow. 'I,' I said. 'I'm... I will never see France.'

I could not possibly admit, given what had happened to Amy, that my scream – the strangest of responses – had been borne of relief. That my husband was safe in hospital with a healing head wound. That my Ernest was coming home.

Francis turns his arm over to contemplate the scuffed, round face of his watch. It stopped ticking a long while since. The

213

minute hand sits at a shiver past the six, trembling but otherwise unmoving, and he knows that it is telling him that soon it will come to a stop. Soon, he will be able to stop. Half an hour and his mind will be free to visit again, if only momentarily, the attic where he and Lily knew with all the certainty of the young that their lives would get better, bigger, bolder. To seek out Busty and look on while the old chap drinks and eats and laughs as though he has a lifetime ahead of him. To stop himself before he throws that last punch at his dear Berto. To choose not to look through the crack in his parents' bedroom door. To check and check again who is nearing before he swings the poker. To reacquaint himself with hope. To persuade himself that he is every part the man he ought to be. To try to forget the sound the guns emitted when he made his thousandth order to 'Fire!' and sent another clutch of unknown Turkish souls to their deaths.

He feels no enmity towards them now. They are only men, lined up behind guns, shooting into the distance. Or they were.

When Francis looks to his target, what he is met by is column after column of rising smoke, guarding the skyline like a series of funeral pyres. That, he supposes, is what they have become; every last one of them; smoke.

He checks his wristwatch again. The minute hand continues to tremble just beyond the six. Not long now. He has only to collect the last of the shells and gee up the men for a final thundering attack. But first, he will retire to his dug-out and allow himself to breathe, just for a trice, alone. He turns and strides away.

Without looking back, he calls over his shoulder, 'Farrelly. Be my eyes. I'll be back soon.'

He hardly realises how sincerely he means the words until they are released. Then, he recognises them as his greatest truth. Time and again, he will come back here, to his men and their ghosts, to the opium moon, to the polished guns and the filthy dug-outs, to Tom Merton's voice and James Henley's hazel eyes, to the shot billy cans and the screams, to the stocked cigarettes and the dry crumble of Huntley and Palmers biscuits in his mouth, to Captain Burrows' orders and his own scribbled, nonsensical letters, to the tireless whisper of the shore.

For the rest of his life, however long or short it might be, Francis House will return to Gallipoli. He belongs on Gallipoli. His men are there, and they are calling to him, and he can hear them.

'Sir,' they beg. 'Sir…'

But he does not turn immediately towards them. He is not quite ready yet, for the end, because a suspicion has come over him – that nothing else will ever matter again, after all of this.

Nothing else will ever matter again.

Nothing else will ever matter again.

Nothing else will ever matter again.

Nothing else will ever matter again.

Nothing else will ever matter again.

And how could any soul tolerate that?

'Sir,' his men plead, but he cannot look to them. Instead, he clambers down into his dug-out, crouches low on the muddy ground, wraps his arms tight around his legs, and listens to the darkness. Five minutes, he tells himself. Just five more minutes. He cannot avoid forever the moment when he will stand in front of his friend, or his ghost, and learn whether or not he is a good man. That is all he has ever wanted to know.

Thirty-Two

It was in that grey cusp part way between night-time and dawn that Berto found him, hunched on the ground behind the stables, his trousers soaked through with dew and his skin white and cold as hoarfrost. His stare was fixed on the body, which lay in the same flat-backed position it had fallen into. He had not tried to lift her, and she had not tried to lift herself. Her eyes, wide open in fright, were the exact same stony shade as the sky she stared unblinking up at. Of all the bad names Frederick had called his son, and of all the grand titles Francis had thought to give himself, no one's lips had ever fallen around the word *murderer*.

And yet, here he was.

He had forgotten how to move.

In the ink-line trees, three crows opened their beaks to the morning and shrieked to anyone who might listen about his crime. He imagined the police would arrive soon, and that they would duly haul him up and out of the litterfall to arrest him, so he did not trouble himself to recall how his ankles might bend and flex to push him upwards until he was standing, or how his legs might be shifted, one in front of the other, to convey him back to the barracks. He only looked at the girl. And listened to the clapping of the birds' wings: an echo, repeated over and over again, of the sound her neck had made when Francis had broken it.

'House?'

Francis was certain, when Berto finally knelt before him and grasped his shoulders and shook him hard, that he must have been there for a long while. His feet must have thudded over

the ground as he searched out his friend, but Francis hadn't felt
him coming. He must have screamed or yelled out, when he first
discovered the body, but Francis hadn't heard his voice.

'House. Look at me.'

Francis could not. He must not take his eyes off the girl. It
was his punishment, to look and keep on looking. He pushed
his tongue between his dried lips, to better peel them apart, and
spoke through the bloodied flakes of skin which tore loose.

'It was supposed to be Hancox,' he said. His voice was the
final crackle of a turned-off wireless. 'I was waiting for
Hancox.'

'I know. I saw you leave the note on his pillow. I threw it in
the fire.'

'Why?'

'Why?' Berto laughed. The sound was empty – as joyless and
empty as the expression painted on the girl's china face. She
was sprawled at a difficult angle, her arms thrown out by the
impact of the blow, her knees and feet buckled inwards. At near
sixteen, Francis was more than half a foot taller than she and
twice as broad. He was training for the army, and she was just
a slip of a thing: light as a shed feather; delicate as a dropped
eyelash; pretty as lace.

'Yes. Why?'

'Because… Listen.' Berto shook him again, but he could not
jar Francis' attentions away from the girl, the girl. She would
never be anything but a girl, because Francis had stolen her
future. 'Listen!' His hands were on Francis' face now, the palms
warm and slick with sweat. He pulled at Francis' head but could
not shift it. 'You don't need to fight for me Francis, all right? I
can look after me. I'm used to it. You just fight for yourself.
That's all you need to do. Just fight for yourself.'

'But, who was she? Why was she –'

'Her sister works in the kitchens,' Berto replied brusquely.

'How do you know her?'

'It doesn't matter now.'

'Yes,' Francis said. 'I need to know her name, so that I can tell... So that I can explain. Do you know her name, Berto?'

'It doesn't matter now,' Berto said again. And it hadn't occurred to Francis to wonder, then, why Berto could not bring himself to speak it. 'And you won't be able to explain anything. They won't believe you, House. She fell, that's what. Look now.'

Releasing Francis' face from his grip, Berto stood and stepped carefully around the girl. He chose a branch which reached out from the nearest tree – a branch of perhaps four inches in diameter and two feet in length – and, wrapping his hands around it, heaved and dragged and hung from it until it snapped loose with a loud, gunshot crack. Above, the crows flustered into flight. Berto paid them no heed. He laid the branch on the ground, just above the girl's head. And then, as gently as a mother, he scooped the girl up, turned her slowly over, and laid her facedown across it, the branch positioned like a pillow beneath her flower-stem neck. From Francis' new perspective, the borrowed greatcoat she wore appeared to be completely empty.

'See. She might only have rushed into it, in the dark. The impact...' He trailed off, glancing about himself. 'And especially if she tripped.' Acting quickly, he selected a twine of knotted weeds and hooked them about the toe of her right shoe before setting her foot tenderly down. 'You see. She tripped, Francis. That's what happened. An accident.' At that, Berto's voice finally broke. He put his hands to his hips and breathed deep – in, out, in, out – to steady himself. 'A very sad accident,' he whispered.

'It was,' Francis agreed. 'It was an accident.'

'I know,' Berto sighed. 'I do know that, Francis. I should never be helping you otherwise. Now, stand up. Come on. You need to get back into your bunk before anyone wakes.'

'But you are awake,' Francis murmured as Berto slipped a shoulder under his arm and hauled him upright. Francis' legs were foal-weak and trembling. He could not support his own weight, but Berto held him steady. Francis turned finally to take in his friend's kind, cheerful face. His blue eyes were made bulbous by tears. His mouth was a tightly-stitched hem. He looked moon-paled, but the moon was not shining tonight.

'Why were you awake, Berto?' Francis asked.

And without looking back at him, Berto replied, 'It doesn't matter now.'

I woke up in a warm bed with a good nurse beside me.
She was good and I'll never forget her.

Thirty-Three

Francis lies sprawled across his camp bed, his long feet dangling off the bottom end, and stares up into the shadow of the pointed marquee roof. For the past three hours, he has been trying to catch hold of the transition, to witness the turn from light to darkness. There is nothing else to do here except think, and Francis has spent so long thinking that he fears he might have permanently lost the knack of it. In some neglected part of his mind, he remembers that story about Lily going off to Rotherwas. But he does not recall where from: a letter of hers? A telegram from their mother or father? A tale he contrived to occupy the minds of his men on Gallipoli? For all his trust in it, he might just as well have played through that scene with Lily laid on the stretcher and being carried towards an ambulance wagon with half her face missing. He has no means of distinguishing the truth from fancy.

Beneath him, the planks of the circular wooden tent base spring under some chap or lady's footsteps, and, based on the frequency of the sound, Francis supposes they belong to a woman. He hopes it is his usual woman, but he does not turn to look. To his right and behind him, the entrance flap ripples open then shut, open then shut, like the repeated crack-crack of light gunfire. To his left, the marquee wall strains against its pinned ropes. Beyond the taut, pale fabric, a man and a woman flit by in urgent conversation. Francis listens to their footfalls but blocks out the shapes of their words. He does not want to know where such hastened steps are taking them.

Outside, snow mutes the scrubby ground. The light is a weak half-effort. It reminds Francis of himself. He should rather have lost an arm than be diagnosed again with pleurisy. He wants his pain to be visible, unstoppable. All that and it was only sleep deprivation, pleurisy, and too much opium. It's an embarrassment.

At the entrance flap, a figure appears simultaneously with a sharp cut of wind, and Francis rolls his eyes around to consider its outline. He recognises it immediately: the bright white skirt, the cream knitted cardigan, the starched-stiff long cap. He begins the lengthy process of pushing himself into a sitting position; the pain in his side flares; the simple movement is more taxing now than once was the swim from Valletta to Sliema.

'Nurse,' he says, by way of greeting. The word is ground out from between his teeth.

'Stay where you are, patient,' Nurse Adams replies. 'Rest. I've no want with you.'

'Ah, but perhaps I've a want with you.'

Nurse Adams stands a tad straighter. She knows her codes of conduct. Francis, however, has no immediate designs on her. He only misses the company and chatter and raillery of existing amongst so many rowdy souls, and the water. 63 General Hospital is too quiet and too dry by far.

He smiles gently to show her that he is teasing. He is only trying to recall what it was to be a boy of seventeen, admired by all those Welsh girls and confident enough, carefree enough, to flirt with them. He is practicing being who he used to be. He is checking that boy is still there, encased in the man he has been sculpting around him all these years.

Nurse Adams' shoulders drop. 'And what might that be, Sergeant House?'

'Conversation,' Francis groans, finally achieving a sitting position.

Nurse Adams smiles back at him across the tenebrous tent.

She continues to strip the sheets from the adjacent camp bed as she speaks, and the sight of her busy hands brings such easy relief in the midst of all that stillness. 'About what?' she asks.

'About a boy called Francis, and where he came from,' Francis offers. 'And about a girl called...?'

'Nurse Adams,' Nurse Adams answers.

Francis cocks his head in admonishment and tries again. 'And a girl called...?'

A pause. Then, 'Frances,' Nurse Adams concedes.

'Frances,' Francis muses. 'We share a name. And where did Miss Frances Adams enjoy being a girl?'

Before Nurse Adams can respond, a sudden wail issues from another tent. It goes up, explodes, and fizzles away in the abrupt manner of a kamuro firework. Francis winces against it.

'A newcomer,' she explains. 'Surgery was required.'

'Ah.'

For some minutes, there is only the susurrus of Frances Adams' fingers over and around the sullied sheets, and the beating of the entrance flap, and the occasional short outburst from the invisible patient.

'Liverpool,' Nurse Adams says, when the quiet grows too loud.

'Liverpool?'

'Liverpool. I was a girl in Liverpool, but I didn't much enjoy it.'

'No?' Desiring a better view of his new friend, Francis turns into the incessant hurt at his ribs. There is no pose which allows relief from it. 'And why was that?'

'Surely nobody enjoys being a child,' Nurse Adams returns.

She has finished her task now and stands watching Francis from five paces. Her flecked gold-green eyes are set in a soft sparrow's face. The exact shade of her chestnut hair is only hinted at in wisps along the line of her cap and about each ear. She is a flighty looking thing, Miss Frances Adams, but there is a whimsical way about her lips and her lashes which matches that of her working hands. Francis' nurse is good. Whatever follows, he vows that he will never forget her.

'I did,' Francis replies, though of course he means only to a point, a most distinct point, when it was all thrown into such confusion.

'Did you? Really? Or is it only easier to imagine you did now that it's over?'

Francis catches Nurse Adams' glance and holds it still. He needs her to look and keep looking. He needs her – he needs someone, in the absence of Lily or Berto – to truly see him. He isn't Sergeant House anymore. How can he be, when he remains laid up here whilst other men hunker in dug-outs and ready the guns, or share the last of their bully and tobacco, or borrow better clothes from dead men? Sergeant House would be amongst them, regardless of circumstance. But Francis is not. Francis does not want to be. Not any longer. And not because he has finally received word from Dad Rymills that Busty was captured by a gang of young enemy soldiers just under a year since and, cornered and alone, beaten to death before being needlessly dismembered. That knowledge would only spur Sergeant House to action. But Francis has nothing left to give. He is an empty kit bag, a bullet-less gun, a discarded greatcoat. He shall have to start again.

'What's your best memory of Liverpool?' he asks.

'Waving goodbye to it.'

'Then I'm sorry for you,' Francis says quietly. 'Don't you think everyone should want to go home?'

Nurse Adams' deliberation on the question brings a momentary squint down over her eyes. She crosses her arms and begins to smile, evidently pleased with her conclusion. 'It depends what you think home is,' she says.

• 'What do you think home is?' Francis enquires.

'Home is any place that makes me smile.'

'And Salonica makes you smile, does it, Frances?'

As if in string-pulled response, her lips spread into a full beam. She nods. 'Yes, it does.'

'Why?'

'Because I'm useful here,' she replies, and balling the soiled bedsheets up against her stomach, she strides across the tent towards the flailing flap. For a breath, she is the echo of Lily. She pauses fleetingly in the pale glare of stolen outdoor light. 'But you should want to go home, Francis. I understand it, and there's not one trace of shame in it. Promise me you'll believe that. You should want to go home.'

With one last nod, Nurse Adams ducks away through the flap and disappears into the day. Her bird-light footsteps are silent over the tamped down snow. Francis lowers himself slowly back onto his pillow and gropes around for a pen and paper with which to write Lily. As he sets about composing the words in his mind, though, he cannot help wondering whether that lovely nurse had entered the tent at all or whether his medicines have simply started talking to him again. He does not consider himself predisposed to delirium, but given how little he knows about the soldier laid in this bed, he supposes anything might just be possible.

He might still be sitting on the Struma's winter bed, searching for his scales.

He might be asleep in his dug-out, a bullet whizzing towards his eye socket, or his kneecap, or his heart.

He might not have woken up.

He might never have made it off Gallipoli.

He might have been shattered to atoms.

Thirty-Four

Some shapeless days later, Francis catches sight of another angel. Tom Merton had been the first. Then came Henley, who had kept him safe. Then there had been Bill Farmer, who had stayed to make the men laugh at Heliopolis while his mates rushed off to the inns without him. Then Nurse Adams, the major modulations of whose voice Francis had woken from his stupor to on his second night at Salonica's General Hospital. Angels, all. And now, as he lies awake at day's break, he is approached by another, and another. What he had thought only tendrils of light about the tent, he knows now to be hundreds of perfectly formed beings. The closer he looks, the more of them he discerns. Edwards, Captain Burrows, Sergeant Saunders, Lieutenant Cruikshank, Dad Rymills, Busty. They are reminiscent of blown dandelion seeds, scattering outwards to stipple the tent, and Francis understands then that the angels belong to the very same dust which had stippled his parents' attic as he, six or seven years of age, whipped his broomstick sword around his body in long, quick arcs. Whoosh!

'I'm going to be a soldier,' he'd declared. 'Like Father.'

But he isn't. He isn't like father. Who could tell what kind of soldier Frederick had been, excepting a broken one? A broken soldier. A broken man.

'Father hated being a soldier,' Lily had said, from her perch atop the leather portmanteau.

'No, he didn't!'

'Yes, he did. Why else would he be the way he is?'

And, oh, Francis knows now. Lifetimes too late, he has found his answer.

'Because, Lily,' he says, 'pain was the only thing that could silence his memories.'

Dreams, dreams, dreams – he and Lily had spoken of nothing else. It was the future, never the past. And they'd sworn themselves to dreams all the more devotedly after that night when they had finally understood the sound which issued from behind their parents' bedroom wall. Because dreams might carry them across the world, and speed them into all the freedoms of adulthood, and march them into war. Dreams might transform them into an animal or morph them into a god. Dreams might so flourish in a body still overfed with opium that they bring angels before your eyes. Beautiful, winged angels. Creatures borne on their kindness. Creatures as elegant as a declaration of love or the vanishment of fear. Creatures who soothe. And always they appear with Nurse Adams – for isn't she one amongst them? Isn't she greatest amongst them?

'Nurse Adams,' Francis mutters into his slumber. Or 'Nurse Adams!' he calls as he wakes.

Though he hides the need as best he can in his tucked blankets and his nightmares, he grows more desperate for her companionship moment by moment. It is only an angel who could come to him now. And comes she does, over and again. And she does not ask who he speaks to in his sleep, or who he cries for, or who he writes to day after day.

Lily, he writes. *I have found my woman. My mermaid. My truth.*

'Nurse Adams! Thank goodness! I thought you'd reneged on your promise for a terrible moment there.'

Nurse Adams, just appeared at the flapping tent door, tries to hide her shy, flinching smile, but cannot resist Francis' daft exaggerations. She needs good company as much as he.

'I was on the very verge of death by boredom.'

'House!' She reprimands him as she steps into the shadows,

leaving a stark winter sun at her back. 'Don't joke about that. I told you I had to finish my shift first.'

She moves across the tent floor and begins fussing with his bedsheets, flicking them into the air so that they billow themselves flat, then tucking them neatly back into place. Francis has rumpled them into a creased globe to bring about this very action. He's been ribbing her with it. Nurse Adams is forever fretting, and to give her something to fret over is the easiest method of keeping her longer in the room. There are only so many hours a guilty man can spend alone in an empty tent, staring down the trembling walls.

'Shall we pick up where we left off?'

He shudders across to the table he's spent such a time setting up and takes his seat, his back slightly hunched still and a blanket shawled about his shoulders in a way that reminds him of his grandmother. It is a tender point of shame, this recognition, but he's had to concede to it in the end. Salonica in November is colder than fear.

'You're keen,' Nurse Adams observes.

'Well, I am winning.'

'You're mistaken, House. I am winning.' She removes her long cap as she approaches the table. Her tight chestnut curls, previously centre-parted and pulled back behind her ears, burst loose in relief. She does not fluff out her hair, but only smooths down the electrified strands and straightens her cardigan about her shoulders. Nurse Adams fusses with everything but herself. And Francis smiles at this commendable quality, imagining what it might be like to notice the same in his wife. Written on Nurse Adams' lovely face are new dreams...

Of the war's end, when he might be posted to R.G.A. Ripon to act as Schoolmaster. Of the depot shifting to Great Yarmouth and Francis making the decision to take his new wife home. Of securing teaching work on Plymouth's windblown coast and setting up house not three miles distant from his difficult but well-intentioned parents. Of deciding that that boy who sat cross-legged in the darkness with his sister and spun a painted globe to determine which countries they would visit has seen quite enough of the world before he sprouts his first grey hair, and refusing to explore any place that cannot be reached from his own foreshore. Then, Frances Adams, his Madam, as he will dub her, will ask for nothing for herself but the affection of her husband.

When she births their only child, and on instinct Francis gathers up his bundled boy and carries him away from his mother to the window, to show him the silver barbs of the approaching tide and say, 'There. See that? That's home,' she will not ask that he be brought back, but only smile from her sweat-damped sheets to notice that the balled-up paperweight of newborn Michael Francis House leaves his father in perfect balance.

When he purchases a shining seaweed-green notebook and decides, during their first dust and clutter weeks in their new house, to write his story, Madam, still nursing Michael, will only pull her spring-loaded curls into a ribbon and bustle about, enforcing order on the mess whilst Francis bends furiously over one white page after another and writes and writes and writes.

When, years later, they walk home from The White Lion along the Hoe, hand in hand and both glad of the light wind skidding in over the waves after the muggy heat inside the pub and the clammy exertions of their dancing, she will tell him that all she might ever need is him and Michael. In the darkness, Plymouth will be only the glimmer of lamplight against the roar of the sea. He'll gather Madam into a close embrace, ready for the slow dance they have both been craving since too much lindy hopping rendered them breathless, and she will tuck her fleshier self into the lean crooks so much swimming has carved into his body, and as they begin to sway she will murmur, 'Just you and Michael. Just that. Two men, of all the people in the whole world. That's not so much to ask, is it?'

But naturally, it will be. She will be left with only one man.

'I have four of your pawns, a bishop, and a rook,' Nurse Adams says.

Francis glances over the board. 'Ah, but you're mistaken, Miss Adams.' He fixes her with a look of round-eyed innocence. She squints back at him, trying to figure his mischief. Every day this week he has charmed her into returning to play chess with him at the close of her shift. Some days, she arrives with a smile in her cheeks. Other days, those cheeks hang grey and tired off her bones, drained of the effort even to lift themselves towards happiness. Nurse Adams works herself raw. And yet, she comes when he asks her to. She will always come.

She notices his trick only when she leans in, scrapes forward her chair, and settles to resume the game.

'You've flipped the board!'

'Certainly not.'

'You have. I was white; you were black. You've flipped it.'

'Flipped is such an accusatory word. I might have twisted it slightly. But I'm sure the wind had begun the rotation. I just straightened it up, really, to save it from falling off the table.'

Nurse Adams raises her eyebrows and tightens the corners of her mouth, adopting the look of a mother chastising a naughty child.

'A man can soon be turned into an imp when he has nothing to occupy himself with, you know,' Francis says.

With a practised tut, Frances submits to his wickedness and lifts the black knight from amongst his losing pieces. She is a better chess player than he. She will win whatever the starting circumstance.

'Well, you soon will,' she says, hovering the bishop over the board as she decides on her first move. Francis' view is of the neat parting of her hair as she bends over her tactics. Are they sending him back, then? Is that what she means? He cannot ask. Suddenly, he cannot locate the words. All he can think is that the blanket wrapped around him is going no way to keeping him warm.

Nurse Adams drops the piece. 'Your move... House?'

'Yes.'

'It's your move.'

'Where to?'

'What?'

'You said I'd find myself occupied soon enough.'

'I did? Oh, I just...' She lowers her hands into her lap. She is the patient mother again. 'I meant the game, Francis. I'm sorry I worried you.'

They sit a while in easy silence. Wind wallops the tent walls, causing them to pulse inwards and back out again with the regularity of a beating heart. Beyond, the occasional groan or shriek catches a gust and rides it around the hospital, scaring men out of their dreams and easing others into darkness. He has moved from one mental asylum to another.

'Although, you can't stay here forever. They'll soon send you home or back to your company. Is it possible you've been hiding out a little?'

His face, he supposes, has betrayed him. He feels himself paled, his skin slackened. He hadn't thought about it in those terms, and yet, maybe he has been hiding. But, home or back to his company? If he returns home, he is coward; if he returns to his company, he will surely find himself entirely alone. He isn't the same Sergeant House who held a clear head in deafening noise, and issued orders so confidently that his men were calmed into action, and made certain that boys like Tom Merton were finally allowed to find their rest. That man fell into the sea and neglected to clamber back out. Or perhaps that man never truly existed. Perhaps he is an only an opium hallucination. Perhaps he is only an idea a foolish boy thought up in the cobwebs of his parents' attic.

'Which is it you want, Francis?' Nurse Adams' voice flutters about him like a moth, bumping up against his thoughts, refusing to settle. He cannot think straight. He doesn't have the answer.

'I'm a failure either way,' he replies.

Nurse Adams offers him another smile. 'You're mistaken, House,' she says. 'You have never been a failure and you never shall be, but you're not well. Any fool can see that. I can persuade them to send you home if that's what you want... Tell me.'

'I can't.'

She knows not what she is dangling before him. Home is all he wants now. The iron cut of the Plymouth sea; the stifling fire heat of his parents' cottage; the chance to sit in bed and sip tea and read a book; a long soak in a hot bath; to share a silent pint with his father at the Crown and Anchor; a bite of Lily's fresh-made rhubarb crumble. When he closes his eyes, he can practically feel the wind whipping in over Tinside Beach, grainy and spray-damp and familiar.

He intends to swim there into old age, front crawling steadily until he reaches that spearhead of quicker current which arrows away from the Plymouth shore, then tumble-turning about and butterflying back across the two-mile stretch he traces out for himself over the years. Every morning he will swim that stretch, as if he is a lifeguard on patrol. Every morning, however deep the winter, he will converse with the mutable tides. Later, a lido will be built near the place where he wades in – a great, curving, ship's bow of a thing, with bright blue tiles and painted white walls and, through the summer, hordes of splashing children. Francis will never use it. The Tinside Lido will cast a shadow on Tinside Beach that he cannot forgive. And besides, those waters hold none of the sea's wild beauty. He cannot imagine where the joy is to be found in diving into stillness.

'You can. I've been trying to muddle it out, whether you want to stay or go, and I haven't been able. You're like, I don't know... You're like the tides, Francis House. You're always shifting. But listen, I can help the doctors decide what to stamp on your record. Just tell me where you want to go. Back to your men or home?'

Francis opens his eyes and presses them to the even black and white checkers of the chessboard before him. To stay and fight, or to return home. He cannot utter it. Never will he be able to look his father in the eye if he asks. Never again will he be able to call himself a soldier.

Besides, he has a promise to keep. He cannot put it off forever.

With his left hand, he reaches across the table and offers his palm to Nurse Adams. She meets it with her own small, warm palm and a questioning look, which he holds as tightly as he does her fingers. Perhaps he can say it without the words. Perhaps he can say it with his thoughts only. In the silence, he chants his answer over and over again, and with his right hand, he lifts the white knight and lets it hover over the board.

He says nothing of the girl who sits, arms locked around her knees, deep in the shaded corner behind Nurse Adams. He does not mention her piercing grey eyes, or the kindness in her smile, or what they have spoken about hour after hour. It is between Francis and Estelle, why she is waiting for him.

*On March 21st 1918 while still in a weak condition we
− i.e. about 300 similar cases to myself − boarded a
train at Salonica bound for Braila, in the south of
Greece. Unknown to us, on this same day the Germans
had started their great offensive, and we were nearly
made reinforcements in France at a later date. Our
train travelled on the new Greek line, across the Varda
Marshes, around Mount Olympus, and then through
very mountainous country to Braila via Larissa. Rain
poured down all the way and was still falling when we
were put into a tent camp at our first stopping place.*

Thirty-Five

Later that night, when the hospital falls quiet, Francis retrieves his laundered clothes from where they are folded beneath his camp bed, winces as he coaxes them over his strange, spindly limbs, and sneaks towards the tent flap. Nosing past the fabric, he opens his lips to gorge on the brisk clean air. Without, a colossal snow moon illuminates the frosted ground. Francis pauses and listens for a nurse on a late round or a doctor tending to an emergency case. Nothing. Only the tent fabric, breathing in the gentle wind. Francis bends to tie his bootlaces then steps outside. He has on a pair of reasonably-soled hobnail boots, wool trousers, a matching tunic, a peak cap, and a greatcoat. Each item has likely known several owners, but they are Francis' now. He has claimed them. Just as he is staking claim to this life of his. For years, he has existed on the edge – of the land, of his sanity, of himself. Now, he is headed for the heart.

As he walks between the tents towards the unknown swathe of black land beyond, he taps at his breast pocket. Sensing a thickness there, he pushes his fingers inside and plucks out a letter. It is short. But one page. He does not need to open it and glance over the words to know what they say: *I've met a girl, Francis. Her name is Carina and, well, I've only asked her to marry me, haven't I?*

He blenches as his mind, unbidden, replays the sign off.

Your Old Pal,

B.

Francis rolls the words over his tongue as he steps out of the hospital compound and into the dark. 'Your old pal.' The oldest, in fact, excepting Lily. And look how poorly Francis has treated him. Look how much he has to make amends for. He tucks the letter back into his tunic pocket and steps quicker over the rimy ground, counting his crunching paces to ensure that he does not slow down. He does not turn back in the direction he has travelled. Not even when the hospital has grown small and doll's house-like. Not even when there is nothing at his back but a long trail of his own footprints. He must keep moving forwards. He has a promise to fulfil and he means to keep it.

The next day we sailed on a tiny ship through a rough sea to Toronto, Italy – which we reached safely after much seasickness.

Thirty-Six

'You came back, then.'

Farmer is sitting on the jetty, one bootless leg swinging over the water and the other bent up so that his heel hooks the splitting wood. On his knee, he rests his elbow. The hand holding his cigarette dangles loosely down, making a dancing firefly of the burning tip which is twinned on the sea's black surface. Moonlight leaks down the back of his neck and along the curve of his spine.

Francis paces down the beach towards his lost friend, his feet slipping in the sand. He had walked until he'd seen clifftops in the distance, then followed their rugged path until he'd discerned those familiar crosses, silhouetted against the low winter sun. It has taken him weeks. He has removed his boots to let the blisters heal and they hang over his shoulders by their laces, beating against his chest like the fists of a wronged love as he walks. He doesn't mind the blue-map bruises they will leave. He has no flesh left to protect him from their assault. His bones press closer and closer to his skin, as though they are searching a way out. Whatever it was he last ate, he cannot remember it now. The rumblings and cravings he used to endure – for crisped bacon and sweet tea, for steaming leek and potato soup, for chocolate and cigarettes and soft cheese – have been replaced by indifference. He cannot imagine how it would feel to rest a hunk of bread or a slice of apple on his tongue, and taste it, chew it, swallow it.

Reaching the furthest end of the jetty, he sits down next to Farmer.

'Of course I came back. I said I would.'

'And I suppose you've never broken a promise, House,' Farmer sulks.

'I've tried not to.'

Farmer does not lift his head from the mirror of the sea; he watches his own face distort and ripple beneath. Francis watches with him.

'They've all gone, you know.'

'Who?'

Farmer shrugs. 'Everyone. There's only us: me, you, Henley, Farrelly, the others. It's too quiet.'

'That's not such a bad thing, is it? I think we've earned a bit of quiet.'

'Maybe.'

They sit a while, their thoughts accompanied only by the wash of the tide: her slurp and crash, her gather and fall, her whim and hiss. Her orchestral subtleties lull them. Farmer sighs.

'We looked for him,' he says. 'Like you asked.'

'And?'

'He's waiting for you.'

The words send an urge for action stampeding along the sorry remains of Francis' muscles. His head throbs. He wants to leap up and rush off in search of the man he has longed and dreaded to see. But he does not know which direction he needs. And he does not want to abandon Farmer, so forlorn and unlike himself, on the jetty. Francis resists the impulse by biting at the inside of his cheek. He grinds his teeth together until something fluid – whether blood or saliva, he cannot say – spills from the tissue.

When he next speaks, his voice is a croak. 'Where?'

Eyes aimed down still, Farmer lifts an arm and points along the sweep of the cove towards a horse wagon, angled into the sand and partly submerged by the incoming tide. A lone horse remains hitched in. She lies on her side, baring her ribcage to the moon. Her bones throw sickle shadows on the sand.

'I'll come back,' Francis says, gripping the ball of Farmer's shoulder.

'Will you?'

'Always,' Francis answers.

In reply, Farmer puts a finger to his nose, hocks back all the phlegm he can muster, and shoots it into the rollers. Francis knows then that he is forgiven – for his absences, for his mistakes.

As he walks the silver-lapped rim of the cove, sea mists murk in: damp, and emphatic, and stinking of cockles. He grapples with the temptation to run but does not concede to it. He is unsure of what he will find when he reaches the horse wagon. It is better he approach slowly. He does not want to spook the man, the echo, the soul who waits for him there.

'Hello…' he offers when he comes within ten yards of the wagon. He is taking an arcing trajectory, to avoid passing too close by the dead horse.

There comes a movement from inside the wagon. A shuffling. Francis halts. His instinct is to drop into a crouch, but he refuses to be spied looking supplicant. He stands as erect as the hairs on his arms and stomach, and he waits. He is chilled to his core. He is a harp seal, an orca, an arctic tern, a sea otter. He is all that is white and cold. Until…

'Nellie!'

And then the warmth, the thawing.

Berto appears from behind the wagon, grinning like a fool, his arms held wide. He is expansive. At ease. His greatcoat hangs open. He has on a vest and no tunic, but he does not seem to notice the temperature.

'Albert,' Francis breathes.

Berto's hoot of laughter echoes along the cove, but Francis' fear of waking the Turks has dissipated entirely. They will not visit this place. 'Albert?' Berto repeats. 'Since when I have been Albert? Jesus, House, what's come over you?'

'Nothing. I just… I'm glad to see you.'

'It has been too long,' Berto replies, dropping his smile. He moves closer to the horse's skeleton and gently places a palm on the highest point of her domed ribcage. He strokes the smooth bracket of bone. 'Poor soul,' he murmurs to himself.

'I did look for you,' Francis offers.

'I know.'

'And sometimes … I didn't.'

Berto turns to find his eye then. 'I know.'

'But you knew where I was?'

Berto nods.

'Then why didn't you…?'

'It had to be your choice. It was your guilt.'

'The greatcoat?'

Berto shakes his head. 'It was never me.'

'But… Should I have felt guilty?'

'Oh, that's not a question I can answer. You have to figure that out for yourself. But let's not talk about that now. Listen, how about a swim? We've missed out on that much larking, you and me.'

'Not yet,' Francis answers.

'When then?' Berto asks. He is close enough to touch and Francis waits for him to bunch a fist and drive it playfully into his upper arm, as he always used to. He braces for the impact, but it does not follow.

'When I've worked it out.'

'What?'

'Whether I'm dead or alive.'

Berto's laugh is hollower than the first. 'Is it difficult to tell?'

'It's becoming so. Increasingly.'

'Then march it out,' Berto suggests. 'Or box it out. Or swim it out. You were always better in action than held still, Francis.'

'That much is true,' Francis replies. 'Or it used to be. I'm not so sure anymore.'

'Who could be sure of anything, here.'

It is not a question. Francis hums his agreement.

A little way up the beach, a length of driftwood has been fashioned into a bench. The evidence of a fire scorches the sand before it. Francis moves to settle himself on its central dip; he's not certain he trusts his legs.

'Do you think about what else we could have been?' he asks eventually.

Berto lowers himself onto the driftwood alongside him. They still have not touched, and Francis' suspicion that, if he were to offer his hand for a shake, it would slide straight through Berto's, renders him stiff and awkward with his old friend. The beginnings of a cramp are tingling along his foot. He spreads his bare toes until they ache.

'Now and then,' Berto replies.

'And what we might still be?'

'All the time,' Berto admits. 'You know, I think about taking Carina home and us having all these little ones. Pasty, Italian brats. And they'd have names like Renzo, and they'd have little ones of their own, and by the time I was a wrinkled old toad, I'd be surrounded by them.'

Francis smiles. It's a wonderful idea. It reminds him of Nurse Adams, and, at the unexpected thought of her, that cold twinge goes through him again, like a drop of hail. He wishes he hadn't had to leave her.

'What would they be like?' Francis asks.

'Exactly like their mother, I'd imagine,' Berto considers. Though he has met her only once, Francis knows Carina to be an effusive girl: all thrown arms and flicked hair and wild laughs. Though her confidence makes it hard to believe, he knows her to be only fifteen years of age, and he wonders again how old Berto really is: he always suspected that he was very much underage when he arrived at Woodlands. That Carina and Berto do not share a language does not seem to matter. They communicate with glances, gestures, barely completed thoughts.

Berto slumps back so that his backside hangs over the driftwood and gives a cheery snort. 'Can you imagine?'

'You – a father? Certainly not.'

But, in truth, Francis can see it clearly. He can imagine how their lives will unfurl, if ever they make it off Gallipoli. He's seen it all, in those darkest moments when the sea has taken possession of him, and held him, and in her pulse and her music, showed him all the living he might yet have to do.

Year after year they would meet on the same rickety bench on the Plymouth Hoe, Francis House and Berto Murley, always on the day before Francis' September twelfth birthday, just early enough to watch dusk skim in over the sea, but late enough to ensure that they are usually alone. There, they will exchange news and drinks. They will have returned home together, rocked in the belly of the same ship, their bodies variously starved and injured and infected and ravaged and tumbledown. Parts of them will have recovered by the time they come to sit on the worn and splinted wood of that bench, hands resting on the scuffed brass-effect arms, trousers snagging on the chunked-away section of the frontmost slat, while they tease and laugh and pretend. Parts of them never will.

They will eat an ice cream cone each, however cold the weather. September, though, will be kind to them. Rarely will they arrive wearing anything more than shirtsleeves, Berto just in from the station and carrying his overnight bag, and Francis holding the two ice cream cones.

The ritual will go unbroken for decades.

In later years, Francis, wincing onto the bench to await his friend, will apply himself with scholarly concentration to studying the changing sky. Sometimes, it will be flat and pale as paper. Other times, he will watch clouds clamshell closed over the last of the flamingo light as it throws out its defiant dying display. Less often still, night will fan in like a peacock's tail, silk and blue and shining. Hours he will spend trying to identify the spot where the feathered light fades into the waves, but the transformation will prove too soft, his eye too ignorant to catch it. He will never know the sky as he knows the sea.

But he will have to familiarise himself with it if he is ever to make real sense of the pictures that will come to haunt him: a Hurricane, taking a hit and beginning a nose-dive; a fattening funnel of smoke; the whirring desperation of a struggling engine.

'It's a good night,' the older Berto will say, tipping back his head.

Francis will mirror him, and there it will be, the trace of a Hurricane breaking the clouds to whine downwards, downwards, and ca-*cuuusssssh*, be swallowed by the frothing chalk-and-fog waves. He will shake the picture loose. One day, a long while into the future, it will be an old picture, but it does not belong behind his eyes yet. First, there is joy ahead of him. So much joy. And so much grief to follow. But all of it worth knowing.

'You can't possibly be pleased to see me,' Francis says.

'I am,' Berto replies. 'I've missed you.'

Francis does not contest the statement. He should rather stick with his premonition and go on believing that he has his best friend back and that they will grow old together. That he will find Frances Adams again and inform her, without a doubt, that he is taking her as his wife. That the new Mr and Mrs House will welcome the little boy he has foreseen – their Michael – into a briefly peaceful world.

He'd suspected Madam was the woman for him from the moment she'd stepped into his hospital tent and saved his sanity with a word, but it will only become more apparent as they giggle into parenthood, and joke towards middle age, and slow-dance through their deepest fears. Madam will know everything she need know about Francis, and he everything he ought to know about her: everything, in the end, except whether or not they anticipate the same nightmare as they curl into spine-to-spine sleep each night, a wall apart from their son's permanently empty bed.

Francis closes his eyes to it momentarily.

Only the rounded tail of the Hurricane remains visible as water swamps the cockpit and drags the plane below the waves. The red, white, and blue stripes work like depth indicators as it plunges downwards. Inside, made invisible by the underwater murk, the pilot will pummel his fists against the surrounding glass as his lungs fill; his head will pound; his heart will drop out of sync from the terror. He will know, without the slightest doubt, that he is going to die, but he will not stop fighting. As he dizzies, he will start flipping switches, jamming buttons. He will hope, uselessly, that something will spring free. The blood vessels in his eyes will pop before his lungs overflow and cease functioning. He will die slowly, writhing in agony, clutching for his life from inside his own coffin. He might even wonder, as grey-green darkness closes around him, how the telegram his parents will receive will be worded. Missing over the English Channel, it might say. Or, Assumed deceased. Or, Lost to the sea.

Not everything that has been prophesied for Francis is as clear as this, but what his heart knows is that he is meant to father the boy. That the boy, the idea of him, is enough to drag him off Anzac Cove and back towards Plymouth. That the boy will do him proud.

'We ought to be getting home,' he says now.

Berto nods. 'We are late.'

'Do you know the way? I think I've forgotten.'

'I know the way,' Berto answers. 'Do you want a drink first?'

'A drink?'

He turns to watch Berto rummaging in his inside pocket, then straightening up in possession of a silly grin and a dulled silver hip flask.

'What's in there?'

Berto shrugs, opens the lid, and sniffs deep. 'Whiskey?' he says. 'To drink to old friends.' He takes a swig, scrunches his eyes closed, clenches his teeth, then hands the flask to Francis.

'We're not so old.'

Berto snorts. 'Have you happened past a mirror lately? You look like a bad piece of taxidermy.'

Francis laughs. 'And you, my friend, look like a rotten walnut.'

'I'll take a rotten walnut over a dried fish.'

'Ghoul!'

'Sea slug!'

They cackle so hard then that Francis fears the cliffs at their back might crack and begin to crumble onto the beach. Always, it was like this with Berto. In their adjacent bunks at Woodlands. When they were racing up and down the narrow passageways of the *Sudan*. As they traipsed about Malta, searching women and trouble. Berto and Francis were bound by friendship, and Francis has not broken that. There is no breaking that.

Francis barges Berto with his shoulder; Berto barges back. Francis is shocked and elated to feel the contact through his muscle.

'Thank you for finding me,' Berto says.

'Thank you for letting me,' Francis answers.

A herring gull flaps to the ground before them and proceeds to parade back and forth, his chest puffed, his grey feathers worn like a biker jacket. He eyeballs the shining hip flask with an unblinking intensity. Seconds later, he is joined by a couple of dishevelled friends.

Birds, Francis thinks. On Gallipoli. His time here has proved it an impossibility. And yet, the gulls strut about before him, arrogant as you like. He can hear their beaks opening and closing. He can see the occasional stretch and beat of their wings.

'Look,' Berto says. 'It's you, me, and Busty.'

This sets them to cackling again, and the racket sends two of the gulls squawking away in disgruntlement. Berto pulls a shard of dried fruit from his pocket and tosses it to the last brave bird. The bird plucks it up and hobbles into an ungainly take-off, and Francis and Berto sigh into silence as they watch the three birds rise towards the first pearly hint of brightening moon to break the clouds, grow smaller, and eventually vanish.

'That swim, then,' Francis says, clapping his hands against his knees and pushing himself upright. He feels stronger already, at the thought of it. He looks down at Berto, shows him a flickering smile. 'Come on,' he says, and slapping at the top of Berto's head with a flattened palm, he takes off down the beach.

Berto's voice chases him over the sand. 'You cheated!' he calls.

Yes, Francis thinks. I suppose I did. I suppose we all did.

We sailed for England – accompanied by German prisoners – which we reached on April 21ˢᵗ 1918. Disembarking at Southampton, I reported from here to Fort Brockhurst, was 'boarded' marked B'11 and sent on leave for one month.

After a fortnight at home I became in love with a girl, who is now my wife. I didn't ask her to accept me, I just took her, and have never yet regretted my choice.

Thirty-Seven

The sea is the dense grey-green of a toad. Francis plunges open-eyed through the frothy waves, his feet pinned together to form a single fin and his arms working like matching propellers to haul his head, his shoulders, his chest out of the water, then pendulum it back below in a perfectly measured butterfly stroke. His body is one long ripple. His heaving breaths are lost to the thundering tide. The pleurisy attempts to crumple his lungs still, but he remains the very same merman. He times the undulations of his stroke to the beat of his heart: a practised slow and steady.

Though the day's first light is late in penetrating last night's chimney-smoke clouds, he does not feel cold. He is duetting with the sea, and her voice is a sustained whisper in his ears, and her weight is a tight embrace, and he knows she will do him no harm.

He stops just short of an approaching cramp and pitches himself up to tread water and look back across the beach. It is mantled in a thin grey light. The morning will arrive eventually, and then he will have to depart.

Berto surfaces besides him.

'Well, you haven't slowed down a jot,' he complains, breathless. 'In fact, I'd wager you've sped up some.'

Francis laughs. He has learnt his lessons. He does not swim against the sea now but moves always with her, his gleaming tail leaving an eddying tunnel of water in his wake.

Berto's mouth gapes as he attempts to refill his lungs. He is pale – worryingly so. He looks like a man who, if caught in a new slant of sunlight, would simply fade into invisibility.

Francis swipes a few salty beads of water into his face and, with a snort, sinks below again. He will lead Berto safely back ashore. He will look out for him now as he should have then.

Minutes later, they footslog along the cove side by side, sometimes bashing shoulders or elbows when the sand tips them towards each other, sometimes tilting apart. They dress as they go, shaking the sand from the messy folds of their uniforms. It is only fitting that the rain should begin then. It is nothing more than a billowing mist, but it obscures their way enough that, as they talk, they veer accidentally back into the shallows. Seeing another opportunity for mischief, they kick at the soft grey ripples and shatter them. They reach down and scoop the water up with their cupped hands. They flick it over their own heads and each other's until they are as much salt-stained as soaked. They splash and stomp and squeal until they are panting with it. They have months of teasing and mad plans to catch up on. More. They have the ends of their child-hoods to see out. They are playing. And encouraging them into it are the waves, surging into boundless adventure, and Francis and Berto are as in thrall to their soothe and shush as Francis and Lily once were.

Finally they stop, breathless, and stand side by side, keen only to listen for a while.

'What do you suppose it would be like,' Berto muses, 'to wade in and start swimming and never turn back?'

Francis is still for a long time before he answers. 'Wonderful,' he decides. His voice is small, considered. 'I doubt there's any other way to feel true freedom.'

They slop down, a puddle of clothes and skin and joy and regret, and lie side-by-side. Pale mists are draped about them, and Francis wonders whether this is his idea of heaven. Seawater drips from every inch of his skin. Salt crusts gently around his nostrils. Here, now, he is heavy and exhausted and as untroubled as perhaps he ever will be again.

'It's stories you'll be asked for, you know,' Berto says finally.

Francis shakes his head. The stories are not for sharing. They are his alone.

He will make the mistake, though, of telling them to Madam. He will punctuate their courtship with recollections of trench wounds and dead bodies and the taste of rotting flesh on the air. How could he imagine that he might need to protect her from the most gruesome truths of his war, lest a son of theirs be packed off to fight another? How could he, not quite yet a father, envisage lifting an envelope addressed to an eighteen-year-old Michael F. House from the mantle and, having noted the stamp which records – no, boasts – that it has been sent from the 'Ministry of Labour and National Service', opening it with hammering heart? How could he, still not yet fully recovered from his own fight, foresee finding that a slanting blue-ink hand has decorated calm black lines of type with oversized whips and loops, and understanding that *in accordance with the National Service (Armed Forces) Act, 1939,* Michael will be *called upon for service in the Royal Air Force and required to present himself on Thursday day, 5 April 1940, between 9am and 12pm, or as early as possible thereafter on that day, to: No. 1 RAF Recruit Centre, Penarth, South Wales?* How could he, twenty-three years old and still weak to the bones, imagine being forty-eight and running strong through the dirt-rain – the scuttering dirt-rain he has almost forgotten – of a lately bombed Plymouth, where flames already quiver on the pier, and smoke shins directly up towards the gape-mouthed moon, and all across the city corresponding columns of smoke rise out of craters of ruin, and at their blind bases people are dying? How could he, a young man who has not yet married his wife, predict that in the tumbling dawn that follows the Plymouth Blitz, he will tuck the telegram which spells out the fortune of their only child into his top pocket, unopened, and keep the news from both she and himself for three full days?

Even he, for all his recent premonitions, cannot see so clearly into one possible future.

Oh, but he'll regret the stories, then. All but the one he writes for Michael in a seaweed green notebook and deposits on his son's pillow when war is declared for the second time. It will end with flowery exactitude, the pen swooping satisfyingly full circle into the final *s*: *I am now the father of a fine son...*

'I don't have a story,' he tells his friend. 'I just fought a war. The same as everyone else.'

Berto sighs. 'But what comes next?'

'Who could say,' Francis answers.

'You're all right. You've done what you set out to do. You always wanted to be a soldier, like your father.'

Francis nods. 'But I didn't want to be my father.'

'And you're not!' Berto shifts his head around, so that he can better frown at Francis.

'Are you certain?'

'More certain than it's decent to be.'

Francis laughs again. 'Is that so? Well, then, I'll have to accept your word on the matter, I suppose.' Though he isn't certain Berto is right. It seems to him that he grows more similar to Frederick with every passing breath. In the quiet between his stories, his father waits with a huff in his nose and anger on his lips and nothing whatsoever behind his eyes. And yet, for all Francis has yearned to make his father proud, he realises now that he is unconcerned with proving himself a man. Rather, he wonders if, given time, he might find his way back to aspects of that hopeful boy he used to be; that little lad he'd left behind in an attic. He'd been ready to go at life, that boy. He'd been worth admiring. He'd been brave.

But Francis is not he. Everything has changed since. Every last thing.

'All right then, old friend,' Francis says eventually. 'Enough is enough.' He can hardly bear to stand up and break the moment. He wants to stay here forever, watching the moon and laughing with Berto. But he knows that he cannot. They have reached their goodbye. 'Time we were getting on.'

Francis stretches out his back as he glances around for the wood he will need. The driftwood they've been sitting on is too large, but a smaller piece... Or a slat of broken jetty, perhaps. He wastes an hour, stepping around the beach, lifting detritus and discarding it: too rotten; too soft; too short; too ugly. Nothing is good enough for Berto: the man he has opened his heart to so many times over; the only man who knows Francis' inner being and has always been worthy.

As he searches what he needs, he tells Berto of all that has transpired since last they saw each other. He needs to fill the silence. He pauses to pull a sodden scrap of paper from his pocket and, from its ruined aspect, pretends to read Lily's last letter.

It was the last Swansea train that restored him to me, soaked through and smaller than ever I'd seen him and still buttoned into his stinking uniform, but smiling. Smiling through his sobs and not giving a damn if the other men heard him or laughed. They didn't, of course. They knew. As you must. But Ernest would have cried even so.

I waited until he was close enough to touch before I said anything, so that I could breathe the Welsh I'd learnt especially against his lips. He clung to me, there on the station platform, and everyone else moving around us, and neither of us saying anything until we were good and ready.

Then, in the end, I got up on my tiptoes and I whispered, 'Fi yma. Fi adre.' Because I was here. I was home. With Ernest. And it was promising me all the adventure I could want.

'He was lucky,' Berto says.

'He was,' Francis replies.

Eventually, he settles upon two slender lengths of driftwood, salt-paled, which swell as though caught by a passing wind. He wants this monument to have a sense of movement. That will suit Berto perfectly.

Francis moves away from the horse wagon and the unfortunate beast tethered to the afterlife by her tattered leathers.

Better the sloop. Better a vessel one might sail on than an upturned wagon one might only drown in when the tide comes in. He uses his hands to dig a narrow hole, then, thrusting the longer piece of driftwood down into it, twists it to left and right until it feels secure. He gives it a kick, to test its fortitude. He finds it as fine as its intended owner. Next, he retrieves the shorter piece of wood and spends a moment holding it up against the first, deciding where it will sit best.

Berto watches Francis work in silence. He does not offer an opinion.

When, after many trials, Francis decides on the correct position for the cross, he removes his belt, wraps it around and around the two lengths of wood, then pulls it as tight as he can and buckles it. He stands back, hands to his hips, to assess his work. It's rough, but it's beautiful, too. One end of the horizontal driftwood flicks up, as though about to take flight. The belt, though cumbersome, is an offering; a reminder; Francis is leaving part of himself with Berto. Lastly, he removes his greatcoat and hangs it over the cross.

Before he leaves, he will erect a second, smaller cross alongside Berto's. For her.

'Her name was Estelle, wasn't it?'

Berto cocks his head in surprise. 'I never spoke it afterwards, Francis. I swear it. Who told you?'

'She did.' Francis pushes on before Berto can question the claim. 'How did you know her?'

Berto averts his eyes. 'It doesn't matter now.'

'It does. Very much… She was your sweetheart, wasn't she?'

At length, Berto lifts his eyes to Francis': they well with plum-round tears.

'I'll let her know,' Francis says. 'Carina.'

Berto drops his palms behind him and leans back on his straightened arms, as he always did. 'Let her know what?'

'That you died saving my life.'

Berto's eyes are round and full. 'But … I didn't. It wasn't your fault. I –'

'You did. You saved my life –'

'No. Listen. Francis, please. I got on the ship. You do realise that, don't you? I got on the ship the next morning. I sailed for Gallipoli. I just…' His head drops, as if in shame. 'I never made it out of the shallows.'

Francis hunkers down before him and grips him by the shoulders.

'You saved my life, Albert Murley,' he insists. 'That's the truth, and that's what they'll know.'

'And what if you don't make it, Nellie. It's a long way back.'

'I'll write to her,' Francis replies. 'In case I don't. I'll write her a letter every day, and I'll post it from wherever I am. They'll be able to make a book about what I have to say about you, Berto.'

Berto laughs. 'Is that so?'

'You're my best friend.'

'Well you'll have to make sure you see it through for me then, won't you?'

Berto straightens up and offers his hand for a shake. When Francis meets it with his own, Berto grasps hold of his wrist and drags him into a rough embrace. They stand, pressed together, until the sea washes in over their boots.

'What?' Francis asks finally.

'Life!' Berto replies. He releases his friend slowly. 'Now get on home.'

Francis turns towards the sea, but he finds himself loathe to move any further, because part of him already is home. Somewhere on the wind, voices wing towards him. 'Sir,' they plead. 'Sir…' He was right to think he would never leave Gallipoli. The voices are accompanied by the flap of serge disturbed by a passing draught. He turns to look at the broken sloop, where he knows the greatcoat will be waiting. And there it hangs, its chest rising and falling to its own even rhythm, its one arm raised to beckon him, the peak of its hat lifted as if in question. It has not finished with Francis yet.

'I said, get on home,' Berto says again.

Francis returns his eyes to the sea, measuring her wolf pelt bristle. I am… I am…

'We're such old friends, the sea and I,' he says.

Berto nods. 'Yes. But she hasn't claimed you yet. What happened to you, Francis?'

Francis shapes a deep shrug and exhales long and slow. 'I don't know,' he says. 'I'm not sure it's been decided.'

He steals a glance up at the gleaming brim of the moon, just emerging on the owl light sky. Water courses down his temples and onto his lips and he licks at the salt. So long as he can keep the tides on his tongue, he will know that he is home. Beneath him, his legs begin to tingle and sting and tighten. Soon, he will return to the shallows and wade into the cold. Soon, he will drop his shoulders in and stroke forward and kick himself free. Soon, he will purl below the surface and into the gloom of the silted sea, and he does not know yet how far it will take him, but he is not afraid anymore. He is where he ought to be. He is who he ought to be. He is entirely himself.

I am now the father of a fine son, Michael Francis,
whom I hope, after hearing how his father tried, will
say – 'I, too, will try' – and in doing so gain just
reward in success and happiness.

Author's Note

Francis Albert House was born on the 12th September, 1892. He was a soldier. I met him first by way of a small seaweed-green notebook, slightly torn in the top right corner, which I happened across entirely by accident. I knew him then only as the name scrawled on the first discoloured page of what I soon discovered to be a journal: Sergeant F. A. House. It was not a name I recognised. But I have never been able to resist words on a page, and so I started to read, and the man I soon came to know captivated me.

I reached the last page of the journal, I flipped back to the start, I read it again. And then I set it aside. I was a teenager; I was a reader; I wasn't yet brave enough to admit to being a writer. But I did not forget Sergeant House. The last line of his journal, so beautifully written, haunted me. Years after reading it, I could recite it from memory. It made me tear up every time.

During my university studies, I set out to find out who he was. What I discovered, by his hand and through my research, was that he fought at Gallipoli – one of the bloodiest conflicts of the First World War. And that he was my great great uncle. His 'favourite sister', Lily Eliza House, was my maternal great grandmother. Given that Lily married into the name Carter, and that her daughter (my grandmother) married into the name Cadogan, I had not recognised House as a name belonging to my ancestry.

But I had felt instantly connected to this voice on a page, and particularly on account of the following phrase: 'I trust my reader to believe…'

His 'reader'. Here, then, was a fellow writer – the only other in my family.

In this novel, I have not attempted to faithfully recreate the narrative Francis set down on the pages of his journal. For some time, I tied myself in knots trying to do that. But of course I could not do him justice, this brave man. So instead, I have considered the impact his experiences might have had on him, physically, mentally, and emotionally, and placed those imaginings within a story. Storytelling is my business, as soldiering was his. I saw this project as a collaboration, between myself and my great great uncle; between two people who never met, but who are connected by bloodlines and pages; between two writers.

Naturally, this novel is not truly Francis' story. A novel demands a structure, a character arc, rising tension, a plot. It cannot reflect a life so directly. But many of the events described here are real: Francis did go ashore in the dark at Gallipoli; Bill Farmer, from Gippsland, did offer him friendship; an army doctor did dose Francis up with opium when he suffered from pleurisy; Francis did have a best friend called 'Berts' Murley (which I originally misread as 'Berto' and couldn't quite bring myself to correct); and Tom Merton really did see a man 'shattered to atoms' as he waited in line for water. Between chapters, I have inserted some of Francis' own words – words which inspired my version of this story.

And, while other elements of the story are my own invention, that phrase – 'I trust my reader to believe' – has persuaded me over and over again of my duty to bring Francis to these pages. I only hope I have done him justice.

Rebecca F. John

Acknowledgements

The author wishes to acknowledge the award of a **Literature Wales Writer's Bursary supported by the National Lottery through the Arts Council of Wales** for the purpose of developing this novel. I am also indebted to the **Society of Authors Authors' Foundation**, who provided me with a grant for the same purpose.

My sincere thanks go to Jenny Savill, who found me tangled up in Francis' story and took the time to unpick the knot; to Siân Collins, for being an early and always supportive reader; to Sarah Reynolds, who read this novel when it was an entirely different one and offered her perceptive, intelligent, and kind reflections. And, as ever, to those patient family members and friends who listen to me talk and talk and talk about books ceaselessly, and almost without complaint.

Through the many hours spent writing this novel, I was kept company by my three little dogs, Betsy, Teddy, and Effie, who are some of my very best friends: they deserve my heartfelt thanks for always offering a wagging tail in times of doubt.

My greatest thanks go not only to Francis, for choosing to set his story down in his own hand, but also to all those other men whose names I've borrowed from his journal: Berts Murley, Busty Leonard, Tom Merton, Bill Farmer, 'Dad' Rymills, Lieutenant Cruikshank, Captain Burrows, Sergeant Saunders, Sergeant Patterson, Doctor Marks, Hancox, General Birdwood, and Hodgson. I do not know your stories, but I truly hope that, somewhere along the way, you all knew happiness.

And finally, as always, to my readers. I hope that Francis' story captures your heart as it has mine, and that you will join me in remembering him.

Rebecca F. John was born in 1986 and grew up in Pwll, a small village on the south Wales coast. Her first short story collection, *Clown's Shoes*, was published in 2015 and her stories have been broadcast on BBC Radio 4. Her short story 'The Glove Maker's Numbers' was shortlisted for the *Sunday Times* EFG Short Story Award. She is the winner of the PEN International New Voices Award 2015. Her first novel, *The Haunting of Henry Twist*, was shortlisted for the Costa First Novel Award. She lives in Swansea.